Project Ordell

Susanna Hays

REAMSPINNER
PRESS

Published by

DREAMSPINNER PRESS

5032 Capital Circle SW, Suite 2, PMB# 279, Tallahassee, FL 32305-7886 USA
www.dreamspinnerpress.com

Project Ordell
© 2016 Susanna Hays.

Cover Art
© 2016 Stef Masciandaro.
http://www.stefmasc.com/
Cover content is for illustrative purposes only and any person depicted on the cover is a model.

ISBN: 978-1-63476-867-2
Digital ISBN: 978-1-63476-868-9
Library of Congress Control Number: 2015952698
Published February 2016
v. 1.0

Printed in the United States of America
∞
This paper meets the requirements of
ANSI/NISO Z39.48-1992 (Permanence of Paper).

Thank you to those who have helped me with Project Ordell: Sera Trevor, Samantha, and Olivia Helling. Also, a special thanks to my best friend, Kathy, who keeps me sane during the writing process, and to Lee Todd for participating in the Hop Against Homophobia contest.

CHAPTER 1

BLACKWICK WAS a small town where it seemed to only rain. When it wasn't raining, it was damp and muggy. Still, the town had its charms; if you looked to gothic architecture for inspiration, Blackwick was a veritable gold mine, chock full of gloom. The tall buildings, each adorned in the finest grays or blacks (and nothing else) did little to help the town stand out against the sky, which itself seemed trapped in perpetual silver. It wasn't a particularly nasty place, mind you—not if you enjoyed the rain.

Ordell did not enjoy the rain.

He crawled out of his small bed and walked over to the window. Another restless night, despite the fact that he should have recharged his energy. The drizzle of rain fell from the cloudy sky and collected alongside the windowsill outside. Mr. Lynch played his accordion down below while the children danced around him. Mrs. Briggs would come out soon after to hit him with her broom and tell him not to play that ruckus so late at night. The two would banter here and there, and then Mr. Lynch would go play his accordion elsewhere.

Then there was the elderly lady who sat in her rocking chair on her front porch and hummed to the music. No use talking to her—she wouldn't answer, only give a small smile and continue rocking. She rocked from nine in the morning to ten at night. She'd go inside from time to time throughout the day, but she'd always come back—like a moth to a candle.

Rumor had it she waited outside for her son to come back from war. The war that had happened twenty years ago. The same war her son died in.

Of course, that was just a rumor. Perhaps she truly enjoyed watching the people go about their lives, like Ordell did. She also seemed to enjoy watching the children dance around while Mr. Lynch played his music and sang one of his whimsical songs.

The gas streetlamps lit up the dark cobblestone street and the soft wind rustled the hanging clothes that were no doubt still wet from the rain. A white shirt flew off the clothesline and down to the small puddle, which had formed near the shallow stairs that led toward the wealthier part of Blackwick.

The wind blew again, and the shirt rustled near one of the children dancing. The little boy grabbed it and wrapped it around his neck like a cape. He grabbed the little girl's hand, and they continued to dance in a circle around Mr. Lynch, singing their own little tune.

Ordell wouldn't change his room for the world. It was a cozy place in the attic above his father's shop. Resting alongside the stairs going up to the wealthier part of Blackwick, Ordell saw everything.

Even the things the world didn't want him to see.

He saw Mrs. Combs's and Mr. Harrison's illicit affair down near the grocery stand every Friday night at exactly six thirty in the evening—that was around the time Mr. Combs went down to the city to collect supplies for his store. Many of the others knew of the affair, but no one told Mr. Combs of it. Or, if they did, Mr. Combs shrugged it off and carried on with his business.

He saw how Mr. Galloway struggled with money and went through illegal means of obtaining a small profit. Usually he met with a mysterious stranger between Mr. Harrison's house and the pub, where there was a tiny nook in which no one could find him easily. When the deed was done, he looked over his shoulder twice and then scurried off into the night.

He also watched how his father would mingle with clients who seemed to have other agendas on their mind.

It was something that concerned Ordell very much. Not for his own well-being, but for the well-being of his brothers and sisters, who were not sentient enough to take care of themselves. Who didn't understand when they would be abused or taken advantage of.

It was Ordell's responsibility to take care of them, to make sure no one could hurt them. Even his own father.

They were just going to a new home.

That was the only thing his father would tell him when he asked where his brothers and sisters were going.

Later on Ordell pressed the topic further, but his father shut him down each time. He knew what they were used for. Manual labor or jobs the humans didn't want to do. At least that was what his father told him.

For the most part, he believed it, but there were times he felt there was more going on between his father and his clients.

"Don't worry, Ordell," his father would say, "they're going to a loving home. They have more potential there than they do here."

"Then why don't I go with them? Why am I still here?"

His father would then place his large hand on Ordell's shoulder and give one of his famous crinkled smiles. "Because you are too special to give up."

It didn't make much sense to him. His father created him at age twenty-one, which was the typical age for his other siblings. Sure, there were some as young as eighteen and some much older, but it was only when a client specified those requirements.

If he pressed further, his father would say that Ordell was too human. Octavio often joked that Ordell was more human than most humans, and he was beginning to believe it. Aside from the few kinks here and there that showed he was a machine, Ordell felt more connected to the humans than the automatons. He liked to mimic them and live his life like the other citizens. He would recharge in a bed rather than prop himself up against the wall like he used to. He would socialize and complain about being hungry when, in reality, he didn't have an appetite. Ordell even shared his fears of aging, which was something that would not affect him.

It was just those tiny things that made him feel like he belonged in the community.

Ordell pressed his forehead against the windowsill and stared back out at the dark streets. Sometimes the clients would come this late at night when his father thought Ordell had gone to bed. He'd see the strangers walk up to the shop when the closed sign was up for the night. They did a strange knock, and his father would come down and open the door. Ordell would then press his ear to the door and see if he could hear the conversation going on in the shop below.

Usually all he could hear were grumbles and sometimes laughter.

Right then he saw the strange man who lately had been coming to the shop around this time. He was a tall and lanky man who seemed to have light-colored hair, but it was hard to tell with the streetlamps. His suit looked expensive, and Ordell didn't miss the shiny gold pocket watch he carried.

Octavio Rutledge, finest automaton creator in Blackwick (and the only inventor left), was not exactly the type of man to mingle with the wealthy. As far as Ordell knew, his father didn't have friends from the upper class. But for some reason, this man was different.

Just like all the other nights, the man first checked his pocket watch, then lifted his cane and knocked on the door three times. Three rapid times. Then he disappeared inside.

Once again Ordell pressed his ear to the door to see if he could hear any of the conversation. Just like all the other times, he only heard the grumbles and laughter.

Ordell could go down and introduce himself. He was allowed to talk to the humans during the daytime, so why couldn't he talk to the customers who came by during the night? There wouldn't be any harm in meeting one of his father's friends, right?

This man wouldn't know he was an automaton. Not many did.

Unlike his brothers and sisters, Ordell was very humanlike. He felt pain and pleasure. He felt sadness and fear. Understood right from wrong.

Physically he looked nothing like his father. Octavio had created him with fine copper-brown hair and smoky blue eyes. His complexion was fair and soft, whereas his father had a crooked nose and leathery skin from the heat of the shop.

He looked similar to his brothers, with their soft features and full lips. Same slender body and small frame. Yet many of the townspeople never guessed he was an automaton himself. They fully accepted him as Octavio's son who had just showed up ten years ago… never aging. Never showing physical signs of fatigue or stress.

Ordell stretched and looked up at the small clock. His version of sleep was powering down after running for a few days. He'd been running for five days now without resting, and he could feel himself running slower than usual. Octavio warned Ordell that he shouldn't push himself that many days, but Ordell couldn't help it; someone needed to help keep the shop in order when Octavio slept. He contemplated again if he should go down and introduce himself. In the end cowardice won out over curiosity. It was a wasted effort to try to listen in on the conversation below, so Ordell walked back to his bed and pulled the covers over himself.

THE MORNING came fast, and Ordell struggled to get out of bed. By the sound of his father's voice down below, he'd overslept again.

Ordell grabbed his button-down shirt and trousers, pulling them on as he raced down the stairs. He grabbed his boots and pulled them on one at a time as he hopped to the counter.

Despite the fact that Ordell helped his father clean the store up less than a day ago, the workshop was already coated, once again, in various blueprints and assorted scraps of metal. An almost-too-large poufy yellow chair was covered with gears and crumpled up papers, which was fine by Ordell, as he always felt that the chair was a bit of an eyesore. He passed gingerly over the loose scraps on the hardwood floor and picked up one of the balled-up pieces of paper.

Octavio's latest invention—an automatic teapot—had not been too successful. The hot tea spurted everywhere once turned on, which was problematic enough on its own, except that the thing even leaked while turned off. Ordell told his father countless times to give up on this particular invention, but Octavio was too stubborn for his own good.

"We can't afford to have you sleep in, Ordell," his father said, narrowing his eyes.

"Sorry, Father." Ordell yawned and rubbed his eyes. "I didn't sleep well last night."

"This is the third time this week that you've overslept. This better not be a habit trending."

"It isn't, Father. I promise."

His father stared at him for another moment, then sighed. "I need you to go downtown and pick up some scrap metal." His father handed him a piece of paper. "If you find any gears, bring those home too. Do not pay for them, though. If I find out you paid—"

"I know, Father," Ordell mumbled.

"Good, now get a move on."

Ordell glanced at the paper as he walked out of the store. They were the typical metals Ordell was used to picking up for his father. They were cheap and rusted easily, but it got the automatons made. They weren't of the best quality, but there wasn't much to expect when one bought their supplies in Blackwick.

He walked up the shallow cobblestone steps and toward the better part of Blackwick. There he saw the glances as he walked by. Ordell forced a nod and a smile, but they just looked away.

He might be accepted as Octavio's son, but even he wasn't foolish enough to be oblivious to the fact that he stood out against the humans here.

A part of him wished to talk to his siblings about it, but they didn't understand his concerns. Really they didn't understand much except orders. Always had that contented smile on their faces, no matter what was said to them. Always so polite and spoke with such simple words.

Ordell used to have a friend. One who knew his secret. She was a little younger than he was supposed to be, but she aged. Grew older as Ordell stayed frozen in place.

Then she grew sick. Something Ordell couldn't comprehend, couldn't fix. And then she was gone. Just like that.

Now there was just his father. Ordell wasn't sure if he wanted to befriend another human. Not if they could die so suddenly.

He'd be nice to them, though. Be considerate to the blacksmith as he received the metals. Smile at the lady who was passing out flowers. Even kindly greet that little old lady who glared at him as he made his way back down to the shop.

Ordell came back to see the tall, lanky man with the light hair. He was arguing with Octavio and looking down at that gold pocket watch. He snapped it shut and turned his attention back to Ordell's father.

"I expect the finest quality, Octavio," the man said. "You promised something more than a mindless sex doll!"

"I gave you what you wanted! You wanted a complacent slave, and that's what you got!" Ordell had never seen his father's face so red before. "You can't have it both ways!"

Ordell's eyes widened, and his father motioned for the man to come to the back room with him. "Let's not discuss this here."

Before the man could turn around and look at Ordell, his father grabbed the man by the elbow, and they went to the back room.

Ordell sat down on the small couch and listened to bits and pieces of the argument. The man wanted a sex slave, yet didn't like his father's design. It didn't make much sense to Ordell, since the man could easily go to another inventor in Goldcrest to make those machines. That was where the pleasure slaves thrived. Why go to a small automaton shop here in Blackwick?

It felt like hours before the two men came back. Ordell looked up at his father, and he could see a strange look on his father's face, like Ordell had done something wrong.

"Ordell," his father said, "go upstairs while I help Mr. Saunders. Take the rest of the day off."

"Who's this?" Mr. Saunders asked, his eyes widening. "You created another one?"

"What do you mean?" Ordell asked. "There's only one of me!"

The confused look on Mr. Saunder's face hardened to an angry expression. "Why isn't he obeying you? He looks human enough to me!"

"I *am* human," Ordell said, crossing his arms.

"Ordell, go upstairs," his father said, his tone harsher this time. "Now!"

"He'll be fine here," Mr. Saunders said before Ordell could get up. "He'll keep me company."

His father stared at them both before giving a slight nod. "I'll be back with the paperwork in just a few minutes."

"It must be nice to help your father out," Mr. Saunders said once they were alone. "I remember when I used to help my father out when I was a boy."

"It's nice, sir."

"Please, call me Ratliff." The man flashed a wide smile, exposing his overly white teeth. "You don't look much like your father. Your mother must've been quite a beautiful woman."

"Do you have a wife, Mr.—I mean, Ratliff?"

"Oh no." He chuckled and sat down next to Ordell. "I have no interest in that. I turn my attention to these machines."

"You mean the automatons."

"They carry out my… fantasies. We all have needs, don't we, boy?"

"That's what they're there for," Ordell said with a sigh.

"I'd be interested in bringing you home with me." Ratliff smiled when Ordell looked at him. "You're exactly what I've been looking for."

"I'm sentient," Ordell said, narrowing his eyes. "That makes me just as human as you."

"Is that so? Maybe you could show me just how human you are." His bony hand touched Ordell's thigh. "I'd love to see it."

Ordell smacked the hand away and jumped off the couch. "Don't touch me!" he said through his teeth.

"Much feistier than your counterparts," Ratliff said, getting up from the couch. "I like the extra challenge."

Ordell took a step back, keeping his eyes on the man. If he could duck around Ratliff, he could get to the upstairs and lock the door. The other option was the front door, to make a run for it.

"Here's the paperwork for the next model." Ordell had never felt so relieved to hear his father's voice. "It should be completed within four weeks, give or take a few days."

"Cancel my purchase," Ratliff said, his eyes still on Ordell. "I have something a little more in mind."

"I told you I can't make what you want. This is the best you're going to get from me. Now I can tell you that the other shops in other areas are going to give you a faulty automaton. I suggest you stick with the model we discussed and take it from there."

"What about him?" Ratliff pointed his cane at Ordell. "Exactly what I have in mind."

"You can't have my son."

"Then make something like him. If you made him once, you can make him again."

"It's not that simple," Octavio muttered. "I don't—"

"I don't have time to argue this," Ratliff said. "When I come back, I better see something like him in the works, or I'm taking my business elsewhere."

"Go ahead," Ordell snapped.

"Go upstairs, Ordell," his father said. "Now."

He glared at Ratliff for a good extra measure, then headed upstairs. Better Ordell got away from that pervert before he did something he'd regret.

CHAPTER 2

IT WAS the same routine each morning. Get up. Help open shop. Say good morning to his siblings. Do errands.

For ten years it had been like that, in that exact order. Sometimes Octavio would ask for a certain item when Ordell went into town, but nothing too extreme. The biggest surprise Octavio threw at him was when he wanted Ordell to visit the fish market and pick up some salmon, which was terribly expensive in Blackwick.

Ordell grabbed his basket and walked up the same shallow steps he'd grown accustomed to for the past ten years. He looked over the small errand list like he did every morning, stepping over Mrs. Briggs's old scruffy dog sleeping on the fifth step.

For Blackwick the day was pleasant. There was a hint of birds chirping in the distance, and the sun peeked through the heavy clouds. The townsfolk were out and about, doing their own errands—Mrs. Briggs out tending the small flower bed below her windowsill, Mr. Combs humming as he swept the area around his shop. Even Mrs. Combs was out enjoying the hint of sunlight. She'd been reading the same romance novel for the past few months while she rocked slowly back and forth in her chair.

Ordell couldn't help but smile along with the people around him. Something about seeing Blackwick come to life with talking and laughter warmed him. Even Mrs. Briggs couldn't be cranky on a beautiful day like this as the children danced around and played marbles on the steps. She tried on her famous glare, but the laughter was too contagious, and she could only sigh and chuckle in the end.

"Good morning, Ordell," Mr. Combs said with a bright smile. "Doing errands today?"

Ordell lifted his basket and shook it. "Just a small list today."

"You and your father should enjoy the warm weather." His bass of a voice filled the air. "You don't know when we'll get another day like this!"

"You know how my father is with his work." Ordell chuckled. "It'll take more than a sunny day for him to leave that shop of his."

"He shouldn't spend his whole life in there," Mrs. Combs said, peering up from her book. "It is such a waste to live inside while the world passes you by. I believe he should get out there and find a nice lady who will bring back his youth."

Ordell couldn't help but feel a twinge of jealousy. Not that it would be a bad thing for Octavio to find a lady and get married, but where would that leave Ordell? They would have a family of their own and children who actually aged.

"Come now, my dumpling," Mr. Combs said, "you know how Octavio is with mingling with others. He would drive the poor woman insane before they reached their honeymoon!" He looked at Ordell and cringed. "No harm meant, Ordell."

Ordell waved it off. It was common knowledge his father wasn't a people person. That might be why he invented Ordell in the first place, really.

"I suppose we've kept you long enough," Mr. Combs said, patting Ordell's shoulder. "Give your father my best wishes."

"Will do, Mr. Combs."

THE REST of the afternoon was filled with Ordell visiting shops and picking up parts for his father. By the time he got to the last errand, the sun was close to setting.

He took the longer way back home, and the smell of the fresh bread from the bakery filled his nose. Ordell had never tasted human food before, but there were many foods he loved the smell of. Mr. Stoke's baked bread had to be at the top of the list of his favorite smells.

Ordell walked in and purchased a small loaf of bread with the leftover money. Even if he couldn't enjoy it, he was sure his father would love it with the churned butter Mr. Harrison had brought over the other day.

Mr. Stokes brought out the loaf of bread and wrapped it up. He paused between folds to adjust his two wooden fingers and grunted out a sigh.

It was unfortunate how Mr. Stokes lost his first two fingers. From what Ordell had heard while eavesdropping, he lost them when he tried to save his little boy thirty years before. Unfortunately his fingers were not the only things he lost that day.

Not much was known about what happened to his wife. The townsfolk gossiped about it plenty enough, but Mr. Stokes never brought it up himself. Rumor was she hanged herself shortly after the accident. Other rumors said she ran off with a rich man, took on a new name, and started a new family.

Ordell, on the other hand, felt she succumbed to illness. It wasn't too far of a stretch, since there were quite a few townsfolk who'd become terribly ill and died shortly thereafter. It didn't make much of an interesting story, though, so the other rumors still lived on.

"Need anything else?" Mr. Stokes handed Ordell the small brown package. "I've just made a fresh batch of sweet rolls I think you'd love."

The smell of the sweet rolls filled Ordell's nostrils, and he couldn't help but take an extra sniff. It was almost cruel that his father gave him the ability to smell but not taste. He'd give anything to try one of Mr. Stokes's vanilla honey cakes; just looking at them in the display made him drool.

"Come on," Mr. Stokes said, "you can have the first one on me."

Ordell licked his lips and nodded. When Mr. Stokes smiled and gave him one of the sweet rolls, he immediately shoved it in his mouth.

He tasted nothing.

The texture was strange, and it made his insides gurgle when it finally slid down his throat. It felt soft and warm, but there was no taste to go along with it. Ordell knew the outcome of trying it, but each time he tasted food, he felt disappointed by not tasting what the humans did. Still, he smiled and pretended it was the most delicious thing he'd ever tasted.

"Would you like to add a few to your order?" Mr. Stokes asked.

"Sorry, maybe some other time. My father isn't one for sweets."

"Then I'd say he's missing out!"

"Thank you for the bread, Mr. Stokes. I must get going, though, before my father starts to worry."

"Come now, Ordell, you can stay a few more minutes. I'm sure he wouldn't mind you staying out a small bit later. Maybe I could teach you how to bake a cake or make bread of your own. That would be a fun way to spend the evening, wouldn't it?"

"I'm sorry, Mr. Stokes. Maybe some other time?" Ordell walked to the door, still keeping his patient smile. "I'll see you later."

"Wait, Ordell—"

"Bye, Mr. Stokes."

Ordell swung out the door and sighed in relief once he was out of the bakery. Mr. Stokes was a nice man, but a lonely one too. He had a habit of talking his customers into the ground about random topics and bakery techniques. Ordell typically enjoyed talking with him, and he felt guilty leaving the poor man behind, but it was already dark out.

Luckily the bakery wasn't too far from Octavio's shop, and Ordell managed to get home before the gas lamps were lit. It was a bit of a silly rule, but his father made him promise not to be out and about when the lights were on.

"I'm back with supper, Father," Ordell said as he walked inside. "I brought home some fresh bread I think you'll enjoy."

Octavio stumbled out of the shop and wiped his forehead with a rag. "Thank you, my boy. I could use some food right about now."

"Have you eaten anything today?" Ordell helped his father to the small table, uncertain if his father would be able to make it up the stairs and to the kitchen. "You're shaking."

"I need to get this project done for Mr. Saunders," he grumbled. "That bread smells delicious."

Ordell felt a twinge of pain in his chest. "You're still doing business with that man? Even after you know what he plans to do?"

"I have very few options, Ordell. Mr. Saunders is a very wealthy man, and I need the money. *We* need the money."

Ordell sat down next to his father. "We can find other ways to make money. There have to be other methods!"

He shook his head. "It's more complicated than that, Ordell."

"Anything must be better than taking this man's money," he whispered. "This shouldn't even be a possibility!"

"Sex bots are the wave of the future, Ordell. They've helped lower crime rates and have opened up a lot of new possibilities."

"For the humans."

"Yes, but these automatons are created to enjoy this. They aren't unhappy with this and love serving the humans. There's no reason to be upset."

"What about the automaton Ratliff wants?" Ordell asked, raising his voice. "He wants someone like *me*. He wants someone who will defy him and someone who will hate being his slave."

"It's just an automaton," his father said with a small chuckle. "It's not like we're taking a human to him."

"I'm an automaton," Ordell said bluntly.

"But you're different."

"How so?"

Octavio leaned forward and patted Ordell's leg. "Because you're my son."

"This is wrong." Ordell pushed Octavio's hand away and got up. "What you're doing is wrong!"

"I'm only selling my creations! We need the money! You shouldn't be selfish!"

"I'm the selfish one?" Ordell let out a small laugh. "I'm not the one creating sex slaves!"

"This isn't as cut-and-dried as you're making it out to be!" Octavio huffed out a sigh and rubbed his temples. "I don't have the time to talk to you about this, let alone argue! Either you accept it or toughen up. Those are your only options, Ordell."

Ordell rolled his eyes and left the shop, slamming the door shut harder than intended. It was better than spending another second with his father.

BLACKWICK LOOKED so different at night. Even up above the stairs, where Blackwick was nicer, sent small chills up Ordell's spine. Shadows formed into monsters, and the people out and about stared at him like they wanted to hurt him. Or worse.

The anxiety increased as Ordell took a step farther into the night. Everything felt so vast and isolated, yet suffocating. It was almost as if there were someone walking right behind him despite the empty streets around him. Every time Ordell looked over his shoulder, no one was there.

Just paranoia talking, of course. Still, he couldn't help but wonder if leaving on the cusp of nightfall was a good idea. Maybe he should've retired to his room instead. At least then he could watch the night from the safety of his bedroom window.

His stubbornness won out, though, and he pursued the streets, the misty air blowing against his skin. Fog clouded the way, and Ordell could only see the silhouettes of the shops up ahead.

As he walked he heard a few wolf whistles but couldn't see who made them; the fog was too thick for him to even make out the simplest features of his surroundings.

"Come on, sweetheart, let's have a little fun," a man's voice said, deep and rough. "A pretty thing such as yourself shouldn't be out this late at night."

Ordell wasn't even sure if this man was talking to him, but it was enough to make him speed up his pace. Whoever that man was, he was bound to cause some trouble.

Finally he reached the pier and sat down on the wooden bench. The lake itself wasn't all that thrilling—didn't even support that many fish, nor was it clean enough to see the fish that were there—but Ordell loved the smell of the wet seaweed and fresh dirt. If he squinted hard enough, he could see the outline of the boats out on the water.

The fishermen there didn't make much of a profit due to the limited supply of fish, but when they did catch something, the townsfolk went wild paying for the small batch. He'd thought about becoming a fisherman himself to help bring in money, but it was too quiet of a job and was away from people. Also it was too much of a gamble as to when he'd get a good haul or if he'd come home empty-handed.

Maybe if he offered to fish for food, Octavio would agree not to go through with making this terrible "product," and they could go back to making automatons for manual labor instead. Even if Ordell didn't agree with that either, it was better than what Ratliff had in mind.

Ordell sighed as he leaned against the railing. He couldn't avoid his father forever.

They hadn't had many disagreements in his lifetime, but his father knew how much Ordell cared for his siblings. He knew how difficult it was for Ordell to part with them after they were created. How could he expect Ordell to sit by as he offered his newest sibling, who was as human as Ordell, to this perverted and disgusting man? Clearly his father had gone mad if he truly believed that!

He looked back out to the lake, but the attempt to see anything was as futile as the first. There wasn't much he could do at the pier, and the shops were all closed.

The only option was to go back home or chat with that creepy man in the alleyway. Both were repulsive ideas, but home was the lesser evil, if he had to pick.

He sighed and made his way back.

ORDELL CAME back home and saw his father still sitting at the table. His eyes were red, and Ordell felt the guilt rise up for storming out earlier.

"Maybe we could talk about giving you taste buds," Octavio said with a sniff. "I know you've wanted to taste Mr. Stokes's cakes, and it shouldn't be too hard to implement."

Ordell sat down and grabbed his father's hand. "I'd love that, but it's not going to change my mind about what you're doing to my siblings."

"I know." He sighed. "That's why I'm not going through with it."

"You're not going to make him?"

Octavio shook his head. "I can't stand to see you this upset, Ordell. If you feel this strongly about this, then Ratliff can take his business elsewhere."

He jumped out of the chair and wrapped his arms around his father. "Thank you. This means the world to me, Father."

"We'll have to find other ways to get money in here, though. Our shop isn't going to survive with the way things are."

"I understand," Ordell said, still smiling wide. "I can get a second job, or I can help Mrs. Briggs with cleaning her house. She's been struggling with the stairs as of late, and I'm sure she'd be more than happy to have my help."

Or he could help out Mr. Stokes in the bakery. The poor man could use a bit of company, and Ordell would most likely get a discount on the bread there. Octavio was sure to enjoy getting fresh-baked bread for supper every night.

"You're such a good boy," Octavio said, cupping Ordell's face. "I'm so proud of you."

He pulled away and furrowed his brows. "Thank you."

"Just remember that I love you very much," he said. "No matter what happens."

CHAPTER 3

WEEKS PASSED by and each day was another struggle.

Ordell got a job at the bakery and did extra work for Mrs. Briggs. When he had free time, he helped his father with the shop and did errands when he could.

Despite his best efforts, the shop was gradually going under. No one wanted Ordell's siblings, not even when Octavio reluctantly cut the price. Each day fewer and fewer people came in. Each day the cash register slowly emptied.

Ordell brought home bread for Mrs. Briggs and for supper, but he could tell his father was becoming desperate.

He tried to comfort his father, but there wasn't much he could say. There were times his father would just sit in the shop and look at the pieces of metal. At first he'd jump up when he heard the bell ring, but it'd only be the postman with the mail. Now even the postman hardly came by unless it was to hand over the bills.

"I could try fishing," Ordell said one day.

"Just a waste of time," his father grumbled. "You won't catch anything."

Perhaps it was a waste of time, but Ordell tried it anyway. He made his own fishing rod and grabbed a few worms from the fresh soil near the lake. He then cast it over the pier and waited.

Not even a nibble.

He tried again on his breaks, after work, before work, before helping Mrs. Briggs, after helping Mrs. Briggs, during errands, and sometimes before going to bed.

Each time was the same. And each time, Ordell grew even more frustrated.

He still refused to give up, though. Not when he saw how much of a toll it took on Octavio to see the shop going under. Now Octavio didn't even bother making automatons.

"You should at least try to make something, Father," Ordell said one time after coming back from another failed attempt at fishing.

"Maybe you can make something new that will impress the people of Blackwick."

"It's no use." Octavio kicked at a gear. "No one wants this shit! No one cares about these stupid pieces of metal!"

"They're not stupid."

"Just go to work, Ordell," his father said. "Mr. Stokes will have better use for you."

During that workday his father's words swam around in Ordell's head. He knew Octavio only said them out of frustration, but it hurt to hear that come from him. To call his siblings stupid pieces of metal.

"You remind me so much of my son," Mr. Stokes said, icing one of the cakes. "Both of you went off in your own little world. He was such a sweet boy, but refused to stay in reality for more than five minutes." He chuckled and shook his head. "Drove my wife insane, he did! She wanted him to do this, and he was too busy skipping off to the pier."

"I would've loved to meet him," Ordell said with a small smile.

"Me too." His voice grew low. "I wish I could talk to him again. Hear those little rambles as he talked about that world of his." Mr. Stokes cleared his throat and looked back up at Ordell. "Why don't you take the rest of the day off? I'm sure your father would love to have some help around the shop."

"Are you sure, Mr. Stokes?"

He waved his hand. "It's been a slow day. You should enjoy the weather while it's still nice. Here." He put a few pieces of bread in a small brown package. "A little treat for you and your father."

Ordell patted Mr. Stokes's shoulder. "Thank you so much. Would you like me to help open up tomorrow?"

"Sounds like a plan."

Ordell gave him one last hug and left. The day was nice out, and Mrs. Briggs was tending her small garden.

"I have something for you," he said, opening the small package and taking out three rolls. "They're a little hot, so be careful."

"Thank you, boy," she said, taking the rolls. "Mr. Stokes's bread always makes my day."

"Do you need any help today?"

"I'm okay for now, unless you know how to get Mr. Lynch to stop playing that ruckus in the middle of the night. Back when I was your age, this town was silent and peaceful without all this noise." She waggled her finger at Ordell. "You know, I think there should be a ban on accordions! It'll make Blackwick a better place!"

"I'm sure it would be, Mrs. Briggs," he said, suppressing a smile.

Over the past week, he had listened to Mrs. Briggs talk about how Blackwick was when she was a little girl. Automatons were prominent and respected, not some piece of equipment. She talked enthusiastically about how every summer the giant automaton would be rolled down the streets for cleanup. She and her older brother would sit on top of the roof of their old house and watch in awe as this giant machine glided down the streets, still huge even with them being up so high.

Not much was known about what the giant automaton did. It was rumored to be made to help in wars, but as far as Ordell knew, it was never used. It had a humanlike head, but the rest of the automaton was too blocky to be a humanoid. From what Mrs. Briggs told him, the arms looked to have guns attached to it, which made Ordell think that it was meant to be a weapon of mass destruction.

Just hearing her stories made Blackwick sound like this magical place back then. Whether it was really as extravagant as she said or not, he couldn't tell. All he knew was he enjoyed hearing about this alternative place where automatons were treated as well as the humans and the humans even enjoyed their company.

Which tempted him to tell Mrs. Briggs the truth about himself.

There were times it almost felt like she knew. Other times she'd bring up the automatons and give Ordell this look, like she knew he was one of them.

And she was okay with it.

"You should get on home to that father of yours before he starts yelling up a storm," she said. "Last time he threw a tantrum, he startled my poor cat."

"Will do, Mrs. Briggs."

When Ordell got to the shop, he could feel the heavy tension around the room.

"I brought home some rolls," he called out. "They're freshly baked."

Ordell took a few more steps until he reached the door to Octavio's shop. He took a deep breath and turned the doorknob.

"Father! What happened in here?"

Papers were scattered around the shop, blueprints torn and metal tossed around. Ordell found his father hunched over the workstation with his beefy fingers threaded through his peppered hair.

He raced over to his father and grabbed his shoulders. "Father! Are you all right? What happened?"

"I can't find the damn blueprints! That bitch must have them!"

"What blueprints?"

"The ones for the—" Octavio sighed and pushed his hands through his hair again. "Forget it. I don't need another argument with you."

"You said you wouldn't!" Ordell narrowed his eyes. "I can take on another job! I can—"

"I need the money, Ordell!" he snapped. "The shop needs this! How can you not understand this?"

"You said you wouldn't do this," Ordell said again, punctuating his words slowly. "You promised."

"I won't be bullied by my own creation!"

"Now I'm just your creation?" He swallowed hard. "I thought I was your son."

"Ordell—"

"Just forget it." He took a step back. "Do what you want. They're your creations, right? Don't let me stop you from earning a quick profit." He turned on his heel and stormed out of the shop.

THE WALK down to the pier cleared Ordell's mind. By the time he reached the bench, his good mood had come back enough for him to enjoy the smell of the lake.

Fishermen were out on their boats, and Ordell wished he had his pole so he could see if he could get a small bite.

What's the use?

It wasn't like him bringing home a fish would help change Octavio's mind. He made it clear he didn't think much of Ordell or his siblings. Just his creations. Just some stupid gears and pieces of metal.

The anger rose through Ordell. Even if Octavio had said those words in a bout of anger, there was some truth behind them. Maybe Octavio should just sell Ordell off to that pervert instead. At least then Ordell could kill the bastard and get out of there. Start a new life somewhere else where automatons were still respected.

Maybe he could go to Mrs. Briggs for help. Confess to being an automaton and get it out in the air. She could help him make sure his father didn't create this… sex bot. Or maybe when Octavio finished creating his latest sibling, they could go in and steal it before Ratliff came to collect it. Ordell had always wanted a little brother who was as sentient as he was. Maybe he could teach him how to survive and mingle with the humans.

A small smile crept across Ordell's face. Each new plan of his sent a spark of adrenaline through his body. He'd destroy the blueprints so Octavio couldn't make another automaton for Ratliff.

Mrs. Briggs would be asleep by then, but once he explained everything, he knew she would more than understand why he woke her up. Maybe even be happy Ordell had finally come clean about everything and trusted her enough to help him.

He left the pier and ran through the dark streets. The steps leading down were in his view; he could even smell the flowers from Mrs. Briggs's windowsill.

Before he could make it past the first step, he tumbled over something and landed flat on his face.

Not something. Someone.

He heard the poor lady groan, and Ordell immediately got up and helped her. It was just like him to run over a poor elderly lady.

"Are you all right?" Ordell asked, helping her up. "Do I need to take you to the doctor?"

"I'm fine, I'm fine." She used his shoulder as leverage as she got to her feet. "Just a little shock to the system, is all."

"Are you sure? Let me at least walk you home—"

"I said I'm fine." She brushed away the stray white hairs that fell out of her bun. "Just because I'm old doesn't mean I'm useless, boy!"

Ordell took a step back so he wasn't hovering over her. "Sorry, I just feel awful about trampling over you like that."

"You're fine." She coughed and then looked up at Ordell, her beady eyes widening. "I never thought I'd see you again." Her tiny brass glasses slipped down her long nose as a smile grew across her face. "You're better than I imagined!"

"Excuse me?"

She grabbed Ordell's hands. "Much prettier than I designed, but I wouldn't put it past Octavio to design you for *those* purposes." Another blink. "I thought he sold you off to Goldcrest. Just to see you here... walking around just like us."

"Do I know you?"

"Of course, my boy," she said as her eyes lit up. "I'm the one who created you."

WINIFRED GRIFFITH, inventor who turned to the stage after automatons slowly grew out of style in Blackwick. Now retired and living in the same house for decades.

Ordell thought he knew everyone in his little town, but apparently he'd missed one.

All his life Ordell had thought his father had created him from scratch. It seemed plausible, and his father shared so many stories of how much effort it took to create Ordell. To hear someone else had created him first was.... Well, Ordell wasn't too sure of what to make of that.

"Make yourself at home," Winifred said when they reached her small, broken-down home. "Don't mind the mess. I don't get many visitors these days."

He couldn't believe all the little gadgets she had made over the years. Her house was filled to the brim with automatons Octavio could only dream of creating.

"You created all of these?" Ordell asked as he wound up a small music box. "Wow."

"I even wrote that melody," she said. "Was a small trinket I planned to give to my father before he passed away."

"All these are amazing! My father would be jealous to see all these inventions!"

"He was," she said, sitting down on the old floral armchair. "I was the one who made automatons popular forty years ago. Amazing how time flies by."

"What got you into creating us?"

"I wanted to create a subrace." Winifred coughed again. "Automatons who were so human that they could coexist with the humans and no one could even tell the difference. One of my most ambitious projects, but I knew if anyone could do it, it'd be me."

Ordell picked up one of the pictures. "You were friends with my father?"

"Octavio and I were the closest of friends," she said. "He was the only one I could trust with this project. The plan was to make an automaton so humanlike it could help the human race with diseases." Winifred got up from her chair and went over to the wall safe. She opened it and pulled out a roll of blueprints. "You were created from our prototype."

Ordell looked down at the blueprints. The design was too complicated for him to understand, but he understood a few of the notes. "You and my father created me?"

"When we brought to light what our plans were, it came with great praise. At the time humans wanted to coexist with automatons." She lowered her eyes and rolled the blueprints back up. "Unfortunately it didn't last. The humans slowly grew to wanting automatons as slaves, not friends. I had no choice but to abandon the project."

"Then why am I here?"

"You were already in progress by the time I left. In fact, you were so close to being finished that, with only a few tinkers, you would've been good to go." Winifred patted his shoulder. "Octavio grew interested in the sex bot craze in Goldcrest and took you for himself. Honestly I don't know why he didn't sell you. I truly thought he did." She smiled then. "I'm glad to see that your human implements I made are still in place, though."

"So I was meant to be a sex bot." Ordell's throat closed in. "And to think he spent the last ten years calling me his son."

"It's possible he had a change of heart, Ordell," she said. "He's not an evil man. Just a misguided one."

"You don't expect me to forgive him for this, do you?" He took a deep breath when he realized he'd raised his voice. "How can you forgive him for stealing your creation? For stealing me?"

"I don't, but I also didn't spend the last ten years seeing him as my father." Winifred walked back to her armchair and plopped down. "You have, Ordell. That is part of what makes you human. You don't see him as your master or creator, but as a part of your family. Don't ever lose that."

"But anger also makes me human," he said. "So does the option to not forgive someone for betraying you."

"I've known Octavio for a long time. He's done so many things to hurt me, but there is a good chance that he might've changed. He never sold you, which speaks volumes to me."

"He might be back to his old habits," Ordell said with a sniff. "There's this man who came over to the shop. Ratliff Saunders. He wanted my father to make a sex bot who was just like me. He wants the automaton so humanlike for God knows what!"

"Ratliff," she said, sneering at the name. "Yes, I know of him. He's the man who got the idea for these sex bots in the first place. I do not like to curse a person's name, but if he were to die terribly, I wouldn't mind."

"My father agreed to do business with him."

"Octavio must be out of his mind! He knows what this man is capable of! Knows his opinion on automatons. He's a dangerous man, Ordell. You must stay away from him at all costs."

"My father wouldn't let anything happen to me," Ordell said. "He plans to create another automaton as human as I am to sell to Ratliff. I've tried to talk him out of it, but he won't listen to me."

"Ordell," she said with a small sigh, "your father can't create another version of you."

"Why not?"

"I'm the one who gave you the human qualities. Your father just made the exterior." She rubbed her temples. "There is only my version of the blueprints. Even if Octavio somehow got a hold of them, I doubt he'd be able to make heads or tails of it."

"What should I do?"

"Run. Run before your father does something even he'll regret."

Ordell chewed on his lower lip. "I need to at least pack."

"Fine, but you need to leave before morning. I don't know how desperate Octavio is, but I don't trust him."

He nodded and left, unsure if he should heed Winifred's advice.

Octavio had done many things to upset him, but he was still Ordell's father. Had been his father for ten years now.

He could stay with Mrs. Briggs for a little while until things cooled down. She'd more than likely enjoy the company.

Ordell reached for the key and opened the front door of the shop. The moment he stepped inside, his eyes widened.

Ratliff was there, talking to Octavio. No laughter this time around. No, by the look in his father's eyes, Ordell knew he'd made a huge mistake coming back home.

Chapter 4

"WHAT A coincidence that you showed up now!" Ratliff lifted his cane and a wide grin spread across his face. "We were just talking about you."

Ordell felt the color leave his face. "About what?"

Two armed men in strange uniforms came out from behind Ratliff and Octavio. When Ordell turned to run out the door, two more blocked the front entrance. Ordell's eyes then focused on these figures and their guns.

The men—were they men?—were covered head to toe in crimson, save for the black gloves gripping their steam-powered rifles and large, round globular helmets, almost alien in appearance. At first Ordell thought they might have been automatons, but the glass of the helmets was opaque, so there was no way to be certain.

"Father," Ordell said, almost whimpering, "what's going on?"

"I'm sorry, Ordell." He didn't even look at Ordell, just the worn-out wood flooring. "I need the money."

His eyes widened as he took another step back. "You sold me? To him?"

"The boy has a bit of a tongue on him," Ratliff said between chuckles. "I'll make sure to change that very soon."

"I'm sorry," Octavio said again. "I didn't have any other options."

No time to refute that; the armed men moved closer toward Ordell, and he had to think fast, or else he'd....

Well, he didn't want to think about what Ratliff planned to do once he got his slimy hands on him.

"Is there a way to deactivate him?" Ratliff asked. "It'll make travel easier. Don't want to deal with taking him to Goldcrest with him fighting me every moment."

"No," Octavio said, "there's no way to deactivate him. He's... he's as human as you and me."

"Maybe your next creation should have an off switch."

"I thought this is what you wanted," he snapped. "I'm giving you my own son, and that still isn't good enough?"

"I'm not your son," Ordell said.

"Might cut out that damn tongue of his," Ratliff said with a small huff. "Maybe then he'd learn to mind his manners. I don't have time to listen to some *brat*."

"He's here now," Octavio said, rubbing his temples, "so where's the money?"

Ratliff handed him an envelope, and Octavio cut it open with his letter opener. His eyes narrowed and he frowned. "This isn't the price we set on! I can sell Ordell for much more than this."

"I'm not paying full price for such a reckless boy!" Ratliff then shrugged. "Either take the money or go bankrupt. I don't see many options for you, Rutledge."

At first Ordell thought Octavio had a change of heart. Maybe he realized his mistake and was going to kick Ratliff out of his shop once and for all.

"Fine."

That one word was the most painful thing Ordell had ever experienced. Not just that word, but the fact his own father looked him in the eye and agreed to sell him to this monster!

Ordell opened his mouth to say something—anything. Maybe curse his father's name or ask why he could even possibly agree to this. Even pleading would've been an option right then.

But nothing came out.

"You won't regret this, Rutledge." Ratliff then glared at Ordell. "Let's just hope I don't regret this purchase."

"You won't!" Octavio cleared his throat. "I know he's a bit fresh right now, but he's a pliant boy, you'll see. Very eager."

"Better be," Ratliff said. "Get him packed up, boys."

The four guards closed in on Ordell, and he ducked around them, running to the stairs. He grabbed the broom and shut the door behind him, wedging the broom within the doorframe.

Ordell made his way to his windowsill and broke the glass with his elbow. He crawled out and onto the roof, almost slipping on the damp leaves that blanketed the top of the shop. He went from the roof to the other side of the shop, Ratliff's yelling heard clear as day. He jumped from the roof to the bins between the buildings, and onto the streets.

He ran as fast as he could, the sound of his feet hitting the puddles on the cobblestone street overshadowing the echo of Ratliff's yells.

The only place that felt safe now was Winifred's.

ORDELL DIDN'T even bother knocking on the door, just walked right on in.

Before he could even call out Winifred's name, he felt something heavy hit the back of his head and he collapsed down to his knees.

"Ordell?" She lowered the cast-iron skillet slowly. "My heavens, boy! You gave me quite the fright! Don't you know better than to waltz right into an old lady's home? It'll be the death of you!"

"Sorry, Winifred," Ordell groaned out and rubbed the back of his head. "I guess I had other things on my mind."

"That doesn't excuse poor manners, boy! If you want my help, you must knock first."

Ordell got up and knocked on the doorframe. "May I come in?"

"Ordell? Is that you?" She gave him a small hug. "Nice to see you again, my boy. Now what is it that you need?"

"Octavio completely lost his mind!" Ordell stammered out. "He sold me!"

"I told you," she said. "Did you at least get everything you need?"

"No, Ratliff was already there. He had these guards—and I had to get out of there! He just stood there while Ratliff said those things about me! He looked at me and agreed to sell me!"

"If I know Ratliff as well as I remember, then he's not going to give up just because you wandered off. The man has an ego so big it could fit an entire village! He no doubt sees this as you testing him."

"I don't want that man's grimy hands anywhere near me!" Ordell pushed his thin fingers through his hair. "I can't believe he sold me. He actually sold me! I'm his son! I've been there for him for ten years! Ten goddamn years! And this is how he treats me? Like some *thing*?"

Winifred walked over and squeezed his shoulder. "You are much more than just a thing, Ordell. You are as much of a person as I am."

Ordell lifted his hand and wiped away the stray tears. "Sorry."

"No need to be sorry," she said with a small chuckle. "Crying is all part of being a human."

He couldn't help but smile at that. "Thanks, Winifred."

"Now we need to get you a change of clothes." She patted his back. "It'll make it a little harder for them to recognize you at first. If you go upstairs, you'll see a chest. It's filled with some clothes and maybe a mouse or two. I doubt they bite, though."

Ordell walked up the creaky stairs and found the chest off in the corner. He was a little hesitant to open it at first; mice were one of the things that frightened him. Finally he took a deep breath and opened the chest.

There he found a ruffled white button-down shirt and a nice pair of dark brown fall-front trousers. He quickly slipped into them and the light brown duster underneath them. He went to grab the boots, but a mouse scurried by and he jumped back.

Ordell grabbed one of the pillows and trapped the mouse in the corner of the chest, grabbing the boots in one fell swoop.

"Took you long enough," Winifred said when he came back downstairs in his new attire. "Those look absolutely lovely on you. Much better on you than on me."

"You used to wear these?" Ordell asked with a small grin. "For what?"

"For this play I did a while back," she said. "Had to dress up as this airship pirate. The man who was originally meant to play the part broke his leg, so they naturally had me fill in."

"They couldn't find another man to play the part?"

She slapped him upside the head. "I'll have you know that the play was a big hit! I played the part flawlessly!"

"Okay, okay," he said with a giggle. "Sorry."

"You're darn right you are," she muttered. "Now we need to talk about where you're going to go. You can't stay here in Blackwick."

"Couldn't I just live with you?"

She shook her head. "Too dangerous. No, you need to go somewhere that treats automatons as equals. Where you don't need to hide who you are."

"Is there a place like that, though?" Ordell asked. "I thought everyone treated automatons the same way."

"There is one place different than the others." She walked over to the dark-wood dresser and opened one of the drawers. Winifred pulled out a map and tossed it down on the table next to Ordell. "Linnesse is a safe haven for automatons and for humans who support the coexistence of humans and automatons. A revolution has been created to help give rights to automatons. Not all of them, of course, but the ones who are like you."

"Wow." Ordell traced a path on the map with his finger. "I didn't even know something like the revolution existed."

"At first it didn't," she said. "Automatons were just creations and the rights belonged to the creator. It wasn't until the automatons became more complex and human that things began to get complicated. There were times I wondered if I was doing the right thing. Maybe we're taking it too far in giving rights to automatons." She then looked up at Ordell. "Then I see you. I see how you're no different than me, and I think, 'Yes, this is the right thing.' Maybe it isn't, but it's what feels right to me and to us."

"And Linnesse will keep me safe?" Ordell asked. "I can be myself there?"

"Absolutely. There's no better or safer place I can think of."

"I don't know how to get there, though," he said. "Even with the map. I've never traveled outside of Blackwick before."

"I suppose that would be a bit of an issue."

"Come with me," he said. "You can create automatons again, and the revolution will benefit with having you there. We could start a new life there."

She shook her head. "No, my boy, my life is here. I was born here, and I plan to die here. There's not much juice in these bones of mine to get back to creating automatons again."

"I don't want to do this alone," he said. "Please?"

"I can't leave here, Ordell." She then sighed. "But I can get you a travel partner."

WINIFRED HANDED Ordell the gas lamp as they made their way down to the cellar. Ordell swatted at the cobwebs strung from the ceiling as he walked down the steps.

"I began working on Project Elias a few years after we started you," Winifred said, seemingly not minding the stray webs. "Octavio never knew about this, and I had no intentions of telling him."

"Why not?" Ordell swatted at another web. "I thought you two were close."

"Even back then my gut told me not to trust him," she said. "I didn't listen to that gut when we made you, but I did when I started working on Elias."

"So you've made him completely from scratch?"

"Almost," she said. "Elias has acted as a son to me, helping me get through the challenging tasks of the day and keeping me company. I never let him travel outside because I was scared."

"Scared?"

"He's as human as you, but there is still that mother's fear of someone finding out the truth. If he were to be taken away from me like you were, I don't know how I'd be able to cope with it. He is twenty-six years old, but someone is bound to notice him not aging if I let him travel around."

"Why didn't you make him older, then?"

She shrugged. "I didn't have many options when it came to the age. I chose what I thought was best."

They made their way down to the cellar, Ordell almost falling over the last step.

"The place is beginning to fall apart, I'm afraid," Winifred said. "It'll do Elias good to get away from this rickety old shack."

Winifred walked down to the end of the hall and opened the wooden door. Ordell followed closely behind as she took the lantern.

"Elias? Are you awake?" She placed the lantern on the table and walked over toward the small bed.

The light from the lantern highlighted Elias's short dark hair and square chin. He looked to be slightly taller than Ordell, with broader shoulders. His skin was light, with a slight tan to it—something Ordell felt a twinge of envy for.

Elias then tossed to his side and brought the pillow closer. He let out a sleepy groan and moved the pillow over his head.

"Wake up, Elias," Winifred said in a harsher tone. "I swear you're the laziest butt I've created!" She smacked his bare shoulder. "Get up, you! We've got company!"

The man yawned and pried himself up off the bed. Wild strands of his hair were all over the place. He stretched out his arms, and Ordell caught a glimpse of his toned muscles.

"I'd tell you he's never this lazy," Winifred said to Ordell, "but I'd be lying to you. We might have to get the cold water."

"I'm up," Elias said through another yawn. "You said I could sleep in today, remember?"

"Change of plans." Winifred went to grab the blankets, but Elias tugged them back, his dark brown eyes widening.

"Ma, I'm naked! I'm not about to give a show to a random stranger!"

"Get dressed and come upstairs when you're done."

Ordell followed Winifred upstairs and waited for his new travel partner. Both of them waited in awkward silence at first, but Ordell then spoke up.

"He seems like a nice guy." Ordell cleared his throat. "Very human."

"Very lazy," she said. "And a brat. If I weren't his mother, I'd never put up with him!"

"Are you going to be okay without him here?"

"This will be good for him too," Winifred said. "He can't stay in that cellar forever. It's as cruel as giving him to Ratliff."

"And he knows how to get to Linnesse? I mean, he hasn't even been out in Blackwick."

She waved her hand. "He's been programmed to know how to get there. I never got to program it inside you due to what happened, but Elias knows the way. Don't you worry, Ordell; he may be lazy, but he's also reliable."

"I'm surprised you completed him," Ordell said. "Are you sure he's an automaton?"

"He better be," Winifred said. "I'd get arrested if I were tinkering with an actual human! I didn't intend to complete him, but I did somehow."

"What are we supposed to do once we get to Linnesse?" Ordell asked. "Do you want us to join the revolution? Are we just supposed to live our lives? Will Elias come back to Blackwick?"

"You two will figure that out once you get there," she said. "I only programmed him to get to Linnesse, not dictate how his life should be."

Elias came up the stairs with a glint in those dark brown eyes. "So who's ready to go on an adventure?"

CHAPTER 5

BLACKWICK FELT grimmer than usual.

Ordell had walked up those shallow steps many times, but this time it felt like the hardest feat. Almost like someone had poured cement in his legs before he woke up that morning.

In an hour he was supposed to be at the bakery to help Mr. Stokes open shop, spend half the day there helping with customers and listening to Mr. Stokes go on about what life was like when he was just a young lad.

"Back in those days," he said once, "we were allowed to go anywhere we pleased without our parents becoming worried. They didn't bat an eye when we came home with scraped knees or broken bones. Children today are too pampered for their own good."

After listening to Mr. Stokes prattle on, he would be free to go and help Mrs. Briggs out around her house. To his surprise he began to see less of a cranky lady and more of a lady who wanted the world to be like she remembered it.

Now it was something he wasn't going to experience again. No more listening to Mr. Stokes's stories. No more listening to Mrs. Briggs rant about the modern world. He wouldn't be seeing the pier again or the fishermen struggling to catch one nibble.

He wouldn't see his father again.

At Winifred's it was easy to discuss going to Linnesse with this stranger (albeit an attractive one) and to have this grand adventure. Now that he was at the border of Blackwick, following closely behind Elias, it felt more like a struggle.

Not that Elias was bad company, just not someone Ordell was used to. Hell, he didn't know this man existed a week ago!

Elias would stop along the way and look at the flowers or chase a bird. An odd thing to see a grown man do, Ordell thought to himself.

The moment they stepped outside Blackwick, Ordell caught Elias lying in the grass and staring up at the clouds.

Another distraction.

First it was the flowers, then the grass, then the birds, then a rock, of all things! Now he was impressed by the damn sky! The day wasn't even that cloudy. With each distraction Ordell felt his patience grow thin.

"We can't keep stopping," Ordell said. "It'll take us years to get to Linnesse at this rate!"

"Relax a little," Elias said. "We can take a few detours along the way."

"Detours? You're going on a whole different path!"

"We're still on the right path, little Ody, just at a slow and steady pace."

"Did you just call me 'Ody'?"

Elias plucked a piece of grass and chewed on it. "It's such a nice day out. Come and bask in the sun with me."

"We can bask in the sun once we reach Linnesse," Ordell grumbled. "There will be plenty of nice days there."

"No need to hurry," he said, closing his eyes. "Linnesse will still be there when we reach it."

"Not if we keep going the pace you're going!"

Elias opened his eyes and then propped himself up on his elbows. "You have quite the temper. I hope this isn't something common with you."

"Humans get angry."

"But you're not human."

"I'm as human as they come," Ordell said bluntly. "You won't find another automaton with accurate human qualities such as mine."

"Except for me, of course."

"Except for you?"

"Correct."

Ordell rolled his eyes and huffed out a laugh. Such an intolerable man! He would've done better to just travel to Linnesse alone! "That isn't possible."

"With me Winifred wanted to make an improvement on your design. There is no need to feel offended. We're here to help the humans. That's all that matters, is it not?"

"I doubt you are just an improvement on me," Ordell said with a sniff. "Are you able to feel emotions properly? Do you know how to feel anger? Love? Happiness?"

"Yes to all those."

"Pleasure?"

"Absolutely."

"Can you get…." Ordell stopped and his face heated.

"Yes," Elias said with a laugh. "I can get an erection."

"That wasn't what I was about to say!" The heat grew to his ears and knots formed in the pit of his stomach. "I would never ask anything so inappropriate!"

"Then why are you blushing?"

"I'm not!"

"You are," Elias said, "and you're shouting."

"I'm angry! You made me angry!"

Elias cocked his head to the side, which only added to the churning in Ordell's stomach. "How did I make you angry?"

"If you're more human than me, then why don't you figure it out?"

"Winfred didn't make me a mind reader, Ody."

"Stop calling me that!"

"Would Ory be better?"

"No!" Ordell pushed his hands through his hair. "Just call me by my first name. I don't want a nickname or a pet name."

"All right." Elias rose up to his feet, then walked over to Ordell. "I will only call you by your first name." He smiled and pushed his fingers through Ordell's coppery hair. "If that's what makes you happy." By the time Ordell closed his eyes, the fingers were gone and Elias had walked away. "We better get a move on. We're wasting sunlight."

IT HAD been hours since they departed, and Ordell was ready to get to their next destination with no more distractions. Elias, however, was still a ball of energy. He would whistle along with the birds or make random chitchat over how pretty the trees looked.

And Ordell was close to losing it.

He wasn't sure how Elias was programmed, but Ordell only had about five days before he began to slow down. He could go up to two weeks without powering down automatically, but doing so would make his insides heat up. Elias causing them to get sidetracked only felt like wasted energy.

"I'd love to see the snow," Elias said. "Winnie told me all about it and how people would make these snow angels. Have you ever made a snow angel?"

"No," Ordell grunted out, rubbing his back.

"One place I've always wanted to visit is the mountains. Maybe we could go together someday. Climb the largest mountain and then slide all the way back down. I've heard sledding is a common hobby in the snow."

"Maybe we should focus more on getting to our destination before we lose our energy," Ordell said as he rested against one of the trees. "I'd like to keep powering down to a limit if we can."

Elias furrowed his brows. "What's the hurry? If you need to rest, I can keep a lookout. Perhaps even carry you while you sleep soundly in my arms."

"You might have to. Being around you is exhausting."

"It's not much longer, I promise."

"Where are we going?" Ordell asked. "We can't be close to Linnesse already."

"Silverfield."

Ordell's eyes widened. "Why are we going there?"

"There's this man Winnie's good friends with," Elias said. "He can help us out."

THE FIRST things Ordell saw when entering Silverfield were the tall buildings.

The evening sky was lit up by the lights and smoke that crept toward the large white mountains in the distance. Light rain drizzled on the buildings and dark roads as people walked down the streets, protecting themselves with umbrellas and briefcases.

Ordell's eyes widened when he saw the motorized carriages zoom down the roads, splashing the cold rainwater onto the sidewalks.

He jumped when the loud ring from the large clock tower echoed through the busy streets. The people seemed to pay no mind to it, but Ordell felt the urge to get closer to the tower.

There were many people in Blackwick who had small clocks, including Octavio, but none as massive as this one. In fact, it was about tall as three of Blackwick's homes placed on top of one another.

"Ordell!"

He blocked out Elias's shouts and walked over to the tower. He ᵈ out and touched the cool marble and brick.

fore he could even consider climbing the tower, Elias grabbed 'ers and spun him around.

"You can't wander off like this!" he said. "You don't know this area!"

Ordell frowned. "You're scolding me?"

Elias blinked. "No, I didn't mean it like that. I just don't want us to get separated."

"Just remember that I'm technically older than you." Ordell tried to keep a straight face but a small smile slipped out. "I should be the one getting on you for not keeping up with me."

"I suppose I should work on my stamina, then."

Ordell held his smile a little bit longer and then pushed away from the clock tower. "I can't believe how big this place is."

"The best inventors moved here from Blackwick," Elias said. "After the plague hit there, the healthy humans didn't want to risk staying around. That's probably why Blackwick is slowly dying."

"What plague?"

"You don't know about the plague?" Elias laughed. "That's why we were created, Ody—Ordell."

"I don't know anything about it."

"The plague hit forty years ago." Elias leaned against the clock tower and pushed up his sleeves before crossing his arms. "Winnie wanted to make something that would help detect and cure the plague. Her idea was to make automatons who did more than just one or two tasks."

"She wanted to make an automaton as close to a human as possible."

Elias nodded. "There is a slight odor to those who have the plague that only we can sniff out. We're programmed to be able to find the source of the plague and help stop it before it grows and infects other people."

"And to cure those who have the plague, right?"

Elias cleared his throat. "Anyway, Project Ordell—that's you, by the way—was in full swing when the plague hit Blackwick. You were to be as human as possible so you did not cause alarm to the humans who had it, and then you were to terminate the plague."

"Then why did things turn out the way they did?"

"There was some controversy about how to handle the plague," Elias said. "Many didn't want to accept us, and Winnie grew frustrated trying to convince people that this was the right method of handling the situation. I was meant to be an alternative method for handling the rioters, but fortunately that wasn't needed."

Ordell looked at Elias and gulped. The man didn't seem like a violent type, but maybe it was possible.

"Oh, don't worry, I never hurt anyone," he said as if he had read Ordell's mind. "Besides, by the time I was in action, you were gone and the plague was taken care of."

"That's good, then. I mean with the plague being gone—but it's good that you haven't hurt anyone either."

"Well, I wouldn't say that the plague is gone, just covered up."

"What do you mean?"

"Ratliff made this 'cure' as the answer to the plague. It's how he got so prosperous in the first place, and no doubt the only reason he made the damn thing in the first place. The problem with his medicine in a perfume bottle, though, is that it doesn't last long. Since he has a monopoly, he gets to keep selling the junk unless we come in and take care of the plague once and for all."

"Then he goes out of business," Ordell said.

"Which isn't exactly a bad thing, now is it?"

They continued onward in silence.

"ARE YOU sure he will be of any help?" Ordell asked when they reached the house. "I think we can figure out how to get to Linnesse ourselves."

"Is that your way of saying you want to be alone with me?"

"Ring the damn bell," Ordell said, narrowing his eyes.

Elias chuckled and then rang the bell. Moments later the door opened, and there stood a petite man with wild white hair.

"Buford Moore?" Elias extended his hand. "I'm Elias Griffith, and this is Ordell Rutledge. Winifred sent us."

Buford pulled his goggles down past his bushy brows. "So she finished you two, did she?" A smile crept across his thin lips. "I was a bit worried that you boys wouldn't see the light of day!" He shook both their hands and stepped aside. "Come in, come in! How is sweet Winnie these days?"

"Doing well," Elias said as he stepped inside. "A bit tired, but has enough energy to hit me upside the head."

"I'm sure you deserved it," Ordell said with a smile, and Elias nudged him.

"I can't remember the last time I spoke to her," Buford said. "She became a recluse once those original blueprints were stolen."

"What blueprints?" Ordell and Elias asked at the same time.

"The ones long before Project Ordell took place," he said. "Would you like some tea? Maybe a sweet roll?"

"There are other blueprints?" Ordell asked as he sat down. "She never said anything about that."

"It was tough on her," Buford said. "At first we thought she simply lost them, then those… love bots started popping up, and they looked so similar to her design. Ratliff plastered his label all over them, but to this day, we don't know how he got her design."

"No doubt my father," Ordell said with a small huff.

"Octavio didn't know about these. At the time only Winnie and I knew these existed. Granted, we didn't plan to have these automatons do much except manual labor. Nothing of what Ratliff ultimately made them for. We'd never do something like that."

"Maybe Ratliff didn't steal them," Ordell said. "My father creates automatons for manual labor all the time, and I've heard of many others doing the same. It isn't as complex as creating something like us."

"Maybe you're right, but Winnie insists that it's her design," Buford said. "And if she believes that he stole her design, then I believe it too."

Ordell nodded, but he still had his suspicions. He had watched Octavio design his blueprints for the manual automatons, and it wasn't too far-fetched that someone had a similar idea as Winifred and sold the design to Ratliff. Hell, even Ratliff could make the bots with his own two hands if he had a simple enough design.

Not that he wanted to defend that waste of life, but he wasn't going to blame the man for something he might be innocent of.

"Just to think he turned those poor automatons into slaves," Buford said. "Should be illegal, you know. I don't care if he created them with his own bare hands, he shouldn't do this to them!"

"How sentient are they?" Ordell asked.

"Does that even matter?" Buford glared down at Ordell. "If you want to defend this *rat*, then get out!"

"That isn't what Ordell means," Elias said. "He's just curious and likes to ask nonsensical questions. Trust me, I've spent hours listening to those question that lead nowhere."

Ordell made a note to self to punch Elias in the arm once they were alone, but for now, he appreciated the save.

"Well, I'm not too sure," Buford said. "They act more like brainwash victims than actual humans. Make what you will of that."

"Is there a way we can save them?" Elias asked. "Maybe we could take them to Linnesse and have the revolution reprogram them. Maybe even Winnie would—"

"I doubt she'd do it," Ordell said. "She seems to have retired from the automaton business."

"But the revolution would most certainly help!" Buford clapped his hands together. "However, getting there isn't easy. Linnesse is a difficult place to get access to."

"There has to be something we can do," Elias said. "Maybe if they see that we're automatons, they'll let us in."

"That used to be the case, but not anymore." Buford pushed his goggles back up on top of his head and grabbed a map. "We'll have to get passes in Goldcrest."

"Goldcrest?" Elias furrowed his brows. "Why there?"

"There's a small Black Market there that will make passes for those who are automatons."

"So we're getting illegal passes, then." Ordell frowned. "And if we get caught?"

"Don't worry," Buford said, "I trust this person with my life! Now you two should get some rest. I need to prepare the ship before we head on out."

Ordell headed up to the small guest room. There was a bed off in the corner of the room, and he debated whether he should sleep on the floor or take the bed for himself. Perhaps he could bypass resting since he still had enough energy to run smoothly for a few more days. However, it'd be best to reset his stamina and gears while they waited for the next day. Eventually he grabbed a blanket and pillow and made his bed down on the worn-out wooden floor.

"You can take the bed if you'd like," Elias said. "I don't mind."

"Go ahead and take it," Ordell said, turning his back.

"We could share."

"Good *night*, Elias," he ground out.

Maybe having one extra guest on their journey wasn't such a bad idea after all.

CHAPTER 6

ORDELL WOKE to the chimes of the clock tower.

He groaned and rolled out of his warm nest of blankets. He rubbed his eyes and blinked against the bright sunlight. He felt recharged but still a little stiff.

He rubbed his eyes again and looked up at the bed.

Elias was gone.

Probably went out to smell more flowers, Ordell mused to himself. Well, at least now he'd have some time to explore Silverfield.

He got dressed and headed downstairs, where he saw Buford cooking sausage and eggs.

"Morning, my boy," Buford said as he poked at one of the eggs. "Care for some breakfast?"

"No, thank you, Mr. Moore." Ordell sat down on the third to last step and pulled on his boots. "Plan to check out Silverfield a little more before we have to head out. This place is amazing."

"It loses its charm after you've lived here for a while," he said. "Personally I can't wait to get out of this place and have a change of scenery. You can only look at those mountains for so long before you want them gone."

"Why don't you move? Maybe back to Blackwick. I'm sure we could use your skills there."

"Blackwick's behind me, my boy. I suppose I could move, but I've been here for so long that it feels… odd to just leave." He turned around and smiled so wide that Ordell could see his stained teeth. "Of course, I couldn't pass up an opportunity to go to Linnesse. It's not an everyday opportunity, you know."

"What do you plan to do once you get there?"

He shrugged. "Haven't figured it out. I could continue my work there, or I could retire. I'd hate to give up on the automatons, but my age is beginning to catch up with me. Of course, I'd be more than happy to share all my information with the revolution. Perhaps they could put that to some good use."

"What is the revolution, exactly?" Ordell stood up and straightened out his jacket. "I know they help the automatons, but what do they do? Are they inventors?"

"There are many jobs there. Even jobs for you, Ordell. There are inventors, researchers, scientists... you name it. The opportunities are endless."

"Sounds rather ambitious."

"Which is why you and Elias will be great assets." Buford chuckled. "I hope to be a good asset too, but I'm not too confident of that."

"Speaking of Elias," Ordell said, "where is he?"

"Oh, he went out to the lake by the forest. If you head west near the mountains, you should find this small forest. Don't worry, it's impossible to get lost in there. Even I could find the way out of there."

"Why on earth would he be out there?"

"Don't know. Took my fishing rod and told me to prepare for fish tonight. Not sure what he plans to catch there."

Ordell rolled his eyes. "I'll go to the store and pick up some fish there."

"Careful of the cats," Buford said. "I can't tell you how many times I've walked home from the fish market just to have one of those feline furballs steal my tuna."

"I'll be careful," Ordell said, holding back his laugh.

The moment he stepped outside, a wave of warm air hit his face. It wasn't hot enough to be summer, but it was refreshing after the cool and rainy weather from last night.

The streets weren't as busy as the day before, but there were still more people walking about than in Blackwick. Ordell watched as one of the motorized carriages went past, followed by another.

Maybe he could convince Elias to ride in one of them with him.

Another couple went by, and a woman's scarf fluttered behind her as the carriage went by.

"Exciting, isn't it?"

Ordell turned to the little blond woman next to him. "Are you visiting too?"

She nodded. "My husband came to see his sister for the month. While they catch up, I decided to do a little bit of sightseeing. I've heard that there are airships here."

"Airships?"

"It's merely a rumor," she said, "but I hope it's true. Can you imagine flying like a bird? You could go as high as you'd like and feel so weightless."

"I thought only Goldcrest planned to create airships," Ordell said. "I didn't know there were plans to make them here too."

"Silverfield and Goldcrest have been competing on who makes the shinier invention for a few years now," she said. "Quite ridiculous, if you ask me. Ever since Goldcrest made those...." She blushed. "... those automatons, Silverfield's been trying to find a way to make the next shiny toy."

Ordell's stomach churned. "They're not planning on bringing those automatons here, are they?"

"Oh no! Even if they wanted to, Goldcrest refuses to ship any of their bots out. Appears they're afraid of other places copying them. Quite juvenile, if you ask me."

He nodded. "Better if we just get rid of them. The automatons, I mean."

"Well, I better get going," she said. "It was a pleasure, but I'm sure my husband's wondering where I am."

After she left Ordell glanced at the mountains in the distance.

Might as well make sure Elias didn't get lost. Knowing him, he was still out there trying to catch fish.

FINDING THE forest wasn't too difficult. Navigating it was simple enough, with the linear path and large rocks blocking off most of the stray paths.

In the distance Ordell heard the stream of the water and smelled the scent of fresh dirt not long after. Even if Elias had already left, at least Ordell could sit back and enjoy the scenery.

Actually that sounded exquisite. He could sit by one of the rocks and just doze off while listening to the sound of the water. Maybe wade his feet in the water and enjoy the warm air on his skin.

Ordell reached the lake and almost gasped. Smelling the flowers and listening to the birds was one thing. Cloud gazing and talking on and on about snow angels was another. But to bathe out in the open was unacceptable!

Ordell had half a mind to get closer and scold Elias, but then he felt the heat in his ears again. He glanced up at Elias's bare back and the water barely covering his… his….

Damn it, to hell with him!

Ordell turned around, and his face almost felt as if it'd melt right off.

"Going to come in?" Elias called out. "There's room enough for two."

"We don't *need* to bathe," Ordell stuttered out. "What you're doing is unnecessary and inappropriate!"

"It's refreshing," he said, and Ordell heard the splash of the water. "There's nothing to be ashamed of—it's just our skin."

"Yes, but society has standards, Elias. I know you haven't been around the humans to understand what is proper and what isn't, but this isn't something a gentleman would do." Ordell took a deep breath and exhaled. He was embarrassed for Elias. That was all this was. Nothing more, nothing less. "We have standards."

He heard Elias's chuckle. "You need to loosen up. It's only the two of us. Have a little fun for once."

Ordell sighed and turned around. He pulled off his boots and walked over to the edge of the lake. There he sat down on one of the rocks and dipped his feet into the cool water. "Happy?"

A wolfish grin grew on Elias's face. "I would prefer to see a little more skin, personally."

He glared and brought his hand down to splash him. "You're nothing but a pervert!"

"You are a bit confusing, Ordell," he said as he bathed. "I can see your attraction for me, but you act as if you hate me."

Ordell's mouth gaped open. "Excuse me?"

"Well, I mean how you gazed at my body just now." Elias's eyes trailed down to Ordell's lap. "And I can see how it excites you." Ordell quickly folded his hands in his lap. "But you act as if you can't stand me. I don't understand."

"I just… I don't know either. I've never spoken to another automaton as human as I am."

"So we both don't understand."

Ordell couldn't help but laugh. "I have been acting like an idiot, haven't I?"

"I suppose I haven't made it easy." Elias began to walk out of the lake, and Ordell averted his eyes. There was the sound of clothes shuffling. "I've been thinking with the wrong head, and haven't even asked you your favorite color!"

"My favorite color?"

"Isn't that a topic people bring up when they first meet?"

"I suppose," Ordell said. "I'm fond of the color purple. Such a rich color."

Elias finished changing and sat down next to Ordell. "Are we friends now?"

"All right," he said, "we're friends." He extended his hand, and Elias shook it. "Now it's official."

"I'm sorry for my advances," Elias said. "You are just so beautiful and like me. You could say I got a bit carried away." Ordell frowned, and he sighed. "What did I do wrong this time?"

"I'd prefer dashingly handsome over beautiful."

"Fine," he said with a smile. "You are just so *dashingly handsome* and like me. Better?"

"Much."

"When we get to Goldcrest," Elias said, "we'll just find the friend and get out of there as soon as we can."

"Why? Is Goldcrest that bad?"

"Worse. The place is…. Well, it isn't kind to people like us. I'd go as far as to say that Goldcrest will be one of the most dangerous locations we will reach."

"Because of the sex bots? I already know about them. We just need to keep a low profile and we should be fine. Besides, I'd like to see the creation of the airships there."

"We can't, Ordell," he said, voice stern. "Look, Ratliff lives there. Not only that, but he is far more important than you'd think. That cure he created made him loved in Goldcrest. We are walking right into the lion's mouth."

"Then maybe we shouldn't go. We can go somewhere else to get the passes."

"No. This is the only person whom I trust with getting us these passes. We just need to get in there and get out before Ratliff finds out you're there."

"I don't know." He sighed and pushed his hands through his hair. "I just don't know if this is worth the risk. Maybe we could just live here.

Silverfield's nice, and I could set up my own automaton shop here. Or maybe I could make a tiny clock shop."

"And how long will it take before they find out about us? Before they start to realize we haven't aged? Before they notice we don't get ill? Before Ratliff puts out a search for you and this place is packed with guards?"

"Maybe he won't be looking for me, though. Maybe he'll give up and just have Octavio make…." Ordell's gaze dropped to his lap. "Oh. Right."

"I'll protect you."

"What?"

"When we get to Goldcrest," Elias said, "I'll protect you."

"You don't have to do that."

"I'm not letting anything happen to you. That's why I was built in the first place, remember?"

"I thought you were built to silence the rioters."

Elias shrugged. "That too, but mostly to protect you. At least that's what I prefer."

"Fine, but I won't kiss you."

"Hm?"

The heat came back to Ordell's ears. "You know, in those stories. The knight will come in to rescue the princess, and she'll give him a kiss. It—it was a joke. You haven't read those stories?"

"I have, but I don't see how it applies to this situation."

All he wanted to do was sink into the ground and disappear. "It doesn't. Of course it doesn't! I mean, that's ridiculous, right?"

Elias tilted his head. "What is?"

"Just, well, you and me. I mean, not that it is ridiculous in and of itself, but that we'd risk our friendship for something so juvenile. Not that those emotions are juvenile… just in this situation—"

"Ordell."

"Yes?"

"What the hell are you talking about?"

He rubbed the back of his neck. "I don't know."

"We should probably head back."

Ordell hopped up and pulled his boots on. "You're right. We don't want Buford worried about us."

Elias grabbed two apples from one of the trees nearby and tossed one to Ordell. "You should try these; they're delicious."

"Actually I can't taste food. Or anything for that matter."

Elias took a bite out of the apple, then tossed it in his hand. "When we get to Linnesse, we'll find someone to give you taste buds."

"They can do that?"

"Of course," he said as he took another bite. "Then we can have this extravagant meal so you can taste everything. Even the moon."

"The moon?"

"Why not?" he asked with a shrug and threw the apple core on the ground. "You can do anything."

"But the moon?"

"Anything."

"Okay, then," Ordell said. "Should we get ready to head back?"

THERE WERE conversations about the types of food Ordell wanted to try once he got his taste buds.

"Certainly sweet rolls," he said with a smile. "I've wanted to try those for the longest time. Oh, and then those vanilla honey cakes. Have you tried those?"

"I can't say I have."

"They smell amazing," Ordell said. "Oh, and I'd love to try some fresh-baked bread with butter. Maybe even that sweet cinnamon butter that Mr. Stokes sometimes makes."

"Mr. Stokes?"

"Oh, he's the baker in Blackwick. I worked for him before this whole mess happened. He became lonely after his son passed away, but he's a very nice man nonetheless. You'd probably get along with him."

"A shame I never met him," Elias said. "Or anyone from Blackwick."

"Didn't you try asking Winifred if you could go out and visit? Maybe she would've allowed it on special occasions."

He shook his head. "She's my mother and I love her, but she was too protective of me. So scared that someone would take me like they took you, so she refused to let me go out and meet anyone else. I'm a bit surprised she even introduced me to you."

"Wow," Ordell said, lowering his voice. "That must be awful."

"Understatement of the century." He stretched. "But I'm out of there now. Not only that, but I met a beautiful—I mean—dashingly handsome man and get to go on an adventure. Not much else I can ask for."

"Then you're easy to please," Ordell said with a chuckle. "If it were me, I'd want to talk to everyone and try every hobby out there. In fact, I probably wouldn't want to go back inside ever again!"

"Well, the outside is nice. I could probably live out here for a month or two with no complaints."

"Try not to get mauled by squirrels," Ordell said with a laugh. "Those little monsters are vicious!"

They got near one of the buildings and he stopped, eyes wide.

CHAPTER 7

ORDELL RIPPED the poster off the wall and balled it up. "I can't believe this. Wanted posters? Really?"

"You must've cost a lot of money." Ordell glared at him, and Elias cleared his throat. "Which means nothing because you're a priceless treasure."

"Why Silverfield?" he asked. "Is he going to post these all over the world?"

"Well, I wouldn't go that far, but—" He stopped, and Ordell's eyes stung. "Hey, we'll get this figured out."

Ordell turned away before the tears fell. "This isn't fair."

"I'm here to protect you, remember? I know the posters are a bit jarring, but that doesn't mean the people here care. They might not even notice these posters with how busy their lives are."

"I don't want to go there. I don't want to be this man's... *toy*!" More tears fell, and Ordell tried his best to wipe them away before Elias could see, but it was no use now. "My father just gave me to him! After all these years—" His sob cut him off, and he threw the balled-up poster at the side of the building. "I'm his son! How could he do this to me?"

"Hey, Ordell," Elias said, grabbing his shoulders, "you need to take a deep breath, okay? Just try to calm down a little before you go on a rampage."

"I'm not going to—!" He raised his hands and took a deep breath. "Okay, see? I'm taking deep breaths. I just don't understand how someone can be so—" God, he couldn't even form a coherent sentence! Elias probably thought he'd lost his mind. "I'm fine."

Elias wrapped his strong arms around him and pulled him close. "It'll be fine. I promise."

"I guess you're right," Ordell said, trying on a smile. "There's no other choice but to go to Goldcrest. I guess there isn't much of a reason to stay here, then."

"We still need to have Buford set up the ship. Maybe we could walk around and have you clear your head before we go back."

"And have some guard catch me?" He pushed away from Elias's grip. "We should just go back before someone sees the posters and turns me in."

"I think you're being a bit overdramatic," Elias said with a small chuckle. "Ordell, it's not like these posters mean anything. The reward money isn't even that big. Besides, Silverfield's big enough that no one will even recognize you."

"Fine," he said with a sigh. "What do you want to do, then?"

"Why don't we look at the airship designs? They seem to be a great tourist attraction."

"I'm still not too sure. What if Ratliff's there?"

Elias grabbed a hold of Ordell's shoulders and locked eyes with him. "It'll be fine. Let's just have a little fun before we leave."

Not that he had much say in that; Elias grabbed his hand and dragged him toward the exhibit.

"I don't know," Ordell said. "I'm not all that fond of the airships. They seem rather silly and juvenile to me."

"Once you see them, you'll love it," Elias said, tugging his hand harder. "Trust me, Ody, you'll absolutely love it."

"What did I tell you about calling me that?"

"But it suits you so well," Elias moaned. "Let me at least have a little bit of fun. I promise it'll only take a few minutes. Fifteen minutes at the most. If you get bored, we can leave."

"Fine," Ordell said. "But we leave in fifteen minutes."

THE AIRSHIP exhibit was crowded by the time they got there. It took a bit of effort, but Ordell managed to weave past the sea of people and toward the exhibit.

What he saw when he reached the airship made the neurons in his brain hurt. The best way to describe it was a boat—just a normal, average boat, the very same one might see out on the open waters just a short distance away—with a number of balloons attached, each no more than a few feet around. How anyone could think this would ever fly baffled Ordell.

"Do you think it'll work?" Ordell asked once they got up close to the airship model. "Seems rather extravagant." Extravagant was not the word Ordell was thinking of, admittedly, but he thought it best to reserve his true feelings for the moment, given their location.

"I think so." A small smile crept across Elias's lips. "Who knows? Maybe we'll ride in one eventually."

"But with the current design, it'll be much too heavy to lift an entire ship. I just don't see their logic in it."

"Let us have our fantasy," Elias said. "Until we discover giant birds, this is the closest we'll get to flying."

"We believe that we will replace all ships with flying ships in the near future," the lady near the exhibit said. "Our best inventors have worked long and hard on this concept and feel confident that we are one step closer to the clouds."

"Are these like the concepts in Goldcrest?" a man asked. "Are you working with them?"

"No. This is our own design." Her smile widened and eyes sparkled. "There are many flaws in the Goldcrest airships, but our design is a step in the right direction. We have high hopes that we might be traveling through the clouds as early as five years from now."

Ordell took another step closer to the model. As far as he could tell, it just didn't seem plausible. If it were as simple as this, they would've placed a hot air balloon on a ship by now. He wasn't sure what the Goldcrest airships looked like, but if they looked anything like this, theirs were bound to fail as well.

"You must admit," Elias said, "the idea of riding in the sky is rather romantic."

"Until the balloon pops and we all come crashing down in a horrific death."

"Aren't you just the poet in the making. Could melt any man with those words."

"If you're not working with Goldcrest," another person asked, "then why was Mr. Saunders here earlier this week?"

"That is confidential information," the lady said with that same big smile. "Now let us travel to the east wing, where you can see the inside model of the airship."

The group moved away, and Ordell grabbed Elias by the arm. "Why was Ratliff here?"

"You can't be that surprised," he said, pulling his arm away. "Those posters didn't appear out of nowhere."

"I know that, but why would he care about the airship?"

"Winnie told me he's a bit of an investor. He's always looking for the shiniest new toy to come around," Elias explained. "Collects random inventions all over the world and makes them a hit in Goldcrest. In fact—" He lowered his voice to a whisper. "You know the medicine he made for the plague?" Ordell nodded. "Well, that wasn't even his invention. He bought it from this doctor from a small island infected with the junk. Tore the concoction apart and learned how it was made. Took the idea for himself and became rich."

"And how does Winifred know all this?"

"There are some people who used to work for Ratliff. He burned a few bridges with them, so when the revolution came calling, they were more than happy to divulge just about every bit of information they had on the guy. Turns out they want him to come crumbling down just as much as we do."

"I just don't want to be his next shiny new toy," Ordell said with a sigh. "I don't care if he crumbles or not. He can be the richest man on earth for all I care."

Elias frowned. "So he can create even more of these sex slaves?"

Ordell was going to bring up the controversy about whether automatons were sentient enough to be considered slaves, or if they were just equipment, but he let it go. They had just become friends; he wasn't going to ruin it over a man he was already not fond of.

Still, the anger that flashed through Elias's eyes made him curious. Something told him there was a little more to the story than what Winifred had told him. In fact, there were a few things about Winifred that made Ordell raise his eyebrows. Some things he knew he couldn't ask Elias about without triggering an argument, but maybe Buford could answer a few of his questions.

"Maybe we should head back," Elias said. "Buford's probably ready for us."

"I didn't mean—"

"Let's just drop it. We don't need to be having these types of conversations."

Ordell nodded. The truth was he wasn't even sure where he'd draw the line on this. Of course the automatons like him and Elias should have rights. They were just as human as any of the civilians here and could easily hold their own in society and pay taxes and vote. Just like anyone else.

But what about those who couldn't? What about his siblings, who were nothing more than smiling creatures willing to do whatever their owner ordered them to? Did they count as automatons who should have rights? As far as Ordell knew, they enjoyed what they did. They loved their owner no matter how poorly they were treated.

THEY ENTERED Buford's house, and the first thing Ordell heard was the music. The same music his father played in his shop.

"What's wrong?" Elias placed his hand on Ordell's shoulder. "You look as if you've seen a ghost."

He moved away from Elias and walked toward the phonograph.

"One of the most famous songs by Earlene Glenna," Buford said. "Made her debut back when I was just a little boy. One of the most interesting figures in music history."

"Why is that?" Ordell asked, tracing his fingers along the phonograph.

"You see, she created this special music box," Buford said. "Not much is known about it, but apparently the music held a secret. Only one was created."

"What happened to it?"

"Well, no one knows. She was murdered in her house shortly after it was created, but she hid the box somewhere and never told anyone where. Not only that, but no one has found out who the killer was. The police have tried to find out who this person was, but all hints have led to dead ends."

"Are there any suspects?" Ordell asked. "Perhaps a disgruntled fan or another musician? Or maybe she had a relative whom she fought with."

"The police checked all leads," Buford said. "She died from a blow to the head, which made them originally think a robbery gone wrong. However, nothing was stolen from her home. The odd thing about it is that whoever killed her reorganized her bookshelf. Strangest thing, it is. No books were stolen, and there didn't seem to be any purpose to it."

"That is odd," Ordell admitted. "Maybe the killer tried to make a message out of the books? Did they ever look into that?"

"That was what the police first thought as well, but there were no messages they could make out. It has been one of those mysteries that stumped the police and the people for many decades. I wish we could find this monster, though. To kill such a beautiful lady in her prime. She had so much talent to bring to us and could've been someone to change music forever. Now she's gone and we will never know what her full potential could bring us."

"She must be quite popular; my father plays her music in his shop all the time." He couldn't keep the anger from his voice. "Particularly this song."

"This is one of her more famous works," Buford said. "It wasn't the song that made her famous, but it is the one that people associate with her. It was also her first song after she left Goldcrest behind her. Smart lady, she was. I applaud her for leaving such a wretched place!"

"Is Goldcrest really that horrid?"

"Yes," Elias said in a sharp tone.

"For the revolution, it is," Buford said. "Not only do they treat automatons poorly, but I firmly believe that many of their inventions have been stolen from Silverfield. Of course they deny that, but I wouldn't trust an inventor there any more than I'd trust a hungry lion."

"I trust the hungry lion more," Elias scoffed, crossing his arms.

"At least the lion doesn't know any better," Buford said. "I have the ship ready, and we can head off first thing in the morning."

"You're coming with us?" Elias asked. "Isn't it rather dangerous for a man in your… condition?"

"I'm not that old!" Buford snapped. "And it'd be better to have a human with you, especially if we're heading straight into the pit of Goldcrest. Do you have any idea how dangerous it'd be for you two to be wandering around there? Especially for Ordell."

"And why is that?" Ordell asked, narrowing his eyes.

"You expect that doll face to not get you in trouble?" Elias laughed. "It'd be dangerous for you there even if you were human."

"I can handle myself."

He knew he shouldn't get worked up over something so ridiculous, but Ordell knew more about people than Elias did. He'd walked around Blackwick for ten years with no problems. Sure, the occasional stray cat would give him a bit of trouble, but that didn't mean he needed the *mighty Elias* to protect him.

"No need to be offended," Buford said. "We just want to make sure that you're safe. We thought we lost you once, and we don't want to lose you again."

He still had the urge to argue this further, but gave up. It was two against one, anyway. "Maybe it'd be better if we left tonight."

"Is Silverfield that boring for you? I thought you wanted to stay and explore."

"It seems that Ratcliff came by earlier." Ordell paced around the room and sighed. "There were some posters out. Of me. The reward isn't that big, but I don't know if I want to stay another night and risk something happening."

"Nothing will happen," Elias said.

"You don't know that." Great, they went from wanting to protect him from the spooky bumps in the night to thinking Ordell's true concerns were silly. It was like he couldn't win with these two!

"I'm sure Ratliff is long gone, Ordell. If he were still here, we would've seen him. It won't hurt us to spend one more night here."

"Actually it might be better if we left tonight," Buford said to Ordell's relief. "Better to be cautious, yes? Besides, I can't wait to get the old ship back out on the water again."

"Fine," Elias said, pinching the bridge of his nose. "But we take the back way to Goldcrest."

"But that will be longer," Buford said. "We should be all right going the intended route."

"You were the one who said we needed to be cautious. We'll take the back way to make sure that Ratliff or his guards don't see Ordell. We can handle a small detour."

"I don't care which way we go," Ordell said with a sigh. "Let's just get out of Silverfield before a guard comes in here and takes me away."

"A sensitive boy, isn't he?" Buford chuckled. "I don't recall Winnie making him this emotional."

"Clearly it came from his father," Elias said. "We both know how neurotic Octavio can be."

Ordell glared at them both and stomped out, intentionally slamming the door as hard as he could.

Something told him this would be a very long trip.

CHAPTER 8

ORDELL LOOKED out at the vast sea and thought about what Octavio had said. About how he loved Ordell no matter what.

Was money really that important to him? After all they'd gone through?

Ordell didn't remember much about his "birth" except that Octavio had created him in the workshop. He remembered how Octavio went back and forth on how he couldn't get attached and that Ordell was for a client. He remembered being confused, watching his father talk to himself and pace around.

That was when he got up and placed a hand on his father's shoulder to comfort him. Didn't know where he'd learned that gesture meant to comfort from, but it came naturally to him, like getting up from the table and walking.

Next thing he knew, his father was working on his first brother. Looked very similar to Ordell, but was a little smaller and had wider eyes. Ordell would come in and hand tools to his father and provide simple chitchat. He still remembered the first time he expressed a dislike for the color orange, which was a trait Octavio didn't program inside Ordell. He thought the poor man's eyes were going to fall out of his skull!

"You're much more human than I thought," Octavio said, then laughed. "I guess I underestimated my own talent!"

Since Ordell didn't know any better, he assumed Octavio made him from scratch. Octavio never even brought up a Winifred Griffith or that Ordell was made to detect and destroy the plague. No, all he knew was he was Octavio's son and that he was simply helping his father create these beautiful automatons. Stupidly thought they were used for purposes other than… well, what Ratliff had in mind.

With how his body reacted (involuntarily, mind you) to Elias, Ordell was meant for those purposes from the start.

Octavio could've easily given Ordell some physical flaws. Maybe a scar or perhaps mismatched eyes, but no. He kept him in this condition.

Did his father always plan to sell him? Maybe he was just waiting for the highest bidder.

Ordell balled his hands into fists and forced down the bile he felt build up. If he ever saw his father again, he couldn't guarantee they'd both come out alive.

"Ordell?" Elias placed a hand on his shoulder. "Are you all right? Are you seasick?"

"No, just thinking."

"About what?"

He shrugged. "Just about this whole thing. One minute I'm helping my father with his shop. Next I'm here on this boat with people I've never met before."

"I thought we were friends now."

"We are," Ordell said, "but it's still a bit jarring when I think back on all this. You don't feel the same?"

"No."

"But this is your first time outside. How can you not feel overwhelmed by all this? Aren't you at least a little bit homesick?"

"I miss Winnie, but I don't miss the cellar." Elias turned around and leaned his back against the edge of the ship. "I don't think it's a terrible loss to leave Blackwick."

"I grew up there." He looked down at his hands and back at Elias's profile. "I spent ten years living with those people… living alongside them. I spent ten years with my father. He treated me like his own son. Then—" He sighed and dipped his head, his copper bangs falling into his eyes. "Well, you know the rest."

"Don't dwell on the past, Ordell. See this as an opportunity. You get to see places you've never seen and get to experience it with a handsome companion."

"Well, I think Buford might be a little too old for my tastes, but I can see the appeal."

Elias lightly punched him in the shoulder. "You know what I mean."

"That your ego is too big to fit inside this ship?" Ordell teased. "If so, then yes, I know exactly what you mean."

"Maybe I should throw you overboard."

"I'm taking you down with me," he said with a raised eyebrow. "I may not look it, but I can certainly hold my own in a fight."

"A pretty thing like you in a fight?" Elias chuckled. "That I would love to see."

"Come on," Ordell said. "I can get down and dirty too."

"Is that so?" Elias asked with a small grin. "I find it hard to believe that Ordell Rutledge would do something against society's standards."

"And what is that supposed to mean?" He crossed his arms and glared up at Elias. "I'll have you know that I've had my fair share of mischief in the past."

"All right," Elias said, still laughing. "If I remember correctly, you were the one who had a panic attack over me having the audacity to bathe in a lake."

The heat grew from his face to his ears. "I-I was shocked. Startled." He cleared his throat and looked down at his feet. "And why must you bring it up again?"

"Because I like seeing you get flustered over me."

His eyes shot back up to Elias's. "I do not!" he stuttered out. "Y-you can't prove that!"

"What's there to prove?"

"Just pretend it never happened! From here on out, it was just a dream!"

"Well," Elias said, "if it were a dream, you'd be in that lake with me." A glint of mischief flickered in those brown eyes. "Naked."

"Bastard," he muttered under his breath.

"I didn't mean to make you blush this intensely," Elias said with an innocent head tilt. "If it'll make you feel better, I'd be naked too."

"That does *not* make me feel better, Elias!" Ordell snapped. "And I think we should drop this inappropriate conversion!"

"Then what would you like to talk about?"

"Have you ever been to Goldcrest?"

Elias frowned. "Why do you ask that?"

"You seem to have a lot of anger toward the place." He shrugged. "And I'm a bit curious."

Elias was quiet for a few moments, then sighed. "I was created there."

"Winifred created you in Goldcrest?"

"No."

"I don't understand," Ordell said. "You just said you—"

"It's the past for a reason, Ordell," he snapped. "These aren't happy memories for me. I'd prefer to keep them buried."

"I'm sorry."

"It's fine," he said. "Let's just talk about something else. It must be exciting to travel on a ship, isn't it?"

"It would be if there was more than just water to see." Ordell imagined islands or other boats. He'd even take some seagulls over looking at more endless water. "It isn't even clear water."

"Personally," Elias said, "I'd love to travel in one of those airships. I think it'd be rather fun to travel alongside the clouds and birds."

"It'd no doubt be like traveling through fog. I don't think you'd be able to see much."

"One of these days, I'll get you into the beauty of airships," Elias said with a laugh. "You will be in such awe of them that you'll wind up living in one."

Ordell couldn't help but laugh too. "I don't see that happening anytime soon."

"You never know."

"We have a bit of a problem." Buford came up on deck and pulled off his goggles, blinking his beady eyes. "I don't think this will be as cut-and-dried as we thought."

"What do you mean?" Ordell asked. "I thought things were going smoothly."

"Yes," he said, pulling his goggles back on, "but I fear we may be heading toward dangerous waters."

"How dangerous?"

"Well, I'm not too sure of that," Buford said. "Could be something that'll cause some annoyance, or it could be severe enough to ruin our ship."

He didn't like the sound of that at all. Even if it was just some annoyance, Ordell could only take so much, and his patience was already running thin with Elias. Not only that, but he wasn't overly fond of getting dirty seawater on him.

"Maybe we should change course," Ordell said. "We could go and travel the shorter route. We'll also get there in less time."

"No!" Elias said. "We need to stay on this course."

"I'm afraid he's right, Ordell. There's a storm coming in, and if we turn around, we'll head straight into it. It might be even more dangerous to turn around."

"Okay," Ordell said, "then what do we do?"

"We keep heading the way we intended," Buford said. "We just need to be cautious."

He wasn't sure if it was the best approach, but he nodded. Buford walked back down belowdecks, and Elias didn't seem to be too concerned.

Still, something in the pit of Ordell's stomach told him they should turn around and try going the other route.

"Are you sure we shouldn't try going the other way?" Ordell tried. "Maybe we could wait till the storm passes, and then we could travel that way."

Elias shook his head. "This is the best option. Trust me on this, Ordell. You don't want to go to the front entrance of Goldcrest."

"And you won't tell me why."

"No."

Ordell rolled his eyes. He suspected as much.

LATER THAT night Ordell rested on his bed, reading some strange novel Buford packed. Something about whales and the sea life. Truth be told, Ordell wasn't particularly fond of novels filled with adventures—he much preferred the ones filled with romance and politics. Still, it was a nice little escape from Buford's horrid steering and Elias's pacing.

"Why are you so nervous?" Ordell asked as he flipped a page. "I doubt Buford will actually wreck the ship."

"It's not that," Elias muttered. "I'm just a bit anxious, is all."

"Your pacing makes me anxious," Ordell said, peering over the book.

"Sorry."

He sighed and rolled out of the bed, tossing the book on his pillow. "Is this about Goldcrest?"

"I'm not going to talk about it."

"Too bad," Ordell said. "You've been agitated all day and you've paced in that one spot for so long that you might burn a hole in the floor!"

"I'm still not going to talk about it. I know that's not what you want to hear, but these are my memories. Memories that I don't even want to be reminded of, mind you. I'm not about to pry that open just to provide you some comfort."

"I just want to help."

"Then stop bringing it up! I told you that I don't want to discuss this."

"Fine," he said. "Can you at least tell me what Goldcrest is like? That way I can prepare for it."

"It's an awful place," Elias said. "People get wrapped up in the beauty of it and the rich golds. From a superficial standpoint, the place is gorgeous. Far more advanced in technology than Silverfield, though I hate to admit it."

"That doesn't sound too bad."

"It is," he said. "The people there are awful. The bottom of the barrel, if you ask me. They are consumed with greed and selfishness. Wouldn't help someone out of the goodness of their hearts, that's for sure. Ratliff is probably one of the better people of Goldcrest, if you want me to put it in perspective for you."

"Wow." Ordell's stomach turned at that thought. To think Elias would hate a group of people this strongly. "I didn't realize how awful it was there."

"That isn't even the worst of it," Elias said. "The automatons there are nothing more than sex dolls. Just pretty faces. What pisses me off is that Goldcrest goes on and on about how they have the lowest sex crimes due to these automatons, but treats them like garbage. They can just be tossed aside in some ditch and left there, deactivated. You know how devastating that is, Ordell?"

"I can't say I do."

"Imagine that you've been brainwashed to love Octavio and only him. You have to obey every single order he gives you. Somehow, no matter how horrific it is, you end up loving him more for it and justifying each order. No free will, no say in what you want, no expectations. You just do what you're told and are *grateful* that your owner is giving you attention. Next thing you know, the very person you love and would do anything to please has thrown you in some ditch for a newer model because you weren't pretty enough. Tell me, how would you feel about that, Ordell?"

"I don't know," he said. "If we go with your theory that I had to obey him no matter what, then I'd still be happy."

"And how can you be happy if you're deactivated?"

All Ordell could do was shrug. With Elias's fidgeting and the way he raised his voice, no matter what answer Ordell gave, it would be the wrong one. He didn't want to bring up that they were just dolls—about as useful as a clock or a bell ringer. Not just because he knew it'd cause problems, but Ordell felt horrified he even viewed those automatons like that.

"You're lucky Octavio had a change of heart," Elias said. "That he kept you instead of selling you off."

"A part of me thinks he always intended to sell me. Why else would he keep me like this? I bet even if we thrived as a business, he would've sold me off to someone who had enough money."

"I don't think that's true." Elias's gaze burned into his. "There's no doubt in my mind that he loved you, Ordell."

"If he did, he wouldn't have sold me."

"Are you sure there isn't more to it?" He brought his hand up and caressed Ordell's cheek with his fingertips. "If you were mine, I wouldn't sell you for the world."

Ordell felt the thumping in his chest and head, his throat dry and fingers trembling. This was something much more than the moment at the lake or earlier on the ship. He licked his lips and parted them, wanting to say something—anything—but nothing came out.

"If you were mine," Elias said, his voice dropping down to a whisper, "I'd never let you go."

Ordell couldn't take his eyes off of Elias's intense gaze. He pulled himself closer and his eyes drifted shut. He felt Elias's hot breath so close to his lips; his entire body became numb, and nothing mattered right then.

Just this....

"We have a problem!" Buford's voice snapped him out of his trance, and he felt Elias push away. "A very big, disastrous problem!"

"What's wrong?" Elias asked, racing toward the stairs. "Is it a storm?"

"Much worse than that! You need to come up here! Both of you!"

A large crash rocked the ship, and Elias almost fell over Buford. Ordell grabbed ahold of the column as another crash hit against the ship.

"What the hell is that?" Elias shouted out above the loud crash.

Buford ran back up the stairs, and Ordell and Elias followed behind. Once they reached the deck, Ordell's eyes widened.

"Son of a bitch," Elias muttered under his breath.

CHAPTER 9

A LARGE tentacle came up over the deck, shaking the entire ship.

"What is that thing?" Ordell asked, steadying himself. "I didn't think sea monsters existed!"

"They don't, my boy," Buford said, holding on to one of the posts. "This is the border's protector. We must be between Northpine and Southpine. They've been at war for as long as I can remember!"

"I think I need more of an explanation." A large wave hit the ship and soaked Ordell. "Why would anyone think to put this horrific creature here?"

"Northpine has shown an outbreak of the plague, and the medicine is no longer working," Buford said. "Southpine refuses to let anyone from Northpine enter their territory out of fear."

"I knew that medicine was a scam!" Elias said. "That bastard probably never even tested it!"

Another large tentacle came crashing down onto the ship, breaking part of the railing.

"My ship!" Buford shouted. "One of you do something before it tears the whole ship apart!"

Elias ran down to the lower deck, and moments later he came back with an ax. When one of the tentacles came down again, he raised the ax and hacked at it. Oil came out of the damaged tentacle and onto the deck. He raised the ax again, but Ordell stopped him this time.

"Stop!" Ordell said, yanking the ax out of his hands. "If we run into anything that causes a spark, we'll start a fire for sure!"

Buford blanched at that.

"We have no other options," Elias said. "If we don't stop this thing, the whole ship's going under!"

There was a loud thud, and both Ordell and Elias turned around to see Buford had fainted.

"You take care of Buford," Ordell said. "I'll take care of the kraken."

Elias snorted. "I'm sorry, but I don't see how you can handle this, Ordell."

He frowned and narrowed his eyes. "And what's that supposed to mean?"

"Nothing, but I think this is more for someone like…." Elias cleared his throat. "I just don't want you to get hurt, is all. Perhaps you should take care of Buford and I'll take care of the kraken." Ordell crossed his arms and raised his eyebrows, and he could see Elias's eyes widen. "Or maybe you could take care of the kraken."

Ordell patted Elias's shoulder and then went down to the lower deck. He grabbed Buford's toolbox and looked through the screwdrivers. He was uncertain which screws the kraken had, but with the large size, he could take a guess. He grabbed the screwdriver and raced back up onto the upper deck.

Despite Elias's claim to let Ordell take care of the situation, he was still fighting off the kraken with the ax. Ordell shook his head and raced back up to one of the tentacles.

He placed the screwdriver in his mouth and climbed up one of the tentacles. He heard Elias call out his name, but when the tentacle began to thrash into the water, all Ordell could hear were the waves and the sound of the tentacles crashing into the ship.

Once he was out of the water again, Ordell continued climbing up the tentacle until he reached the kraken's head. The metal surface was slick from the water and there wasn't much friction, but Ordell managed to keep his footing as he searched for an opening.

A large tentacle came up and swatted at Ordell, and he grabbed hold of the eyes as it swatted at him again. This time it hit the small of his back and a heavy pain shot through Ordell's spine. He winced through the pain and forced himself to keep searching for the opening.

Finally he found a small area that looked out of place in comparison to the rest of the kraken. He felt it with his fingers until he found the screw. With shaky hands Ordell pulled the screwdriver out of his mouth and placed it on the screw. He struggled to unscrew it with the kraken thrashing around, but he was so close to getting the screw out.

Then the kraken swung its tentacles again and knocked the screwdriver out of Ordell's hand.

"Damn!" Ordell said to himself and then tightened his grip on the kraken as it crashed its head against the waves. He was hit with a mouthful of water and spat it out once they were above the surface again.

Ordell pulled himself back up toward the screw and twisted the rest of the screw free. He used the edge of the screw to work on getting the others free. Finally he got the metal pad away and exposed the gears inside the kraken. Without the proper tools, he wouldn't be able to remove the gears. He dropped one of the screws inside in hopes the gears would catch.

Nothing.

He wiped his brow and tried again with another screw. This time it jogged two of the gears and he heard the screech of the gears working against one another.

Ordell jumped off the octopus and back onto the ship, falling face-first onto the deck. He turned around onto his back and heard the octopus chug and finally submerge into the water. He sighed in relief, but then a large tentacle emerged from the water and hit the ship again.

A large wave came up and pushed the ship with a massive jerk. Elias grabbed the steering wheel, but it was no use; they had lost control of the ship.

THE SHIP crashed on the shore and Ordell fell forward, falling overboard and onto the sand.

"Are you all right, Ordell?" Elias called out.

"Where are we?" Ordell grunted out.

"We're in Southpine, my boy," Buford said.

Ordell then turned to his side and choked out some water. "We have a hole in the ship."

"What?" Buford got out and stumbled toward the damage. "My ship! My beautiful ship! Do you have any idea how long it took for me to buy this? It's ruined!"

"We could probably patch it up," Elias said, getting out. "The hole doesn't look that big."

"Now she's going to have a large blemish no matter what I do," Buford grumbled. "There's no way that I can make the patch barely noticeable!"

"Could someone help me up?" Ordell groaned out.

Elias got down and helped Ordell to his feet. "That has to be the most idiotic thing you've done!" Elias snapped. "What were you thinking?"

"I was thinking about saving us," Ordell said. "At least we still *have* a ship."

"Are you hurt?" Elias asked, softening his voice. "Do you need to sit down?"

Ordell waved him off. "I'm fine."

Truth was his back was killing him, but he couldn't show his weakness now. Not when Elias was right there.

He was more than a pretty face. He had to be.

"We're stuck here until I get the ship repaired," Buford said with a sigh. "My poor, beautiful ship."

"Is there another way to get to Goldcrest?" Ordell asked and flinched when raw pain shot through his back.

"Are you all right?" Elias asked.

"We could rent another ship," Buford said, "but it's far too expensive for us. No, the best option would be to stay here until I get my beauty repaired."

"Maybe it's for the best," Elias said. "It'll give you a chance to rest, Ordell."

"I don't need to rest." He didn't mean to make it sound as harsh as it did, and debated apologizing for his harsh tone. "I'm going to look around and get some supplies," he said instead.

As he walked away, he realized he wasn't alone.

"You don't need to come with me."

"I want to," Elias said. "It'll give me time to find my land legs."

Southpine wasn't as extravagant as Silverfield. In fact, it was more run-down than anything. There seemed to be a thick smog that cast a shadow over the town and made it feel as if all color was sucked out. The only animals that seemed to exist were the crows that flew above and the rats that skittered across the broken cobblestones below. A small group of people crowded near the crashed ship and whispered amongst themselves.

"Not the most cheerful place," Elias muttered.

"Imagine what Northpine must look like." If the plague had hit Northpine like Buford said, then there was a good chance there weren't many people left there.

Southpine didn't seem much better, though. There were people around, but they mostly stood in one place or kept their heads down as Elias and Ordell walked by. Many looked sickly pale and their clothes lacked color as much as the dilapidated buildings. The only sounds were the caws of the crows and the occasional cough from one of the civilians.

"They never recovered from the plague when it first hit," Elias explained. "There hasn't been much activity in regards to inventions and automatons here."

"Then who made the kraken?"

Elias shrugged. "There must be someone here who knows a thing or two about automatons."

The kraken wasn't extraordinary work compared to other inventions, but it was built well enough and the supplies used weren't too low quality. "Someone must've given it to them as a gift," Ordell said. "Or someone isn't sharing their work with the town. The first option sounds far more reasonable. Perhaps we could ask around and see who created the kraken."

"It isn't important, Ordell," Elias said. "You're right; it was most likely gifted long ago before the plague, and they stored it away until recently. There isn't much more to it than that."

"But aren't you just a little bit curious about who created it?" Ordell asked. "The work is rather impressive, considering the state of the town. It managed to keep its own in the water."

"You seemed to have dismantled it easily."

"And I happen to have worked alongside my father for all of my life," he said with a frown. "An average person would've struggled with dismantling it."

Elias laughed. "I couldn't get you to bat an eye at the airships, but you can't stop obsessing over the kraken. I just don't understand you at times."

"The airship isn't practical," Ordell said. "The designs have far too many faults, and they wouldn't even get the ship off the ground with the direction they're going."

"One of these days, I will get you to see the beauty of the airships, Ordell. They're the wave of the future, not a silly giant octopus."

"Yes, I admit that the octopus could use some work, but in the right hands, it would make for an impressive weapon. I bet Winifred would be able to create something truly remarkable with it."

"We're not taking the kraken with us," Elias said flatly.

"It wouldn't take up too much room."

"No."

THEY WALKED around Southpine and reached a small area that was lively enough to have a general store and a market.

"We should get some food for Buford," Ordell said as he picked up a few apples. "I'm sure he'll enjoy some dried meat."

"We don't have much money on us," Elias said. "Only grab what's necessary."

Ordell nodded and picked up a few items that were relatively cheap—far cheaper than they would be if he were to purchase them in Silverfield or Blackwick. Unfortunately that meant the quality wasn't the best. He hoped it wouldn't make Buford ill, but from his quick observation, Ordell felt the food passed as edible.

"You know," Ordell said, "if we grabbed the octopus, we could sell the parts."

"If you want to go into the water and fish it out, be my guest," Elias said with a chuckle. "You're not getting me in the water, though."

"It's not like you'll melt," he said. "But if you won't help me, then I'm not going back in that water."

Besides, they still had money left over for emergency use. They walked around the town, and Ordell was glad to see there seemed to be some sort of community in this area. The buildings were still worn compared to Silverfield, but at least there was some color. Not only that, but he could hear people laughing and talking to one another as they walked by.

"Much better," Ordell said with a contented sigh. "At least it doesn't feel like death passed over here."

"Still not as impressive as I once remembered," Elias said.

"You've been here before?"

"Hardly. My memory is foggy at best when it comes to my time here. My master came here for something important, but I can't remember what. All I remember was that the buildings were in better shape than this."

"What was your master like?"

Elias's eyes widened and he turned his face away. He didn't say anything for a few moments but then whispered, "That doesn't matter. There's no reason to bring it up."

"You were the one who mentioned him."

"And I'm ending the conversation about him," Elias snapped. "It isn't something you need to know about me."

"Did he order you to slaughter a million people?" Ordell asked. "You're acting like you've done this terrible thing. Why are you so afraid to discuss it with me? Are you worried I would think less of you?"

"There's nothing to discuss. I can't even remember most of my time there. My clearest memories are with Winnie, and I'd prefer it stay that way."

"There are some things you remember, though," Ordell said with a sniff. "You wouldn't be so defensive if it weren't the case. Do you just not trust me enough to tell me?"

"Why is it so important to you?" Elias closed his eyes and took a deep breath, most likely to keep his voice from rising. "There's no reason you need to concern yourself with this."

"You're my friend," Ordell said finally. "I want to know who my friends are and not have secrets surrounding them."

"You don't need to know everything about everyone, Ordell. There are some secrets I'd rather keep to myself."

"Fine." He wasn't pleased with the answer, but Elias wouldn't budge on this. That didn't curb Ordell's curiosity, but he was willing to push it aside for now in favor of keeping their friendship. "What do you plan to do once we reach Linnesse?"

Elias smiled, clearly relieved Ordell had dropped the previous conversation. "I plan to join the revolution. Even if my help is small, I would love to do what I can to push the movement forward. What about you?"

Ordell shrugged. "I haven't thought much about it yet. I'm thinking about a peaceful life and maybe creating my own small shop. I could even help fix damaged automatons."

"You could use your skills to help us out," Elias suggested. "We could use all the help we can get."

Ordell shrugged. "I suppose, but I prefer to stay out of the action. It just isn't something that calls to me."

"You don't want to help others like us?" Elias furrowed his brows. "We can make a difference for other automatons."

Ordell shrugged again. It wasn't that he didn't support the cause; he just didn't know where the line was drawn for which automatons deserved rights and freedom. He glanced up at Elias, who was now frowning.

"I guess it's your life," Elias said. "I just hope you change your mind."

Ordell opened his mouth to argue, but a figure stepped in front of them, and his eyes widened.

Why would *he* be here, of all places?

CHAPTER 10

"WELL, IF it isn't my toy," Ratliff said with a wide smile. "I'm glad to see there is no damage done to you."

"You don't own me!" Ordell snapped. "I take no part in what you and Octavio agreed to!" Ordell himself seemed taken aback for an instant; on any other day, he would have fled without a second thought. Today, something was different—as though a switch had been flipped.

"But I do own you," Ratliff said. "Without me you'd still be somewhere in a basement."

"Ignore him, Ordell," Elias said, grabbing Ordell's shoulder.

"What do you mean?" he asked, nudging Elias's hand away. He knew Elias was right, but he was tired of running. Tired of being afraid of this man. "I was created for the plague. Even you should know about that!"

Ratliff chuckled and shook his head. "You've always been such an ignorant boy. You're lucky you're a pretty face, or else you'd never get through life."

Ordell gritted his teeth and glared at the older man. A part of him wanted to rip the bastard's heart out then and there. That'd show him what this *pretty face* could do!

Maybe he should. A lifetime in jail was worth it, was it not? At least the world would no longer have this rat to deal with.

He wouldn't even regret killing him. No, he would dance with joy the moment this bastard was buried six feet under. And if Ordell was the one to cause that, then all the better for him.

"Calm down, Ordell," Elias whispered in his ear. "He's doing this for your reaction. Do not give him that satisfaction."

"You need to control that temper, boy," Ratliff said, warily eyeing Elias. "I like a little spice, but if you continue acting like such a brat, then I'll have no choice but to treat you like those other mindless things your father sold off to me."

"You…." Ordell couldn't find a word accurate enough to describe this disgusting and horrid monster!

"Not the best with words, are you, boy? Thankfully your mouth will be used for other purposes. I suppose I overestimated your intellect."

"I will serve no purpose to you!" Ordell snapped. "The only favor I'd ever do for a monster like you is placing you in an early grave!"

"You watch your mouth, boy!" Ratliff pointed his walking stick at Ordell. "I know Octavio gave you better manners than this! I didn't buy you just to be insulted!"

"Then you might as well get a refund because that is all you'll ever get from me!"

"Don't antagonize him, Ordell," Elias said. "We just need to walk away and get out of here before he does anything."

"You think walking away will help?" Ratliff asked Elias. "I am powerful enough to hunt you both down easily."

"I can handle myself," Ordell said. "I can fight my own battles!"

"Now is not the time to fight them." Elias grabbed Ordell's arm, but it was a wasted effort. Ordell refused to leave until he got back at this bastard once and for all.

"I don't know what your relationship is with Octavio," Ordell said, "but I want no part of this! I'm just as human as you are! You can't do this to me!"

"But you're *not* human," Ratliff said. "You think you're important because you were built to stop the plague. You think you're important because you can say a few more words than your counterparts. I've been in this business for a while, boy, and I can tell you that you're nothing more than a piece of property. A toy. And that is all you'll ever be."

"That isn't true!" Ordell's fists tightened, and he debated the odds of killing Ratliff unnoticed. "You're nothing but a liar!"

"Octavio built you for me," Ratliff said. "I came to him asking for a sex doll and told him how I wanted it. Skin as fair as a china doll's. Silky copper hair." He got closer and grabbed ahold of Ordell's chin. "Watery blue eyes full of innocence and naïveté. Slender and soft." He pushed Ordell onto the ground. "I *created* you."

"Don't listen to him." Elias helped Ordell back to his feet. "You know Winnie created you."

Ratliff laughed. "Do you really think that you'd be here if it weren't for me? You and your friend must have some sort of brain on you! That hag left you there to collect dust. She gave up on her little project long ago." He then looked at Elias. "Well, almost."

Elias took a step back. "How do you know about me?"

"That isn't important," Ratliff said.

"The plague is still around," Ordell said. "So clearly I still have more use than you think."

"I have the plague under control," Ratliff said.

"It isn't under control in Northpine. Southpine even has a giant kraken to keep people from Northpine out. Sounds to me that they don't trust your medicine as much as you thought."

"That isn't any of your concern, and frankly, I've grown tired of your jabbering." Three guards came out from behind Ratliff. "Grab the pretty one. I only want him."

Ordell spun around and ran. A part of him debated if he should look back to see if Elias followed him. He slowed his pace and turned his head to see Elias was still there fighting off the three guards.

He couldn't let them hurt Elias.

Ordell headed back toward the guards, but someone grabbed him, and the next thing he knew, he was tossed over a broad shoulder. The man walked toward Ratliff, and Ordell glanced up to see one of the other guards had Elias pinned to the ground.

Ratliff then came into his line of sight with that disgusting toothy smile plastered on his bony face. "There's my boy," he said with a chuckle. "Good thing Octavio didn't make you a fighter, or else this would have been a *challenge* for me."

Ordell glared up at him and wanted nothing more than to spit in the man's face, but he couldn't risk Ratliff killing Elias out of spite. Instead he remained quiet. When Elias was out of danger's way, then Ordell could make his move to escape.

"What should we do with this one, sir?" One of the guards kicked at Elias's side.

"Don't bother," Ratliff said. "He's just useless scrap. I have a very important meeting and will not allow myself to be late."

Ordell sighed in relief to hear they wouldn't kill Elias. He still didn't want to take any chances of escaping while Elias was there, in case Ratliff changed his mind. It wouldn't surprise him if Ratliff ordered them to hurt Elias because Ordell misbehaved.

"Where should I put him?" the guard holding Ordell asked.

"Just take him to my room and store him in one of the crates. He should be fine there until I return."

They walked away, and Ordell watched as Elias forced himself up to his elbows. He reached inside his vest and pulled out a gun. The next thing Ordell knew, a loud shot rang out, and the man holding Ordell collapsed to the ground.

Ordell didn't even hesitate; he ran away from Ratliff and toward Elias. He extended his hand and helped Elias back to his feet, and then turned around to see the collapsed man, a clean shot right through his head.

At that moment everything felt as if it were moving in slow motion. His eyes were locked on the pool of blood around the still body, and then he glanced back up at the guards and Ratliff.

"Murderer," Ratliff said, eyes wide. "Murderer!"

Ordell tugged on Elias's sleeve. "Come on, we need to move!"

"Kill him!" Ratliff screamed out. "Kill him and grab my boy!"

Ordell finally got Elias to run with him, and they fled through the streets, sounds of the guards behind them. Ratliff was still shouting, but Ordell couldn't make heads or tails of it; all he could hear was the thumping in his ears.

THEY RAN until they reached a wooded area behind the abandoned town.

"I think we lost them," Ordell said once they got far enough into the woods. "I don't hear anything."

Elias walked away from him and steadied himself against one of the trees. Ordell saw the tremors run through his arms. Elias was breathing harder than usual—almost a whimper but too quiet for Ordell to be sure.

"Are you all right?" Ordell asked and placed his hand on Elias's shoulder. "Do you need to rest for a few moments?"

"I just k-killed someone," Elias stuttered out. "I actually killed someone!"

"Elias...."

"My job is to protect you, Ordell," he huffed out. "I was created to protect you. But... but I never thought I would kill someone. I-I couldn't even control it."

Ordell placed his hand on Elias's shoulder. "You protected me. You did what Winifred created you for."

"I don't want to be like this!" Elias snapped. "I thought we were meant to have freedom! I couldn't control it!"

"When we get to Linnesse, we can ask them to change that," Ordell said softly. "They'll fix it."

Elias looked at him and then slowly nodded. "They'll fix it."

He didn't understand much of what had upset Elias. In Ordell's eyes it was self-defense. Elias was only doing what he could to protect them. The guards wanted to hurt them.

"Thank you for helping me," Ordell tried.

Elias pulled away from Ordell's grip. "Don't you understand? I *killed* someone."

"I do," he said. "You were just trying to protect me. They were planning to kill you at first, if you remember."

Elias remained silent. Didn't even bother looking up.

"I'm a bit surprised to see a forest here," Ordell said, hoping the subject change would calm Elias down. "It feels as if no one traverses through here."

"They most likely don't," Elias said after taking a deep breath. "This area's been abandoned since the plague. Mainly hunters come through here, but I doubt any would be out now. We should be safe here until things calm down."

They walked farther into the forest. "The plague really took a toll on Southpine," Ordell said. "I'm surprised it even recovered to where it is now."

"Southpine and Northpine depended on one another for trade and other necessities," Elias said as they walked off the path. "It's foolish for Southpine to block off all of Northpine like it has, but fear makes people do stupid things, unfortunately. The only way they're going to thrive like they once did is if they allow trading from Northpine again."

"Where are we going?" Ordell asked.

It was clear Elias had some sort of path planned. He wasn't sure what that path was, but something about how Elias walked through the woods felt rehearsed. Winifred certainly couldn't have directed Elias about this. Southpine wasn't on the map, and the only reason they were there in the first place was because of that blasted kraken!

"Elias?" Ordell tried again when he received no answer.

"Be patient," Elias said finally.

Ordell frowned at that, but he let it slide. He hated not knowing and hated even more when his questions were ignored. If this was going to become a habit with Elias, then they were going to have a long talk about secrets and giving proper answers.

THEY WALKED farther and farther, and Ordell was beginning to grow even more impatient. The sun was close to setting, and Elias still hadn't taken a break from his path. No small talk. No looking at the trees or the animals. Just walking.

And walking.

"Just tell me where we're going," Ordell said. "I don't like following blindly."

"I need to keep you safe," Elias said.

"Fine, but tell me where we're going!" Never in his life had he wanted to punch a man as much as now. "I'm tired of walking and I'm tired of the silence."

Elias pointed up ahead. "There."

Ordell squinted until he made out a small cottage up ahead. "Why on earth would anyone build a house out here?"

They walked up to the cottage and Ordell peered through the tinted windows. It was too dark to see anything, but he didn't want to risk disturbing someone inside their home.

Elias tried the door, but it was locked. Ordell then walked up to the door and knocked.

"No one lives here," Elias said as he turned over the rocks near the house.

"How would you know that?" Ordell asked. "What are you doing?"

"Looking for something," Elias said. "And I know because I'm programmed to know."

"Did Winifred build some sort of crystal ball inside you?" Ordell scoffed. "How would she know that no one lives here? She hasn't even been outside of Blackwick for a while now, has she?"

Elias grabbed a small brass key from underneath one of the rocks. "This is what I was looking for," he said with a smile.

"You can't break into someone's home!"

"No one lives here, Ordell," he said in a clearly annoyed tone and then put the key inside the lock and turned it. "See?"

Elias opened the door, and Ordell stepped inside, a little hesitant at first. When he felt confident Elias was right, he straightened up and squared his shoulders. "It's still rude to enter a house that isn't yours," he said, clearing his throat.

Elias walked over to one of the gas lamps and lit it. "Right now I'm not all that concerned about manners."

"When are you ever?"

Elias rolled his eyes, and Ordell couldn't help but chuckle to himself.

The cottage was small and cramped; it clearly hadn't been lived in for quite some time. Cobwebs decorated the dirty fireplace and the small wooden table. The place was such a mess Ordell was surprised the gas lamp even worked.

He walked over to the fireplace and inspected the logs. If they wanted a nice fire, they would have to get logs from outside. These were too charred to be of any use.

There was a small bed off in the corner. The sheets were stained and Ordell shuddered at the thought of sleeping on it. The dusty wood floor seemed more hygienic.

Besides, he could offer the bed up to Elias as a kind gesture. Maybe he could prove he wasn't as insufferable as he seemed.

"You were right," Ordell said. "This place has been abandoned for quite some time. It looks like the person who lived here was rather slovenly."

"It's meant to look like this," Elias said.

"Why on earth would anyone want their home to look like this? Is it some sort of fashion trend I missed out on?"

To his surprise Elias laughed. "No. This place was never meant to be lived in. At least not up here."

Ordell furrowed his brows. "I don't understand."

Elias felt along the brick wall and a trapdoor sprung from the floor. Brick stairs led down toward the darkness below.

"This cottage," Elias said, still smiling, "is one of the many homes of the underground revolution."

CHAPTER 11

THE TRAPDOOR led to a bunker down below. Much to Ordell's relief, the bed down there was in much better condition. There also seemed to be a storage area for food and a small workshop off in the corner.

"The revolution set up these houses to easily transport sex slaves to safety. It sort of works like an underground tunnel," Elias said. "Winifred gave me the locations of these bunkers so we could easily traverse in case something like this happened."

"And Ratliff doesn't know about these?"

Elias shook his head. "Only the revolution, as far as I know. They've helped many automatons this way, you know. I don't know what's become of them, but it must be better than their previous life."

"Do they all go to Linnesse?"

"Yes. Linnesse is the safest place for automatons. Not even Ratliff can get inside there."

"Then why were you sent to Blackwick?"

Ordell could see Elias cringe at that question. "I don't know what you're talking about."

"Did someone send you to Winifred?" He gave a small shrug and crossed his arms. "Or did you go there by yourself?"

"You're not going to let this go, are you?"

"No."

Elias sighed and leaned back against the wall. "I was first created as a pleasure slave. There wasn't much to me except to follow my master's orders. I don't remember much of that time, but I do remember feeling trapped. I didn't know it at the time, but it was always there."

Ordell nodded but didn't understand what Elias meant. Still, he didn't want to interrupt to ask silly questions.

"I remember that I loved my master," Elias continued. "I was happy to do anything for him. All I wanted to do was please him and obey him. I was built in Goldcrest, but I traveled with my master. However, there was a part of me that hated him. I hated myself. This wasn't programmed in me, Ordell. This was something I developed on my own. The only difference between then and now is that now I have the freedom to express that hatred."

"You shouldn't hate yourself," Ordell said. "You are an amazing man."

Elias scoffed.

"I mean it." Ordell moved closer. "You have a passion to do what's right. Not only that but you have a good sense of humor and try to see the positive in life."

"Doesn't feel like it."

"But it's true," Ordell said. "Honestly I'm rather envious of you. You have qualities I wish I had. If I could be like you and not care as much about what others think of me, I would be much happier."

"You would be," Elias said with a small smile. "I don't think I'm the only slave who is like this, Ordell."

"You don't really believe that these pleasure slaves are developing their own emotions and opinions, do you?" Ordell tried to keep his voice soft. "I've helped my father create automatons for years. It just doesn't seem possible for something like this to happen without the emotions being programmed in somehow."

"I know what I felt," Elias said.

"Are you sure you didn't just put those emotions there after Winifred fixed you? Maybe your memories are a bit clouded and...."

"I know what I felt, Ordell. You don't have to believe me, but do not mock this."

"I'm not," Ordell said, putting a hand on Elias's shoulder. "I'm just trying to figure it out. I want to understand it."

"There isn't anything to understand. Emotions aren't something you can figure out," Elias said. "Sometimes they show up without reason. That's why my master threw me out in the first place."

"What do you mean?"

"He had me created to please his wife while he was away on business trips. He was worried about her not being faithful and thought I could solve the problem. I was created to be attracted to women, but I prefer men. My master and the person who created me couldn't figure out why that is. Eventually they deemed me a 'fluke' and tossed me out. There was already a working male automaton who did prefer women, so they didn't need my parts. I was just an inexpensive model, after all."

"I'm sorry," Ordell said in a soft voice. "That's terrible."

"It's in the past," Elias said. "Nothing I can do to change it."

"I don't know if this makes you feel better," Ordell said, "but apparently my father set me up to be a pleasure slave too."

"Luckily for you, you managed to get away," Elias said. "I'd hate to think what would have happened to you. I wouldn't even wish that fate on my worst enemy."

"I would've fought back," Ordell said, sticking out his chin. "Ratliff wouldn't put one of his bony fingers on me."

"Don't underestimate the humans, Ordell," Elias said. "Despite how much I hate it, we were built by a human. They can destroy us too."

"But they wouldn't," Ordell said. "Not when we're a novelty."

"That doesn't make it better," Elias grumbled. "We are still objects to them. Just pieces of equipment for the humans to use as they please."

"Not all humans are like that."

Elias furrowed his brow. "I don't understand how you can say that when your father sold you to that man."

Ordell bowed his head. He still hadn't forgiven Octavio for what happened. Truth was, Ordell wasn't sure if he'd ever forgive his father.

"I'm sorry," Elias said, almost whispering it. "I didn't mean to bring up those memories. It was rude of me to bring him up."

"No, it's fine."

He didn't want to think about those memories, but they were there. Prominent in his mind and creeping back to the surface each time he tried to forget their existence. It pained him to know he couldn't change the past and could only leave it behind him. The worst part was he'd trusted Octavio. His own father gave him up to that monster! And for what? An extra piece of bread? Did Octavio get a new house out of their deal? Maybe he got to travel the high seas like he always wanted and had enough money to afford a vacation home.

Ordell didn't know, and a part of him wished he knew what his father was doing right then. If Octavio even thought of him, even felt a hint of remorse for selling Ordell.

And that was when it hit him.

Elias struggled with these similar thoughts. Struggled to overcome them and shut them out, only to have them come back in the dead of night.

"You deserve so much better," Ordell finally said. "You shouldn't have to go through with this."

"With what?" Elias asked, cocking his head slightly.

"With the memories. With the past. Just with all of this. I don't get how you can stay sane after what happened to you."

"Sometimes I wonder if I *am* sane," Elias said with a laugh. "There are times when I'm convinced I've lost my mind."

"You're more sane than me." Ordell laughed too. "I don't know if that's much of an accomplishment, though."

"You're amazing," Elias said. "Your father is the one out of his mind for giving you up. I still can't wrap my head around how he could give away someone so invaluable."

Before Ordell could comprehend what his mind was thinking, he leaned in and kissed Elias.

It was just a quick and modest kiss, but Ordell could see Elias's gaze deepen when they pulled away. Ordell opened his mouth to apologize, but Elias brought their lips together again and kissed Ordell harder.

Ordell parted his mouth to let Elias in; his head spun as Elias kissed him harder and pulled Ordell closer against his body.

The kissing grew faster, and Ordell brushed his trembling hand down Elias's chest.

Elias pulled away, and Ordell opened his eyes. "What's wrong?" Ordell asked. "I'm sorry if I'm moving too fast. We can slow down if you don't feel—"

"It's not that. I just don't want you to feel like you need to do this," Elias said.

"I'm ready for this."

"We can wait till we're in a more romantic place," Elias whispered. "We can wait."

"I don't want to wait," he said. "Please. I need this."

"Okay." Elias nuzzled into Ordell's neck; he curled his arms loosely around Ordell, nudging them back onto the bed.

He then stopped Ordell from tearing his clothes away.

"Let me go first," Elias mumbled into Ordell's skin, taking his time undoing Ordell's shirt. He lifted his hands up when the last button was undone, resting his thumbs on Ordell's nipples, rubbing lightly over them.

Ordell felt them stiffen under Elias's touch and a small noise came from his lips. Elias then trailed his mouth down Ordell's neck, kissing past his collarbone. Then down his chest, lightly biting at one of the stiffened nubs before sucking it into his mouth.

Ordell cradled Elias's head in his hands as he gasped, clutching small handfuls of Elias's hair. He felt his trousers tighten slightly as Elias sucked harder on his nipple. Ordell let out a small groan of protest when he felt his lips leave and then moaned again happily as Elias swapped to give affection to the other one, then slid a hand down to gently grasp his bulge.

"Elias…," he couldn't help but moan out, raising his hips eagerly against Elias's hand for more.

"Patience," Elias mumbled against Ordell's chest.

Elias raised his head and looked at Ordell with a wicked grin. He then lowered his head, sliding his tongue up the middle of Ordell's chest and working back up to his neck. He reached his ear, and Elias paused to give it a light nibble.

Ordell felt Elias give his bulge a quick squeeze, and he let out a small gasp before he ground himself up into the hand, grasping him, the feeling of precum appearing where his length was straining the fabric of his trousers.

Ordell could feel Elias smiling against his neck and then felt his hand move up slightly; Elias rubbed his palm against the head of Ordell's cock through the trousers.

"Just take them off already!" Ordell hissed impatiently.

"Not yet. I've done this before—let me work." Elias chuckled into Ordell's skin.

Elias then rose up, pressing a hand onto Ordell's chest to keep him lying back; with the other he tugged down the trousers, exposing Ordell's cock.

"Stay right there, all right?" Elias slid down Ordell's body, planting soft kisses on the way down.

"A-all right," Ordell couldn't help but stammer as he watched, moving his hands to the sheets, clutching them in anticipation.

Elias rolled his tongue over the tip of Ordell's length, and Ordell felt it jump slightly at the attention. It was all he could do to suppress a small whimper as he raised his hips up, feeling Elias curl his lips around the end, sucking lightly.

Ordell clawed at the sheets as Elias's sucking grew stronger. Ordell gasped when he felt Elias curl a strong hand around the base of his cock, stroking him for extra stimulation.

"Elias…," Ordell groaned softly with a small hiss, grinding his hips up into Elias's hand.

"Yes?" Elias called back in a teasing tone, running his finger over the slit of his head.

That damn bastard was toying with him! If Elias thought he could get away with this, then he had another thing coming!

"J-just take me already!" Ordell snapped, sitting up and slightly glaring down at him. "Damn it, Elias!"

"You sure you want it already?" he replied sheepishly, that damn smirk growing on his face.

"Wh… what do you mean? Yes! I want it already!" he huffed out, feeling as if he had become red from head to toe by saying that.

"Are you really sure about that?"

"Elias!" His eyes then widened. "What the hell?"

He caught a glimpse at what Elias had hidden from the sizable tent his trousers were making, a slight sheen showing on the fabric along his length as his own body prepped itself.

To his surprise Elias blushed. "Well… you know how we're the same. The thing is, though…. Well, my master's wife had… she had a 'beefier' taste in a man's girth." He rubbed the back of his neck. "Not that I was any use to her. You should have seen the next guy my master bought."

"So she wanted a man with the cock of a damn bull?" Ordell grumbled and then looked from Elias's bulge to his own. He pouted, a bit envious.

"Not exactly what I meant." Elias chuckled, nuzzling into Ordell's neck as he grabbed Ordell's length again. "It's also why I'm teasing so much."

"Are… are you serious?" Ordell yelped slightly and squirmed against him. "I-I don't think it's going to fit."

Elias pulled back and tugged on Ordell's trousers, taking them off. "That's why I'm working your body, you nut."

Before Ordell could get another word in, Elias pulled him toward him again, his knees resting on Elias's shoulders. Ordell felt his face and ears become heated.

Ordell whimpered when he felt his sac slip between Elias's lips. He let out a small yelp when Elias gently sucked and teased it. Ordell felt his whole body go limp in pleasure as Elias continued to tease him, precum slowly drooling down onto his stomach. Elias then slipped one finger into Ordell's entrance.

Then another finger.

Ordell arched his back and moaned as Elias worked his fingers in, teasing Ordell in every direction. Elias moved his hand and went back to stroking Ordell's length, stopping at the end, toying with the slit.

"C-can we just g-get it over with already?" Ordell groaned, looking up at Elias.

"Fine," Elias said with a small grin. He positioned himself and pressed the head of his cock inside Ordell's entrance, Elias's shaft nearly dripping with his lube rubbing gently around Ordell's hole. "Tell me if it gets too uncomfortable."

Ordell nodded. "Keep going."

Elias settled fully inside Ordell and then pulled back before thrusting forward and speeding up. Ordell moaned and wrapped his arms around Elias's neck.

Ordell's ears rang as Elias continued, the pace growing faster and faster. Ordell felt a large release of pressure, and relief washed over him when his cum coated his abs. Elias slowed his strokes and his biceps shook, and Ordell could see he was struggling to keep his position.

Moments later Elias met his own release with a groan, a flushed look of bliss crossing his face. He slowly pulled out and rolled to Ordell's side. "Sorry," he murmured, looking at Ordell with sleepy eyes. "I thought I could last longer."

Ordell snuggled against his chest and let Elias wrap his arms around him and pull Ordell closer. "No, I loved it. Any more and you really would have been the death of me."

Elias kissed the top of Ordell's head. "Then it's a good thing we stopped."

Ordell laughed and then yawned.

"Go to sleep," Elias said. "We still have time before we need to leave."

Ordell nodded and closed his eyes, feeling satisfied.

CHAPTER 12

ORDELL OPENED his eyes and stretched. He felt safe and warm wrapped in Elias's arms. He'd never thought he would enjoy sharing his bed with someone else, but Elias, once again, proved him wrong.

If he weren't so smitten with this man, Ordell would have punched him for making him question himself yet again.

The cabin wasn't the most romantic place for them to show their love, but it was perfect enough. Ordell loved every minute of it, but he knew if he stroked Elias's ego too much, then he'd *never* hear the end of it.

Ordell felt Elias massage his shoulders, then circle down to the small of his back. Ordell closed his eyes and let out a soft moan at how good it felt.

Well, if Elias was going to make him feel like this every time they made love, then Ordell had no issues stroking the man's ego after all.

"How are you feeling?" Elias murmured and then kissed the top of Ordell's head. "Sore? Need me to do anything?"

Ordell stretched again and yawned. "I'm fine. I'm not as sore as I expected to be."

"Good," Elias said with a small chuckle. "With how you reacted last night, I thought I might've broken you."

Ordell lifted his head and glared at him. "I was startled."

"I think you were a bit more than startled." Elias's chuckles vibrated against Ordell's ear. "I apologize for making you cry."

"You didn't make me cry," Ordell grumbled. "I told you I got dust in my eyes, which made them watery. It had nothing to do with you."

Elias poked Ordell's cheek. "You'd be far more convincing if you didn't blush bright red while saying that. Besides, automatons can't get dust in their eyes."

"My eyes only watered a small bit," he said, frowning. "You make it sound like I was sobbing!"

"Fine," Elias said with a chuckle. "I apologize for making your eyes water."

"Better."

Elias tickled Ordell's ear. "I'm going to spoil you so much."

"I think you already have."

Despite his best efforts, Ordell felt himself falling for this man. There was an understanding between Elias and him Ordell couldn't find with any human. Ordell couldn't deny the comfort he felt knowing there was someone else like him. Someone who struggled with the pained memories of betrayal, someone who could understand not fitting in with the humans or the other automatons.

He nuzzled into Elias's chest and sighed. Yes, that understanding was a big reason Ordell felt drawn in, but there was more. Elias's passion and humor were something Ordell loved—felt envious of. He wanted that too. *He* wanted to draw Elias into a frenzy like Elias did to him. Not with his looks, but with his words. With his emotions.

It amazed him how anyone could toss Elias aside like he was nothing. Elias was so much more than that—deserved more than that. Ordell could only hope he could offer even half of what Elias deserved.

He felt Elias kiss the top of his head. "Did you fall asleep again?"

Ordell shook his head. "No."

"You got quiet on me."

Ordell smiled. "You got quiet on me first."

Elias tickled his ear again and Ordell squirmed. "What am I going to do with such a silly boy?"

"You could kiss him."

"I could do that."

Ordell lifted his head, and Elias leaned down to kiss him, only stopping inches away. Ordell moved to meet him the rest of the way, but Elias smiled and slowly pulled away.

"Don't be mean!" Ordell said through his laughter. "Kiss me!"

This time Elias did kiss him. It was chaste compared to the night before but still satisfying.

If only they could stay in this bed forever. It might not have been the most comfortable bed Ordell had rested in or even the warmest, but it was the only bed he had shared with someone else—someone he cared about. That alone made this bed better than all the others he had slept in.

Elias kissed the tip of Ordell's nose. "I love when you get lost in thought. Your nose scrunches and you purse your lips out."

Ordell's face heated. "I do not!" When Elias chuckled, Ordell narrowed his eyes. "I don't make funny faces, Elias Griffith! I've been raised better than that!"

"Come on," Elias said, still smiling. "You need to lighten up a bit. I didn't mean for it to be an insult. On the contrary, I find it absolutely adorable."

Ordell smiled back at him. "I suppose I do make funny faces when I think too hard. My father used to slap me upside the head every time I pursed my lips. He said no gentleman in his right mind would purse his lips like that."

"I wouldn't trust anything Octavio said," Elias said flatly. "You're perfect the way you are, Ordell. Don't let someone tell you otherwise."

"I know I should hate him," he said. "It'd be logical if I did, but I can't help but still care for him at times. I'll never forgive him for what he did to me, but that doesn't mean the happy memories need to be tainted, does it?"

"If you want to keep those happy memories, Ordell, then you should," Elias said softly. "As long as you don't believe you deserve the bad memories, then there is nothing wrong with keeping the happy ones."

"Do you think it's safe to go back and find Buford? I'm sure he must be wondering where we went off to."

"Ratliff doesn't know we're with Buford. A little farther ahead there is an old dock where some rafts are stored. If Ratliff has even half a brain in him, he'll come to the conclusion that we stole one of the rafts and went on to Redwood."

"Is that one of the places Winifred programmed for us to go to?"

Elias shook his head. "Only as an emergency. I don't even think Winifred's been in Redwood. I don't carry much information about it."

"She's gone to a lot of places, hasn't she?"

"Yes," Elias said with a nod, "she has. I don't know much about her life, but I've seen the maps and drawings of various places. She seems particularly fond of Silverfield. I'm surprised she chose to live in Blackwick instead of there."

"Blackwick's a nice place," Ordell said with a sniff. "It may not be as full of life as Silverfield, but everyone feels like a family there."

"I hope Linnesse feels like home to you like Blackwick did. There are some areas that are smaller there, but it's a bit more like Silverfield than Blackwick."

"I'm sure I'll love it." Ordell smiled. "I'd much rather be in a place where I don't have to hide who I am. That alone makes Linnesse home to me."

THEY WAITED until midday before leaving the forest. To be safe Elias chose a more hidden path for them to follow, just in case Ratliff was still in Southpine.

"What will we do if Ratliff captures me?" Ordell asked.

"That won't happen."

"But if it did. We should have some sort of plan, yes?"

Elias grabbed Ordell's hand. "I promise that he will not capture you."

He knew Elias was trying to comfort him, but he didn't want comfort. He wanted a plan so they were prepared for the worst. Still, seeing Elias smile and try to play protector made Ordell want to not ruin the moment. Trying to correct Elias for his good intentions was like kicking a puppy. Both were highly unacceptable.

The alternate path they took was depressing. There were broken automatons scattered throughout, and some didn't even look that old. Ordell hadn't seen any pleasure slaves walking around in Southpine, but these broken-down automatons were clearly that.

"Southpine got rid of their pleasure slaves," Elias explained, holding on to Ordell's hand. "Owning pleasure slaves became an 'impure' thing for the people here, and many promptly got rid of them. I'm sure there are some who still own pleasure slaves, but they're kept hidden now."

"And they broke down the automatons instead of simply releasing them?" He felt rage boil inside him. "This isn't even practical! Even if the humans do see us as nothing more than machines, it still makes no sense to throw them out here! If anything it wastes precious money."

"I don't understand the logic either," Elias said.

"Will you be all right walking through here?" Ordell asked. "We can take the other path. It'd make no sense for Ratliff to still be here."

"I'll be fine." When Ordell raised a brow at him, Elias cleared his throat. "We can go the other way instead. I'd hate for you to see any more of this."

Close enough. Considering Elias's stubbornness, this was the closest Ordell would get to a compromise.

They went back and walked down the normal path. Once they reached the lively part of Southpine, Ordell felt relief. The sounds of people talking and children playing helped ease the depression he felt when he'd seen those broken automatons. He squeezed Elias's hand, and Elias squeezed back to signal he felt better too.

A child ran under their linked hands, and then another followed shortly behind. A woman chased after the two boys, scolding them for making a nuisance. Ordell chuckled; the children were anything but a nuisance to him. At least their laughter put a smile on Elias's face.

"I wish I knew what that's like," Elias said, still smiling.

"Running?"

"No," he said. "Being a child. Each age holds something new for them. You must have wondered what that was like too, with you being around humans all your life."

Ordell scrunched his nose. "No, I didn't. I never thought too much about growing old. I rather like my independence. I think being a child would be dull for me."

"You don't feel as if you're missing out on something important?"

"No, not really," Ordell admitted. "There are times I wonder if you have the heart of a child, though. Perhaps you already have what you crave." Ordell meant that to be a joke, but it didn't make Elias laugh. "You're perfect the way you are."

That made Elias laugh. "I'm supposed to tell you that, remember?"

"I'll tell you too if that's what gets you to laugh," Ordell said with a small smile. "Your laugh's contagious."

"If you like it so much, then I'll have to remember to laugh more often."

Ordell nudged Elias, and Elias nudged back. They intertwined their fingers, taking the longer path.

"Shouldn't we try to get to Buford as quick as possible?" Ordell asked.

"We can take a tiny detour," Elias said with a sheepish grin. "He won't leave without us."

They walked by a large crowd and watched a man and woman play a glass instrument. Their wet fingers slid over the glass, making such a unique and beautiful sound. The watery sound was so haunting it sent chills up Ordell's spine.

"I wish I could play that," Ordell breathed. "It's so beautiful."

"When we get to Linnesse, I'll buy you one," Elias said. "Well, once I get a job and we're more stable, financially. After all that, though, I promise to buy you one."

"Do you think they have lessons to teach me how to play it?"

"They have lessons for everything," Elias said with a chuckle. "I'm sure there's instructors out there to teach you how to play the glass armonica."

Ordell closed his eyes and let the strange music fill him. He'd never heard anything like it in his life. He had heard other instruments, but this was such a new sound; even Elias seemed to be in awe over the music it created.

"How do you think they learned to play it?" Elias whispered.

"I'm not too sure." The instrument was such a strange contraption, with what appeared to be glass bowls lined up against one another. They spun around as the couple pressed their wet fingers on the glass. "It must have taken a lot of trial and error."

After they stopped playing, Ordell walked up to one of the musicians and asked if he could try playing it.

"We shouldn't bother them," Elias said when Ordell asked.

"It's no trouble at all," the lady said with a smile. "First, what you do is dip your fingers into the small bowl of water like this." She did just that, and Ordell followed. "Now, just run your fingers over the glass while I step on the pedal to make it spin."

When the instrument started to spin, he moved his fingers lightly over the glass and the haunting tune flowed from his fingertips.

"Perfect," she said. "Just like that."

The music didn't sound as beautiful as when the couple played it, but Ordell still enjoyed the sound it made. It was so unique compared to anything he'd ever heard before—like playing a harp under water.

He let the couple take over to play their next song. "Do you think we could get one of those when we reach Linnesse?" Ordell asked.

"It'll be expensive to own an instrument like that." Elias sighed, then smiled. "But you're worth the money."

The music stopped, and Ordell felt disappointed. He wanted to hear more, but Elias was already walking away before the couple could play their next song.

They walked to the dock, but the ship was gone. Ordell felt a twinge of panic stir inside him at the thought Buford might have left without them. They could use the rafts Elias had talked about, but then Ordell would get wet again, and he hated wearing soggy clothes.

"Over here!" Buford called out from four piers down. "Where have you two been?"

"This isn't our ship," Ordell said as they caught up to Buford. "Looks nothing like it!"

"The other ship was too torn down," Buford said with a small sigh. "I had to get this one instead. We don't have as many memories, but she'll do just fine."

"I think it looks nice," Elias said, trailing his fingers along the side of the ship.

"Don't touch her!" Buford smacked Elias's hands away. "How would you like it if I brushed my fingers across *you*?"

Elias raised his brows. "I'm flattered by the offer, Buford, but…."

"Exactly," Buford spat out. "Don't. Touch. My. Ship."

"We apologize for being gone for so long," Ordell said. "We found a cottage in the woods and slept there for the night. Despite how run-down it is, the house was rather cozy."

"Why in tarnation were you out in the forest?" Buford raised his bushy brows. "You're lucky you didn't get lost in there!"

"Mr. Saunders found us," Ordell said.

"Who?"

"Ratliff," Elias tried.

"I haven't the faintest idea who you're talking about, boy."

"The man my father sold me to," Ordell said in an exasperated sigh. "He's the reason why we're going to Linnesse in the first place. Don't you remember any of this?"

"Of course I do!" Buford said. "We need to leave immediately."

"We're sure he's gone now," Elias said.

"Better safe than sorry." Buford climbed onto the ship. "Besides, the sooner we get to Linnesse, the better."

Ordell couldn't argue with that reasoning. He climbed onto the ship and Elias followed shortly behind.

"Wow," Ordell said with wide eyes. "This is much bigger than our old ship. How could you afford to rent this one?"

"Never mind that," Buford said. "Raise the anchor, Elias."

Elias did just that. "There's so much room here," he said as he finished rolling the anchor in. "I bet that kraken couldn't destroy this one."

The gears of the ship spun and the vessel floated away from the pier. Moments later a large man ran out of the small pub near the docks.

"Come back! That's my ship!"

"Buford," Ordell said slowly. "How did you get this ship?"

"I-I found it," Buford said.

"Did you find it *legally*?"

"My, look at that beautiful sun," Buford said. "A perfect day to be out on the sea, don't you think?"

Ordell sighed. He couldn't believe he'd just helped boatjack their new transportation. That was one step away from becoming pirates!

If his father could see the shenanigans he had gotten himself into with these two, Ordell's rear would be raw for a month.

CHAPTER 13

THE SHIP finally reached the docks of Goldcrest.

Ordell's eyes widened as he took in the new environment. The first thing that caught his eye was the large golden waterwheel and the crystal-blue stream that divided the town. The next things he noticed were the crystal sky-high buildings and the houses that looked like miniature castles. The golden bridge, which connected the two parts separated by the stream, had one of the biggest archways he'd ever seen.

The town was filled with vibrant people, and almost everything seemed to be operated by gears and automatons. Fall leaves fell from the trees, signifying fall had arrived.

Ordell stepped off the ship and walked farther into the town. There were so many stairs to get from one elevation to the other, Ordell swore if he climbed high enough he could touch the clouds in the afternoon sky.

Maybe this was what Elias meant when he talked about how free the flying ships would be. To be among the clouds and the birds didn't seem as ridiculous now that Ordell saw the possibility.

A small rectangular machine zoomed past him and toward the leaves, which had fallen from one of the large elm trees. The little wheels screeched to a halt, and within a blink of an eye, the leaves were sucked inside the machine. It then went to the next pile of leaves, and Ordell couldn't help but chuckle.

There were many machines like that scattered through the town. Some sucked up the leaves, others looked to be cleaning the water, and others cleaned the town of garbage and other wastes.

Despite how extravagant and clean the town was, something about it felt off to Ordell. It was like he could smell what he would call death there.

Ordell scanned the town again. None of the people there acted like they felt what he felt. On the contrary, in fact. The streets were filled with laughter, street performers, and children presumably released from the school day.

"Something is off here," Ordell said with furrowed brows. "Do you sense it?"

"I don't feel anything," Elias said as he got off the ship. "Let's just get to the market and leave."

Ordell put his hand on Elias's shoulder and softened his expression. "You can stay on the ship. Buford and I can take care of this."

"No."

"We understand," Ordell tried. "We'll make it quick and—"

"*No!*" Elias inhaled through his nose and rubbed his temples. "I'm fine, Ordell. Really."

"You don't look fine." He crossed his arms and raised an eyebrow. "And I don't appreciate you snapping at me when I'm only trying to help."

"Not everyone bows down to you, you know," Elias grumbled.

Ordell gaped at that. "*Excuse* me? If you think that you can treat me like this after what happened with us, then you've thought wrong, Elias Griffith!" He narrowed his eyes and stepped back into Elias's line of sight when he tried to look away. "You have no right to treat me like trash! If this is how you plan to treat me from now on, then I want no part of you!"

"I'm sorry," Elias said. "I don't want to stay on the ship like some coward. My job is to protect you, Ordell. If I hide in there, then I'm failing my job."

"Fine." Ordell uncrossed his arms. "However, if you throw another fit, I'm sending you back to the ship."

Ordell heard Elias grumble something else, but he couldn't hear it, which was probably for the best for Elias. If that man gave Ordell any more lip, so help him....

Well, at least Goldcrest was nice to look at. It almost made Ordell envious he didn't live there, despite the fate of automatons. If he were human, he would pack up and live in this town in an instant.

As he wandered away from Elias and the dock, he noticed a group of children playing five stones on the bright cobblestone road.

"Mind if I play?" Ordell asked with a smile. "I love five stones."

A little girl with braided hair nodded at him. "Okay. You can go."

Ordell knelt down on the cobblestones and sighed. "I hope I still got it." He tossed the stones up and got three on the back of his hand. It had been longer than he could remember since he had simply allowed himself to enjoy his surroundings. One of the little boys went after Ordell's turn and picked up the stones with such a fast pace Ordell felt a little embarrassed at his speed.

"You're not very good at this," the little girl said finally.

"Sorry." Ordell grimaced. "It's been a while since I've last played."

"You're still not very good."

"What's your name?" Ordell asked.

"Abigail." She pointed to the boy with the cap. "He's John. The one picking his nose is Walter. We just met him today. What's your name?"

"Ordell. It's a pleasure to meet you all."

"Did you just come here?" John asked. "I haven't seen you before."

"Yes, came in by ship."

"I've always wanted to be on a ship!" Abigail said. "I was going to go with my papa, but he's too sick to travel."

"I'm sorry to hear that," Ordell said, keeping his voice soft. "Does he have a cold?"

She shook her head. "He has a bloody nose and throws up blood. My mama's really worried, but she tells me that he'll be right as rain soon enough. She says that once he is, he'll take us all out on a ship ride."

"Ordell!" Elias ran over toward them. "You mustn't wander off in a new area! Something could've happened!"

"We're playing five stones," Ordell said. He was still bitter toward Elias for how he had spoken to him earlier, but he tried not to let that show. "If I sensed danger, I would have come back immediately."

"We can't be wasting time here," Elias said. "There's no time for you to make friends with these hum—children."

Ordell got up and brushed the dirt off his trousers, but not before making a mental note to look into Abigail's father's condition later. Something about it troubled him to his very core. "What's gotten into you?" Ordell asked. "You've been in this horrid mood ever since we got here."

"You know why," Elias said, matching Ordell's glare. "I think I have a pretty damn good reason for not wanting to be here."

"And I said you could stay on the ship." There were times he didn't understand Elias's logic. Ordell had made it clear he and Buford had this under control. "If you're going to behave like this, then I suggest you stay on the ship."

Elias grabbed Ordell's elbow and pulled him away from the children and the people walking about. "You could be a bit more sensitive about this, you know. I poured my *heart* out to you, and all you've done so far is treat it like nothing!"

"I am being sensitive!" Ordell snapped. "I said you could stay on the ship and Buford and I can take care of it. It's not my fault you're so stubborn!"

"That's no excuse for how you've been treating me," Elias said. "How are we going to be something more if I can't rely on you to be there when I need you most?"

Ordell opened his mouth to retaliate, but Elias walked away. The nerve! He clearly wanted to discuss the matters at hand, but didn't want to hear Ordell's side!

Ordell huffed out a sigh and walked back to the docks. He kicked one of the pebbles toward the water and sighed again.

"What has you in a fuss?" Buford asked. "You look as if you ate an entire lemon."

Ordell shook his head. "I just don't get Elias at times. We had this… understanding… back in Southpine, but now he's being more insufferable than usual!" He leaned against the fence between the pier and the water. "Why would he act like this after what happened between us?"

Buford leaned against the fence next to Ordell. "I don't know Elias as well as you do, but I get the feeling he might be hurt."

"I told him he could stay on the ship while we take care of everything," Ordell said with a frown. "But he's too stubborn to listen to me! He even snapped at me when I was only trying to help!"

"I think you should focus more on why he said the things he did instead of what he said."

"I understand that he's upset about being here in Goldcrest, but there is no excuse for his ill behavior! If I let him get away with this behavior now, then it will only get worse later on."

"You must learn to pick your battles, Ordell. You have a lot of fire to you, but sometimes too much."

"So I just let him walk over me?" Ordell narrowed his eyes. "I'm not some compliant doll who will please others at the expense of my dignity!"

"No, but we can agree that Elias struggles with being here."

Ordell nodded. "I can agree to that."

"Then perhaps you should push that dignity aside for now and be there for him. *Show* that you care for him."

"I suppose I could do that." A smile crept across Ordell's face. "So how did you find out about us being together?"

"You two aren't the most discreet; you practically told me just now," Buford said with a chuckle. "Let's hope that no events come up that require your skill in stealth."

AFTER SEARCHING near the docks, Ordell finally found Elias inside the ship's bunk.

Elias sat on the edge of the bed and whittled at a chunk of wood. Ordell leaned against the doorframe and watched Elias's stern profile as he concentrated on the wood. It was miraculous Ordell was with such a handsome man. One who admittedly made him feel safe.

"I didn't know you could whittle," Ordell said finally as he entered the room.

"I can't. This is the third block of wood I tried to whittle. The closest I've come to an object is a smaller square of wood."

Ordell sat down on the bed next to Elias. "I want to apologize for my harsh behavior. I know being here is tough for you."

"It's different now," Elias said. "I don't mind our bantering, but I need to know you care about me as much as I care for you."

Ordell rested his hand on Elias's thigh. "I care. I want to fix this for you, but I don't know how."

"I just want you to be there for me. I want to know that I'm not fighting this alone."

Ordell smiled at him. "You're not. I'm here to fight right beside you. Tell me what you need me to do."

Elias put down the wood and knife, then wrapped his arms around Ordell and kissed the top of his head. "This."

"What?"

"I just need this," he murmured into Ordell's hair.

Ordell didn't know how hugging could help fix things, but he smiled up at Elias. No point in arguing logic if this was what made Elias happy. Maybe not everything needed to have logic behind it.

Ordell reached up and kissed Elias's temple before ducking his head back under Elias's chin. Even though the goal was to comfort Elias, Ordell couldn't help but enjoy being wrapped up in Elias's arms.

"You know," Elias said finally, "you are incredibly headstrong. I think that's what first attracted me to you. I have a feeling I doomed myself by spoiling you."

"I don't see how spoiling me is a bad thing," Ordell said with a sheepish grin. "If you wish to pamper me, I will not stop you."

"I bet you wouldn't." Elias tickled Ordell's ear. "You'll be the death of me, you know that? Headstrong and beautiful is a lethal combination."

"So is being handsome and stubborn," Ordell retorted. "And of course you make me laugh at the most inappropriate times."

Elias leaned down and kissed Ordell's lips gently. "I wouldn't trade you for the world," he whispered as he pulled away.

Ordell felt as if his body melted at those words. If he could have found his voice, he'd have brought up how rude it was to seduce a man and then leave him feeling frenzied. Instead Ordell just gazed up at him, wanting more.

"We can't," Elias said with a chuckle as if he'd read Ordell's mind. "Buford could walk in on us."

That was the thing Ordell hated about the ship. There were no locks on the doors. If there were, he wouldn't hesitate for a moment to take this man and be devoured. Something about having Elias take control in bed made Ordell feel… attractive. Just seeing the want in Elias's eyes took Ordell's breath away.

Which was why he pouted when Elias kissed the tip of his nose and laughed.

"What?" Ordell asked, still pouting.

"You are adorable."

"Dashingly handsome," he huffed out. "'Stunning' is acceptable too."

"You can't be stunningly adorable?"

Ordell rolled his eyes. "Fine, but only on special occasions such as this."

"I can live with that." Elias kissed the top of Ordell's head again. "Thank you."

"For what?"

"For cheering me up," Elias said. "I feel better knowing you're here with me."

Ordell thought about suggesting that they both stay on the ship, but it wouldn't be fair to have Buford take care of everything. Instead Ordell smiled up at him again and kissed his cheek. It wasn't much, but Elias seemed to like it. If he liked it, then Ordell liked it too.

Staying like this reminded Ordell of that night back in Southpine. Just being this close and feeling Elias's warmth made Ordell feel like he could doze off at any moment. Ordell closed his eyes and curled closer into Elias's chest. A small nap would do wonders right then.

"There you two are," Buford said, startling Ordell awake. "You remember that friend I told you about who works in the Black Market? How would you two like to meet her?"

Ordell looked up at Elias and back at Buford. "Maybe we should wait...."

"I'll be fine," Elias said. "We can meet with her. Is she at the Black Market now?"

Buford shook his head. "No, the place is murder to get to without knowing the way. Fortunately she's at her house, which is simple to get to."

"We'll be right up," Elias said over Ordell's groan.

Once Buford left, Ordell frowned. "You should have told him you don't feel comfortable going yet."

"I'll be fine, Ordell," Elias said with a small laugh. "Really."

"I know, but he might have gone to visit his friend without us, then we would have some alone time." Ordell pulled away and grinned. "It would give us time to make up for the fight we had earlier."

Elias leaned in and nipped at Ordell's nose. "We better get going before Buford wonders why we're taking so long."

THEY MUST'VE climbed three flights of stairs before they were at the correct level. Buford seemed to have no trouble navigating Goldcrest, but Ordell became dazed by the elevations.

A group of men walked by who were nude save for simple collars and leashes around their necks. Their hands were bound at the back and their faces remained still. Ordell felt sick looking at them.

"They're automatons," Elias whispered in Ordell's ear. "Slave auctions tend to be rather extravagant in Goldcrest. The automatons are not programmed to run, but the humans still bind their hands and collar them for show."

"This is a common thing?" Ordell asked, his voice rising. "How can this be okay with children running around?"

"Nude automatons aren't as taboo here like it would be in other parts of the world. Goldcrest is one of the biggest places that endorses pleasure slaves, and their slave auctions are a large tourist trap."

"It will be wise for you not to show any signs of being automatons," Buford said. "Even if a human claims to be part of the revolution, you keep your lips sealed. This is for your own safety."

That made sense, but Ordell couldn't wait until he was free to tell others he was an automaton. He'd spent so long pretending to be human that it wasn't hard for him to act human, but there were times he wanted to be honest about who he was.

They reached a tiny house that looked quaint compared to all of the other buildings in Goldcrest. The house almost reminded Ordell of the cottages back in Southpine. Buford knocked on the door, and an elderly lady with short, curly hair opened it.

"Is that my Buford?" The lady's hazel eyes sparkled. "Oh, I missed you so much!" She wrapped her arms around Buford and kissed his cheeks. "It's been too long."

"You look younger than ever, Millie," Buford said with a small laugh. "You still know how to take a man's breath away."

"You've always been the talker, haven't you?" A smile crept across her crimson lips. "And who are these young men?"

"Elias and Ordell, I'd like you to meet Mildred. She's been with the revolution since the beginning."

Ordell shook Mildred's extended hand. "It's a pleasure to meet you, ma'am."

"Such a gentleman," she said with a giggle. "I'm glad to see that Buford hasn't rubbed off on you boys."

"This lovely lady," Buford said, "is the mastermind behind getting pleasure slaves to the revolution. Like Winnie, she used to create automatons. The giant automaton that used to be in Blackwick was from her blueprints."

"I only created the blueprints," Mildred said. "Winnie was the one who did the handiwork. She's the one who brought my ideas to life."

"Now, no need to be so modest, Millie," Buford said with a small chuckle. "I've never met someone as beautiful and intelligent as you are."

"Oh, you stop that!" She smiled again. "You were always the charmer, Buford. I see nothing's changed."

"If you don't mind me asking," Ordell said, "why would you choose to live in a place where humans freely treat automatons like this?"

Her smile faded. "Come in so we can talk about this more privately." They walked inside and Mildred shut the door. "I stay here to keep a close eye on those who are inventing the pleasure slaves. I keep in close contact with the revolution, and we try to gradually get the slaves to a safer place." She looked up at Elias. "I remember you."

"You do?" Elias cocked his head to the side and furrowed his brow. "We met?"

"I remember seeing you tossed out in a ditch, and I contacted Winnie to come get you. She asked me to keep a lookout for any tossed-aside automatons to help her with her next project." She smiled. "I'm glad to see you finally got the freedom you earned."

"Doesn't feel like I'm free at times," Elias muttered.

"And you…." She walked over to Ordell. "You must be Winnie's first invention. You look so different, compared to the blueprints."

"My fath… Octavio changed my physical appearance for a customer." Ordell averted his eyes. "I take it you know him too."

"I know Octavio." By the harsh tone in her voice, she wasn't too happy to know him. "He doomed us to the plague, thanks to his selfishness! We placed a red X on his name thanks to his actions."

"What does that mean?" Ordell asked.

"It means that he is set up to be killed."

CHAPTER 14

ORDELL WOKE up to an empty bed.

He stretched and got out, stumbled to find his trousers, and then dressed as quickly as his still-sleepy body could manage.

He yawned again and looked out the window. Dew covered the grass and windowsill. A thin layer of clouds covered the sun. Ordell thought about opening the window to let the fresh air in, but by how cold the glass felt, he decided against it. It was still too early and he didn't want to get the chills.

Ordell couldn't believe the revolution had put a hit out on Octavio. Even though his father sold him for his own selfish reasons, he was still Ordell's *father*! Ordell couldn't let them kill Octavio for his own stupidity and selfishness. Lock him up, maybe, but to outright murder him? No, the moment they reached Linnesse, Ordell would have a word with the leader of the revolution. If they refused to change their mind, then Ordell would have to *make* them!

After that he wasn't sure what he'd do in Linnesse. Perhaps start a private life with Elias. Maybe Ordell could become a musician or maybe write a novel about his adventure to Linnesse. Teach others about automatons and how human they really were.

Ordell heard some shuffling downstairs and went to investigate. Elias had a few books in his arms and plopped down on the purple velvet sofa. He kicked up his feet over one of the armrests and opened a large leather-bound tome.

"There you are," Ordell said with a soft chuckle. He walked over to the sofa, and Elias lifted his legs up to let Ordell sit down. "I was wondering where you went off to."

Elias rested his legs back down over Ordell's lap. "I hope I didn't worry you. You looked so peaceful sleeping that I didn't want to wake you."

"What are you reading?" Ordell asked, rubbing Elias's ankles. "You have quite a few books piled up there." He turned his head in the direction of the dark-wood coffee table with its small tower of books. "I didn't know you were such a book lover."

"I wouldn't say I'm a huge book lover," Elias said. "I read a lot when I lived with Winnie. I guess it was my own form of escape when I was trapped in one small area for so long."

"You make it sound like Winifred tortured you." Ordell chuckled. "She just wanted to keep you safe."

"I know, but it was torture. I was a prisoner, Ordell. If you hadn't come along, I would've stayed there for God knows how long."

"Did you try talking to Winifred about how you felt?"

"Many times," he groaned. "She wouldn't have any of it. Said that fresh air was overrated and that I needed to toughen up."

Ordell didn't know how to respond to that, so he continued to give Elias's ankles a reassuring rub.

"You still never told me what you're reading," Ordell said with a coy smile. "Something embarrassing?"

"About the plague," Elias said. "It talks about what happened all those years ago and how Ratliff was the sole reason the plague was 'cured.' The bastard even has his own chapter here!"

"Elias, I have a question for you."

"And what is that?"

"Do you know of any illnesses that cause bloody noses and vomiting?"

Elias shrugged. "None that I know of."

"Were they symptoms of the plague?"

Elias shook his head. "No, the main symptoms of the plague were a high fever and blisters. Nothing about bloody noses. There might have been some vomiting, but I wouldn't call that a major symptom of the plague."

"Oh," Ordell said. He was sure he was onto something. "Thank you."

"Why do you ask?"

"You know the three children I played five stones with? The little girl there told me her father was vomiting blood and had a bloody nose. I'm not sure if he's well now, but she said that her mother was quite concerned about it."

"It might be something else. I wouldn't say it has something to do with the plague. See...." Elias sat up and moved next to Ordell, draping the large book over their laps. "Here is the list of the symptoms the plague carried. The ones with the stars were the main symptoms that showed someone carried the disease."

Ordell skimmed through them. There was a small mention of vomiting, but nothing about vomiting blood. Bloody noses weren't even mentioned. Something about that made Ordell even more concerned about what that little girl's father had. Something about it didn't feel right.

"I'm glad to see you boys up," Mildred said, coming into the room. "I had a man make passes to Linnesse for you two. The bad news is he must stay on the ground elevation of Goldcrest, so you two will have to go to him."

"Why can't he come meet us?" Ordell asked.

"It's too dangerous for him," Mildred said. "What he does is highly illegal, and although Goldcrest doesn't arrest those in the Black Market who stay on the ground level, they will if he so much as takes one step toward the upper levels."

"Wouldn't *we* get arrested, then?" Ordell frowned. "This feels too risky."

"The people of Goldcrest don't know you. Besides, the police are more concerned about people selling things in the Black Market than buying things. Mostly their focus is on automaton parts, since it's bad for business. They wouldn't bat much of an eye at the passes."

Ordell nodded, but he still felt uncertain about going through with this. The last thing he needed was to get arrested. His pretty face wasn't going to stand a chance in a prison cell!

"Is he ready for us?" Elias asked, rubbing Ordell's back in soothing circles. "You'll have to give us directions to get there."

Elias and Mildred continued to talk about the Black Market. Ordell glanced back down at the book on the plague. He wasn't sure what was going on in Goldcrest, but he felt the plague was far from over. If only he could meet that little girl's father. Maybe when they got back from the Black Market, Ordell could check to see if she and her friends were playing five stones again. It wouldn't hurt to check, and it shouldn't take too long.

Ordell wasn't sure how he worked when it came to the plague, but wasn't he supposed to detect the plague somehow? Maybe if he managed to detect it, it'd come to him how he could cure it too.

Why didn't Winifred just *tell* him what he was meant to do? It would have made things so much easier if she'd told Ordell precisely what he had to do in order to stop the plague.

"Are you ready to go?" Elias kissed Ordell's temple, breaking him from his train of thought. "What were you thinking about?"

"Why do you think I was thinking?"

Elias tickled Ordell's nose. "Because of that little nose scrunch of yours."

Ordell rolled his eyes. "Yes, I'm ready to go." Before he could get up, Elias poked him in the ear. "What was that for?"

"Just to watch your reaction," Elias said with a tiny grin.

Ordell scowled. Once they were alone, Ordell would make sure to get him back somehow.

THEY TRAVELED through Goldcrest, and Elias didn't make any detours. Ordell at least wanted to look at some of the attractions, but Elias would tug at his elbow to get a move on.

"We can slow down a little bit," Ordell said. "I want to see some things here."

"There's not much to see," Elias said. "They sell automatons as sex slaves and don't even consider hiding it. Everything in Goldcrest is tainted, Ordell. The sooner we leave this hell, the better it is for all of us."

Ordell opened his mouth to argue, but Buford's words came back to him. He had to pick his battles. He had to be there for Elias when he struggled with this rough time. "Lead the way."

He tried to keep his pace up alongside Elias's, but he walked too fast for him. Not only that, but Ordell still felt distracted and wanted to see everything that caught his eye. He wanted to explore the upper levels of Goldcrest, visit the museums, talk with the people who lived there, watch the street performers. He wanted to see the large golden water mill. Wanted to swim in the crystal blue water like a small group of humans were doing, despite the chilly weather.

When they finally reached the ground level, Ordell was surprised at what he saw.

The area was just as run-down as the abandoned parts of Southpine. There were more people there than in Southpine, but it gave him the same feeling. Decrepit market stalls scattered the ground level; the sellers didn't even hide their shady business down here. There were paintings, sculptures, gears, and even documents sprawled out on the tables. The most notable items were the automaton parts being sold. There were torsos, arms, legs, a head, and Ordell could have sworn one market stall was selling an ear.

Still, there were no complete automatons for sale. Ordell was surprised because, with all those parts, they surely could have created a full automaton and sold it for a higher price, right? It seemed like an idiotic business tactic not to have at least one full automaton for sale.

Elias took him to a stall farther away from the others. A hefty man popped up from behind the wooden crate and gave both Elias and him a large toothy smile.

"What can I get for ya?" the man asked, his voice loud and gruff. "I got some paintin's that just came in this morning. I'm sure it'd look lovely above a fireplace or in a foyer."

"Mildred sent us," Elias said.

"Ah." The man's smile widened. "Good ol' Millie told me to look out for ya. Said you be needin' some passes to Linnesse."

Ordell nodded. "That's correct."

"Don't worry 'bout the cost; it's on me. Any friend of Millie is a friend of mine." He handed Elias three small passes. Ordell didn't know what the passes to Linnesse looked like, but he assumed they were authentic. "Shouldn't have any troubles with the guards there with these babies. Make sure no one sees them, though. Even here these passes cost more than you're worth."

Ordell didn't like that phrase one bit. He knew it was just an expression, but it was uncalled for to say it to two automatons who were all too aware of what it was like to be sold to some rich pervert. Ordell kept quiet, but he made sure his icy glare did the talking for him. The man cleared his throat and seemed to get the message not to say those rude things to future clients.

"Thank you for the passes," Elias said as he elbowed Ordell.

Ordell broke his glare but gave one last mean look as they walked away from the man.

"What has gotten into you?" Elias asked when they were away from the man.

"He was rude," Ordell said with a sniff. "He shouldn't have said the passes cost more than us."

"It's an expression, Ordell. He meant no harm in it."

"He may not have, but he shouldn't use those words toward people like us."

Elias rolled his eyes, then chuckled. "Ordell, he doesn't *know* about us. Goldcrest is a dangerous place for us. Millie wasn't going to tell everyone who we really are."

Ordell's face heated. "Oh."

"All she told him is that we were part of the revolution and needed passes to get to Linnesse. He doesn't know anything else."

Well, that made Ordell feel terrible. He gave a man the glare of death for no reason, then. A part of him wanted to go back and apologize for his appalling behavior, but Elias was already climbing the stairs to get to the upper level. Ordell bowed his head and followed behind.

He was relieved when they were away from the ground level, but that strange feeling was back. It was that same feeling Ordell had had when they first arrived in Goldcrest. He wasn't able to pinpoint what it was, but it made him feel anxious. Maybe he should skip seeing the children again.

No, he had to figure out what that man had.

Ordell pulled away from Elias and wandered through the crowd to see if the children were there. He heard Elias call out his name, but Ordell ignored it.

He reached the tiny store the children had been in front of last time. None of the children were there.

Ordell didn't know what to do next, so he sat down on the curb away from the people walking by. He grabbed one of the pebbles and tossed it up and down as he thought of another way he could get in contact with this man.

He couldn't just ask where Abigail's father was. There must be many girls named Abigail. It was possible the store owner knew the children who played there, unless they didn't play by this curb often.

Ordell tossed the stone back up and it landed on the back of his hand. He tossed it up again and this time had it land in the palm. He saw Elias trying to weave through the crowd to get to Ordell. Maybe it was best to go back to Mildred's. Ordell didn't even know what he was looking for, if anything.

A man walked by with a partially naked man wearing a collar. *Must be a pleasure slave*, Ordell thought to himself. *Seems to be a lot of my type around here in Goldcrest.*

The slave looked happy. He had a wide white grin plastered on his face as he followed closely behind his master. Ordell's stomach turned just looking at those two. A part of him wondered if getting tossed aside was the merciful option for a pleasure slave.

The man stopped by the small shop and began talking to a lady nearby. The slave still had that disturbing smile on his face.

Then something else. A hint of sadness? Ordell furrowed his brow as he saw the slave's eyes waver. That smile fell slightly, and if Ordell blinked, he would have missed it.

He saw the slave mouth something. It was quick, but Ordell caught it as if the slave had screamed it in his ear.

"Help me."

CHAPTER 15

ORDELL SPENT the next few days thinking about the pleasure slave. It might have only been for a few moments, but Ordell saw that sadness. There was no doubt in his mind the automaton was trying to find a way to reach out for help.

Help me.

He must have known Ordell was an automaton like him. He didn't react that way to the other humans, at least not that Ordell could tell. The slave went back to all smiles when his master turned around. It was like nothing had happened at all.

But Ordell knew.

He knew there was something else going on. The automatons were more than just pieces of equipment. Even Ordell's siblings could have been pleasure slaves and stuck in this hell they couldn't get out of. That thought made Ordell shudder.

Ordell felt someone wrap their strong arms around his waist and then felt Elias's warm breath on his neck.

"What are you thinking about?" Elias murmured and then caressed Ordell's neck with warm kisses.

Ordell closed his eyes and moaned. He leaned into the kisses and his entire body felt like it'd melt in Elias's arms. "Nothing," he panted out.

"You're scrunching your nose again," he said between kisses, the words caressing him just like his soft lips.

Ordell wanted to tell Elias, but all he could think about was how aroused he was. Ordell licked his lips and just took in the kisses. He placed his hands over Elias's and leaned into his body.

He could get used to this.

"Not going to tell me?" Elias whispered.

"I can't when you drive me crazy like this," Ordell whimpered. "I can't... can't wrap my head around anything with you being so... so...."

"So?" Elias pried.

"So damn amazing," Ordell breathed out. It wasn't the word he was looking for, but it'd do.

Elias chuckled into Ordell's neck and pulled away. "Sorry, I didn't think I'd put you in a frenzy."

"Don't apologize," he said, catching his breath. "I loved it."

"Now what got you in such deep thought? You looked as if you were in another world."

"You were right."

"About what?"

"About the automatons," Ordell said. "I saw it myself. We need to help them! I can't believe it. I was so stupid not to believe you!"

"Whoa there, calm down." Elias grabbed both of Ordell's hands. "Take a deep breath and tell me what's going on."

"The pleasure slaves have emotions, Elias. I'm sure of it! When I went out by that curb the other day, I saw a man with a pleasure slave. At first everything looked typical, but then I saw his expression. He looked sad despite the smile."

"Are you positive about this?"

"Yes, and that's not all," Ordell said. "He asked me to help him. He mouthed the words to me. Elias, these automatons are trapped in this 'happy to serve' state and cannot help themselves. I think he knew I was an automaton, like him."

Elias frowned, and then it turned to outright anger. "I'm going to kill every bastard who owns an automaton! Hell, I'll burn all of Goldcrest if that's what it takes!"

"Let's not turn to criminal activity," Ordell said. "We should find a way to free the automatons instead of resorting to murder." When Elias's mouth formed a tight line, Ordell squeezed Elias's hands. "We need the humans to trust us. Not every human is bad. Just look at Buford and Mildred."

Finally Elias sighed and nodded. "We should probably get their help with this. We can't do this alone."

They walked down stairs and saw Buford and Mildred hand in hand.

"What are you two doing?" Elias asked with a crook of an eyebrow.

They quickly dropped their hands and Buford's face turned bright red. "I-I was just helping Millie out with... with the table!" He knelt down by the coffee table and wiggled it. "This darn thing can't support anything!"

Ordell chuckled. "You don't have to hide anything from us. I think it's great you two are rekindling your... friendship."

This time Mildred blushed. "I could never resist Buford's charm. The man has a way with words."

"I know how you feel," Ordell grumbled as he nudged Elias with his shoulder.

Elias looked even more confused. "What did I do?"

Buford got back on his feet and put his hand around Mildred's waist. "Sadly she rejected me until now. I must admit I'm not too sure what I did right this time, but I'm glad I did it."

Mildred smiled her crimson smile and touched Buford's nose. "You've done everything right. It'd be foolish of me to reject you due to my own pride."

"We're sorry to bother you two," Elias said, "but Ordell came up with a theory that is rather unsettling."

"What is it?" Mildred pointed to the chairs and sofa, and they all sat down. "It's about the automatons, isn't it?"

Ordell nodded. "I believe they're developing their own emotions. I saw an automaton the other day and he asked me to help him. I could see the sadness in his eyes."

"This isn't good," Buford whispered.

"Is this even possible?" Ordell asked.

"Yes. There's a strong chance that the automatons are developing their own sentience over time and becoming aware of their own emotions. We don't know what automatons are capable of. Just look at you and Elias."

"But Winifred programmed us to be free."

"True, but there are many traits you two carry that weren't programmed," Buford said. "Some things are there inside you both that humans aren't even capable of programming! Ordell, your theory is more than viable."

"Automatons are very complex creatures," Mildred said. "We humans don't give them enough credit."

"There's a good possibility that the automaton you came across sensed you were an automaton too, Ordell," Buford said. "These pleasure slaves may show their true selves to both you and Elias, since you're both automatons."

"But if that were the case, why wouldn't they do this with any automaton they've come across?" Ordell asked.

"We don't know that they don't," Buford said. "Even then, perhaps they knew you were free and thought maybe there was a chance that you two could help them."

Ordell wasn't so sure that theory was accurate. It seemed rather far-fetched to him. He didn't exactly know who was an automaton and who was not. The only reason he knew that man was an automaton was because of the collar around his neck.

"What can we do?" Elias asked.

"It'll be best if you two go out and see if you can speak with a pleasure slave without their master," Mildred said. "It'll be a difficult task, but being able to see how they react to another automaton without their master watching will be useful to us."

The more they talked about putting this plan into action, the more Ordell lost confidence in the plan working. Elias's idea of burning the town was even beginning to sound like the more reasonable option! No, he needed to remain optimistic that this plan would work. Even if it didn't, they could always create a plan B.

"It's settled," Buford said finally. "You and Elias go out and get a better view of the slaves. Make sure the humans do not know what you are."

Elias nodded. "Got it."

"Make absolutely sure that you two do not discuss being automatons or part of the revolution," Buford warned. "Either one of those topics will bring nothing but trouble."

Mildred handed Elias a small square with a button in the middle. "If you boys run into any trouble at all, use this button to page us. We will come immediately to help."

Ordell gulped. "Is that really all that necessary? We've traveled around Goldcrest before and nothing bad happened to us."

"This is just a safety measure," Buford said. "I highly doubt you two will even need to use it."

Ordell could agree to that.

SPENDING TIME with Elias was amazing. They walked with their hands entwined together, and Elias even started swinging them as they walked. This time Elias didn't mind making small detours, which was a huge relief to Ordell.

They even got to look at the large water mill, which sparkled from the water and the sun shining down upon it. The water seemed so clear up in person, and Ordell felt tempted to drink it despite his lack of taste buds and thirst.

He felt a twinge of jealousy that if Elias wanted to, he could drink it and get satisfaction out of it. Once they reached Linnesse, the first thing Ordell would do would be to ask for taste buds so he could finally experience the same satisfaction as humans when they ate or drank something.

"I love when the sun's out," Elias said with a content smile. "Really brightens up this town."

"I'm surprised you'd say anything good about Goldcrest," Ordell said, laughing. "I think this might be the first good thing you've said about it!"

"Well, once we get everything situated, this town will be a nice place to live," Elias said. "The gold sparkles in the sun and the crystals look like diamonds. Don't you think so?"

"Yes," Ordell agreed, smiling. "I think that too."

They walked around Goldcrest and explored the different elevations. By the fourth elevation, Ordell felt dizzy. He looked over the fence at the people on the elevation below. They looked so small from up there.

"If it weren't for the automatons," Ordell said, "I'd love living here."

"I think I prefer Linnesse more."

Ordell laughed. "You haven't even been there yet."

"Yes, but automatons have as many rights as humans there," Elias said. "They're even allowed to marry in Linnesse."

"I've always dreamed of that," Ordell said with a small smile. "Ever since I could remember, I've wanted to marry a man who was kind and treated me well. Someone who would be my best friend and companion for many years to come. Octavio said it was an impossible dream and I should stop thinking such foolish things."

"You marrying the man of your dreams may come sooner than you think," Elias said with a sheepish grin. "I hope you're prepared for that."

"Only if he's prepared to spoil and pamper me." Ordell grinned back. "I expect the best and want to live in a castle of diamonds."

"Not sapphires?"

"Why sapphires?"

"Because," Elias said with a smile, "it'll bring out the blue in your eyes."

Ordell's ears heated. "I see you're taking lessons from Buford."

"Whatever do you mean?"

"You know what I mean," Ordell said, pursing his lips. "You're charming me and making me melt inside like you always do. It's not fair."

Elias leaned down and kissed Ordell's pursed lips. He then pulled away with a large grin on his face.

"See?" Ordell complained. "Just like that! You know it makes me…."

"Aroused?" Elias arched his brow.

Ordell flushed and looked around to see if anyone heard that. "You brat!"

Elias chuckled and kissed Ordell again. This time deeper and longer.

Ordell moaned in Elias's mouth and grabbed ahold of his shirt. Ordell pulled himself closer to his warm body and kissed Elias harder.

Then Elias took a step back.

"Wha—?" Ordell stammered out.

"We don't want to make a scene in front of all these people, do we?" Elias teased. "Unless you like that sort of thing."

"You're doing this on purpose," Ordell said, glaring.

"Doing what on purpose?" Elias cocked his head to the side and gave Ordell an innocent puppy-dog look. "I don't know what you're talking about."

Ordell opened his mouth to retaliate, but then he saw another master with his slave. It must have been a different slave, since the master was an elderly man this time. Still, the similarities between this slave and the other one were uncanny.

It was the same thing that happened the other day. The slave appeared to be happy, with that wide smile on his face. Then, when the humans were not looking, he turned to Elias and Ordell and gave them a look of sadness.

Just seeing that look in the automaton's eyes sent chills up Ordell's spine. This automaton didn't say anything like the other one, though. Instead he smiled wide again when his master turned around to look at him.

Then they walked away.

"You're right," Elias said. "There's something wrong with these automatons."

ORDELL AND Elias continued to walk around Goldcrest. This time, things were much quieter between them. Ordell could see the anger in Elias's eyes, but he didn't know how to comfort him. The best he could do was squeeze Elias's hand to reassure him. It wasn't much, but it seemed to make Elias calm down.

"We'll figure something out," Ordell finally tried.

He wasn't sure what they could do at this point, but there had to be something. There were always multiple paths to get to the same location. That was what his father taught him.

"We should get to Linnesse as soon as we can," Elias ground out. "They'll make those bastards pay for what they've done."

"The humans don't know the automatons are developing sentience on their own," Ordell said. "We can't hate them for their ignorance. It only means we need to correct them on their behavior. If they still fight us, then it'll be fine to hate them."

"We need to get the revolution involved," Elias said. "That's the only choice we have. We can tell Buford to set up the ship immediately. We can leave tonight."

"No," Ordell said. "There's something else going on. I need to figure it out."

"What do you mean?"

"I don't know what it is yet, but I think going to Linnesse right now might be a bad idea. There have to be other options."

Elias sighed. "I suppose we could go back to Blackwick and ask Winnie for her help. I doubt she'll do anything, but what's the harm in trying?"

"Besides wasting precious time getting there? Maybe Buford and Mildred can think of something to help without us going to Linnesse right now."

"I don't understand why you're so opposed to going to Linnesse now."

"Just for right now," Ordell corrected.

"Right, but I don't understand why you don't want to go right now. We have the passes to get there, and it shouldn't take too long to get there by ship. It's just straight up north of Goldcrest."

Before Ordell could answer, a man came running down the road, screaming. Blood fell from his nose and covered his mouth. He looked ghostly pale, and Ordell could see the sweat dripping off him.

Then the man collapsed. People gasped and crowded frantically around him.

"Because," Ordell said above the talking crowd, "the plague has come back to Goldcrest."

CHAPTER 16

"WHAT DO you mean the plague's back?" Elias asked as they entered Mildred's house.

"All I know is that I had this strange feeling. I didn't know what it meant at the time, but now I know it's due to the plague."

"This is a bold thought of yours," Elias said. "If the humans find out about this, they'll go into a frenzy!"

"We need to stay quiet about this for now," Ordell whispered. "I know we need to do something about it, but I'm not sure what to do yet."

"Winnie built you to stop the plague. If anyone knows how to stop it, it'll be you."

"She didn't give me an instruction manual for this, Elias. You were the one who told me I can detect it and somehow stop it. I don't even know the first thing about stopping the plague! Why can't you tell me what I'm supposed to do?"

"I don't know what you're capable of. All I know is what Winnie told me. There has to be something you know," Elias said. "For example, I don't know these places, but Winnie programmed it inside of me to know what directions to take. It's almost like I do it on a subconscious level."

Ordell closed his eyes and thought. There wasn't anything that stood out to him on how he could possibly stop the plague. The closest thing he felt was that sick feeling of the plague being present. So he knew the plague was here. That was fine, but what exactly was he supposed to do with that information?

"Do you feel anything?" Elias asked.

Ordell shook his head. "I still only feel that it's present. I don't know how to stop it, though."

"Try thinking a bit harder."

"I am!" Ordell huffed out a sigh. "I just don't know how I work when it comes to the plague! I need help with this, Elias."

Buford and Mildred walked in, and Ordell apologized for his outburst.

"Don't worry about that, my boy," Buford said. "Just tell us what the fuss is about."

"Ordell says the plague is back," Elias said, and Ordell glared up at him. So much for keeping this information quiet.

Mildred gasped. "Are you sure about this?"

"This isn't something to joke about," Buford said slowly.

"I know what I feel," Ordell said. "I just don't know what to do with that. Winifred never told me how to stop the plague or that I needed to do it."

"How odd." Buford sat down in one of the satin chairs. "She didn't give you any hints?"

Ordell shook his head.

"Not too odd when it comes to Winnie," Mildred said. "She has a bad habit of being vague or letting important things slip her mind. Drove me insane when we used to work together!"

"Maybe we should go back to Blackwick," Elias said. "We can ask Winnie what she knows about the plague, and she can show Ordell how he can help stop it."

"That isn't possible," Buford said with a sigh.

"Why is that?" Ordell asked. "She must be willing to help when it comes to the plague!"

"That isn't the issue."

"Then what's the problem?" Ordell pressed. "Is it dangerous to go to Blackwick? Maybe we can send her a letter or—"

"She's gone," Buford said. "I just found out this morning that she went missing."

"What do you mean she went missing?" Elias asked, raising his voice.

Before Buford could get another word in, Elias stormed out.

"I'll talk to him," Ordell said.

ORDELL FOUND Elias out by the piers. Elias threw a stick in the water, and Ordell could see he was upset.

"We'll find her," Ordell said as he leaned on the railing next to Elias. "She couldn't have gone far."

"I just don't know what could have happened to her," Elias said. "She's always so cautious. What if she's hurt? Maybe we should go to Blackwick to find her."

"She might not even be in Blackwick anymore. Buford just got the news this morning. Who knows how long she's been gone. We should wait to see what Buford and Mildred say. They know her the best."

"No," Elias said. "*I* know her the best. I'm her son. I should know where she is or who would've taken her, if anyone." He lowered his eyes and looked down at the water. "I should've stayed in Blackwick. I knew leaving her alone was a bad idea."

"Hey," Ordell said, squeezing Elias's shoulder. "Winifred knows how to take care of herself. If she couldn't, she wouldn't have had you leave."

"I still can't help but regret leaving."

"She wanted you to leave." Ordell moved his hand in small circular motions across Elias's back. "She told me how much she regretted keeping you trapped inside. Before we left, Winifred told me that you deserve more than what she has to offer. She wanted you to go to Linnesse to be free. If she knew you regretted all this because of guilt, she'd no doubt slap you upside the head and tell you to stop."

Elias smiled. "Yeah, she would do that, wouldn't she?"

"Absolutely," Ordell said with a small laugh. "Probably dump cold water on you for good measure."

"I still can't help but feel guilty, though. I don't understand what anyone would want with her. She's hardly active in the revolution anymore."

"But she has those blueprints, correct?"

"Yeah, but why would anyone want them when the pleasure slaves are so obedient? It's not like many humans want us to be sentient."

"We don't know that," Ordell said.

"We know by how they treat us," Elias said. "It's pretty damn clear they just want a sex toy and nothing else. If they really cared about us, they'd try to put us to better use. They'd try to see how we operate. They'd try to see if we're sentient enough to form our own opinions and emotions."

"They're just ignorant."

"Yeah, well, they can't hide behind that excuse forever."

Ordell sighed. He wished he knew what to do to comfort Elias, but he couldn't think of anything. He didn't want to say everything would be okay because he wasn't sure if it *would* be. Ordell moved his hand over Elias's and intertwined their fingers. It was the only thing Ordell knew to do to show some comfort.

"I just wish I knew what happened," Elias said. "Did she leave on her own? Did someone take her? I can't imagine that she would just up and leave on her own. She's been in that house ever since I can remember. Why would she suddenly leave now?"

"Maybe since you're gone, she went exploring on her own?" Ordell shrugged. "She was quite worried about leaving you alone, you know."

"Do you think she's all right?" Elias whispered. "What if she's hurt?"

"I'm sure she's fine." Ordell tried on a reassuring smile. "And if someone did take her, you know she will be fighting tooth and nail to escape. Hell, she probably escaped by now and is heading back to Blackwick."

"You think she's been captured, then."

"I didn't say that," Ordell said. "I'm just tossing out the worst-case scenarios. That doesn't mean I believe them."

The truth was Ordell didn't think her getting captured was too far-fetched. Ratliff could have captured her if he knew she was helping Ordell. Still, it wouldn't be good to tell Elias that theory when Ordell didn't have any evidence to back it up. It'd only worry Elias more, which he had already done enough of.

"Go back to Mildred's and get some sleep," Ordell said. "I'll keep a lookout and see if I can find information on what happened to Winifred."

"Should I really be sleeping when she's out there?"

"It's better than you staying up and making yourself sick with worry."

Elias nodded. "You'll tell me if you find anything?"

"Of course."

Elias squeezed Ordell's shoulder, then walked off toward Mildred's house. Now that Elias was resting, Ordell could go around and ask about Ratliff and possibly find some information about Winifred's whereabouts.

ORDELL WANDERED around town, visiting shop after shop, asking if anyone had seen Ratliff or a lady similar to Winifred's appearance. Finally Ordell came across a small inn on one of the middle elevations. He walked inside and noticed how cozy the place was—almost like a tiny cabin. A fire was lit in the waiting area and there was laughter and discussion among the humans. He went up to the front desk and rang the tiny bell.

A petite lady walked behind the counter with a bright smile on her face. "Hello there. My name's Lee Todd and I'm the owner of this small inn. Do you have a reservation, or is this a walk-in?"

"Neither," Ordell said. "I'm looking for a friend of mine and was hoping maybe you've seen her."

"Many outsiders stay here for the night or two. If she's a visitor, then she might have a room with us."

"Her name's Winifred Griffith. She has long white hair that she usually wraps up in a bun. She's usually dressed in brown and is about your height. Slim, with hazel eyes."

"Are you a friend or family?"

"Family."

"Do you have proof of this?"

"Excuse me?"

She sighed. "I can't give you information on my clients unless you can prove you're a family member." Before Ordell could say anything, two men broke out in a fight. "Will you excuse me for a moment?" She grabbed her broom and walked out from behind the counter. "Henry! Burt! You two stop that!" she said as she hit them with the end of the broom. "I will not have another fight in here!"

Ordell snuck behind the counter when the attention was on Henry and Burt. He found the large leather-bound book and skimmed through the list of names. Finally, he found the last name Griffith, who had checked in the previous week. There was no first name in place, but there was a mention of a Mr. Saunders who had checked in the same week.

Why would Ratliff and Winifred check into the same inn together? They checked in at the same time and had their rooms side-by-side. Unless these were two different people, there was something strange going on.

Ordell left the inn, convinced Winifred and Ratliff were involved in something. Either Ratliff had her hostage somehow, or they were working together. Unfortunately the second option seemed more plausible at this point.

ORDELL WAITED until Elias woke up. He pondered how he was going to tell Elias his discovery. Ordell didn't want to believe Winifred would work with Ratliff, but he also couldn't rule that out as a possibility. There was also the possibility of Ratliff blackmailing her, but with what?

This whole situation was one big mess.

Elias came down the stairs, buttoning his shirt. "Did you find anything?"

"Winifred's safe," Ordell said. At least that part seemed true.

"You know where she is? Is she back in Blackwick?"

Ordell shook his head. "She's here in Goldcrest."

"What?" Elias asked. "Did she come to check up on us? Is she going to help us with the plague and the automatons?"

"She's with Ratliff."

Elias's eyes widened. "Ratliff has her?"

"Well, I don't know. She's currently staying at that tiny inn just left of the water mill. She was with Ratliff. It doesn't seem that he's doing anything to hold her hostage."

"You can't honestly believe that she's with him of her own accord."

"I don't know. It's a possibility." When Elias narrowed his eyes, Ordell added, "But she could also be blackmailed into helping him. It's not clear at this point."

"Buford, Millie, and I will go check out the inn and see if we can find Winnie," Elias said. "There must be some reason why she'd even consider helping a snake like Ratliff."

"Shouldn't I be coming with you?" Ordell asked. "I'm the one who found all this out."

"No," Elias said. "You stay here where it's safe."

"What?"

"You'll be safe here. Make sure you lock the doors and windows. We have the keys to get inside, so don't open the door for anyone, even if you think it's us."

"No," Ordell said, crossing his arms. "I'm coming with you."

"Please don't do this now." Elias sighed. "We really have to make sure you're safe. It'll do us no good if we're too busy worrying about you."

"I'm not going to be treated like some child!" Ordell snapped. "I can handle myself. Did you forget who deactivated the kraken? Not only that, but I've managed to escape from Ratliff twice already."

"And one of those times was with my help," Elias shot back. "Ordell, please just stay here so I don't worry about you."

"Why worry about me?"

"Because I love you, damn it!"

That shut Ordell up. He wasn't sure what to say after that. It was implied, but neither one had actually said that word. Ordell wished the first time Elias said it had been on a less aggressive level, but it still had the same impact as if Elias had said it while lying on a bed of roses.

"Just please stay here," Elias said, softer this time. "Do this for me. I know you can handle yourself, but I'll worry about you even if you are with us. I just don't want anything to happen to you."

"Fine," Ordell said with a small nod. "If it means that much to you, I'll stay here."

Elias closed the space between them and kissed Ordell on the tip of his nose. "Thank you."

"Elias."

"Yes?"

"I love you too," Ordell said with a lopsided smile.

Elias smiled and kissed Ordell's lips. "I'm glad."

Buford and Mildred came in and Elias explained all that had happened. The three went to go find Winifred, and Ordell was left by himself.

The house felt so much bigger when no one else was there. Much quieter too.

Ordell walked over to the shelf and glanced through the books Mildred had. Many tomes were lined up, from history dissertations to educational texts. She had a few scrolls as well, but Ordell didn't open them for fear he would tear them. Instead, he grabbed the large leather-bound book on the plague. If he was to stop this thing, he at least needed to be better educated in what the plague was.

The plague was deadly and contagious. The most dangerous thing about it was it traveled through the air and water. This made areas close up their borders, similar to what Southpine did to Northpine. Rats and insects were killed as well, out of paranoia that they carried the plague. There wasn't any evidence to support that, but fear did crazy things to people.

Ordell searched through the book for any hints of a bloody nose and vomiting blood as a side effect to the plague. If not, there was a chance the disease had mutated.

Before he could get to the list of side effects, Ordell felt someone grab him from behind.

CHAPTER 17

"YOU LOOK just like him," Ratliff said in a breathy tone.

"Who?"

"My first love." A small smile crept across his face. "His name was Abraham. He was about three years older than me and had soft copper hair just like you do. Such soft, beautiful features and an elegant face. In all my years, I've never met anyone who could match his beauty."

"You better leave," Ordell ground out. "It isn't below me to scream for help."

"I'm not here to take you," Ratliff said and then lightly touched a piece of Ordell's hair with gentle fingers. "You are his visage in everything. Octavio truly is a master of beauty."

Ordell pulled away. "If you love Abraham so much, then go bother him! I want nothing to do with you."

"Such a cheeky boy," Ratliff said, and then, to Ordell's surprise, he laughed. "Abe was like that too. Sometimes I admired it, other times I wanted to shake the man! Alas, the fantasy of being with him will always remain an unattainable dream."

"Why is that?"

"He's dead."

"Oh." Ordell's voice softened. "I'm sorry for your loss."

"Even if he were still alive, it would be impossible for us. Abraham fancied women, and a little too much so, if you ask me. Every night it felt like he had another woman on his arm. However, someone as beautiful as him should have had a man's touch...." Ratliff smiled again. "My touch."

"It sounds like you set yourself up for a broken heart," Ordell huffed out. "Why fall in love with a man who doesn't even fancy men? Rather idiotic, if you ask me."

"You can't choose love, Ordell," Ratliff said flatly. "I didn't plan to fall in love with him. When we first met, I was in the orphanage, and he would see me every weekday when he walked home from school. His parents were one of the wealthier families, and eventually they allowed me to live at their house if I worked for them for free. We grew closer, and I charmed Abraham's father to the point where he adopted me.

"It was a fantasy for me. I received the proper schooling and made it my goal to make humanity a better place. I saw the worst of humanity, Ordell. I saw the murderers, the rapists, the overworked, the hungry.... I had to do *something*.

"Abraham and I came up with a plan. We were going to replace dangerous human labor and sex crimes with automatons. They wouldn't take the jobs the humans needed in order to thrive, just the ones that were already so underpaid and too dangerous for a decent human to do."

"What happened to Abraham?" Ordell asked. "How did he die?"

"He died from the plague," Ratliff said, his eyes wavering. "Even when he suffered through it, he was still so beautiful. I wanted to find a cure for him—make him better—but nothing I did worked. I spent sleepless nights looking for a way to stop this disease.... Anything at all that could save my friend."

"Is that why you made the medication?"

"At first," Ratliff said. "I didn't want anyone else to die from the plague. I didn't want anyone else to lose someone they loved dearly. I didn't expect it to bring me fame and wealth like it did, but I cannot deny that I enjoy every minute of it."

"Where's Winifred?" He was done with story time. It was time to figure out what he and Winifred were doing.

"I haven't the slightest idea."

"I know she was with you earlier," Ordell spat out. "Are you two working together? Did you blackmail her? Answer me!"

"I don't know where she is."

"Look," Ordell said, "as much as you don't want to believe it, the plague is back with a strong vengeance. I'm sorry you lost your friend to it, but you can't keep being in denial about it and hope that it'll eventually go away. We need to do something."

"I know," he said.

"You know?"

"Winifred came here on her own terms, Ordell," Ratliff said. "I knew she somehow figured out a vaccine for the plague long ago. We thought the plague was under control with my medicine, so her vaccine was deemed useless. When I saw that the plague had grown immune to my medicine, I came to her for help. To my surprise, she said you were the answer."

"I can sense the plague," Ordell said, "but I don't know what I can do to stop it."

"She went out searching for you," he said. "She was going to explain everything to you."

"Why can't you tell me?"

Ratliff shrugged. "She didn't tell me. She said this was between you and her. I protested at first, but she isn't one to back down. I eventually gave in and decided to help her find you."

"Is my father here too?" Ordell asked. Even though Octavio sold him off, Ordell wanted to see him. He had so many questions to ask and so many words to say—most of them unpleasant ones.

"Octavio didn't want to see you again," Ratliff said matter-of-factly. "He says you bring too many painful memories."

"*I* bring *him* painful memories?" Ordell scoffed. "I swear if I ever see him again…."

"Don't bother," he said. "Octavio's back to creating and doesn't need you distracting him. He's one of the most prolific inventors for pleasure slaves. The only reason his store's going down is because he's too stubborn to move to Goldcrest, where his business will boom."

Ordell felt sick to his stomach. He'd helped create those pleasure slaves. Octavio told them they were just workers and would be treated well. How could he be so stupid?

"If he makes more like you, he's sure to be a success regardless of where he lives."

Ordell balled his hands into fists. By the tone of Ratliff's voice, he was oblivious to how insulting those words were. It seemed like the man was attempting small talk but was failing miserably. Ordell thought to glare at him but remained quiet and demure instead. He was alone with Ratliff, and he didn't want to risk angering the man, especially if Ratliff genuinely thought he was making harmless chitchat.

"Octavio did good with your programming," Ratliff said with a nasally chuckle. "We love complacent slaves." He hooked his slender finger under Ordell's chin. "We'll have to change your name, though. 'Ordell' is too much of a peasant name; you'll do much better being called 'Abraham.'"

Ordell pulled away from Ratliff's touch. "I like my name."

"You'll get used to your new name. We can discuss that later, though. Right now we need to discuss how you're going to help us with this plague."

Ordell remained quiet.

"Ms. Griffith didn't tell me much," Ratliff continued. "She said that we needed to find you as soon as possible so we could get you ready to stop it."

"And if I don't do it?" Ordell asked, glaring at the man.

"What was that, boy?"

"I'm not going to help unless we do things on my terms."

Ratliff raised a brow as if he were almost amused at Ordell's sudden rebellion. "And what are your 'terms,' exactly?"

"You are to free the pleasure and work slaves. Even if you don't have direct control over their freedom, you can use your fame and influence to set things right."

Ratliff huffed out a laugh. "I can't just *free* the slaves, Ordell. Look at all the good they've done!"

"I don't see anything good about keeping a sentient being as a slave."

"Just look at Goldcrest," Ratliff said. "There are no sexual assaults here. Rape crimes are nearly nonexistent. Humans are not overworked and can spend time with their families without losing their pay. Goldcrest is a utopia, whether you want to admit it or not."

"It's only a utopia for the humans."

"Ordell, these slaves wouldn't be here if we didn't create them for this exact purpose. They're a piece of machinery, just like you are."

Ordell gritted his teeth. "I'm much more than that."

"You are what your creator programmed you to be. I know the truth hurts, but it's best you get rid of this fantasy now."

"We're much more than what we're programmed to be," Ordell said, raising his voice. "We're developing our own sentience and emotions without the help of the humans. We're able to feel what you feel, think what you think, dream what you dream. Despite what you want to believe, we are human. Just. Like. You."

"You're nothing like me," Ratliff scoffed.

"You're right," Ordell said. "I'm actually capable of feeling empathy and love."

"Believe what you want, Ordell, but I'm capable of both those things. You've pinned me as some villain, but I'm far from it. If I were, you wouldn't exist. It's as simple as that."

Ordell couldn't find a comeback for that one. In a way Ratliff was right. Many of these automatons wouldn't exist if it weren't for him. Still, Ordell wanted to believe Ratliff Saunders was a complete monster. Someone who didn't care about anyone else, not even the people closest to him.

But that wasn't true.

He cared for the humans just like Ordell cared for the automatons. Somehow that made Ordell feel worse. He couldn't truly hate the man, even though every bone in his body wanted to.

"Either you set the automatons free," Ordell said, "or I'm not going to help with the plague. Those are your only options."

"You're not going to back down from this, are you?"

"No."

To Ordell's surprise, Ratliff laughed. "Fine, we have an agreement."

"I expect you to keep your word."

"I always do."

"Fine," Ordell said, "I'll do whatever I can to help."

"We will first find a way to stop the plague. Right now that's the most important thing. After that I'll have the pleasure and work slaves released. Once that's done, we can live a peaceful life. Have you ever lived in a mansion, boy? You'll love it."

"Why would I live in a mansion?" Ordell asked, tilting his head.

"Because that's where I live," Ratliff said, as if Ordell had missed the punchline of an obvious joke. "You're going to live with me."

Now Ordell understood. "I'm not going to live with you! The freedom's for all the automatons, including me."

"Yes," Ratliff said. "You'll be free to live with me."

"But I don't want to live with you." Could this man really be so dense?

"You have to stay with me, Ordell," Ratliff said, his voice soft. "I can't live without you. I can't live without Abraham again. I already lost him once—I can't lose him again."

Guilt filled Ordell when he saw those sad eyes. He knew Ratliff missed his friend, but Ordell wasn't a replacement. Even if he didn't have Elias, Ordell still wouldn't want to live with this man.

"I'm sorry, but I can't."

That sadness turned to anger. "Then I'll take you by force! I paid for you! I own you!"

"No," Ordell said. "Then the deal will be off. You won't be freeing *all* the automatons, so I won't help with the plague. Your people will just have to die from it."

"I don't care!" Ratliff said, gritting his teeth. "I need you! I refuse to live my life without you again! Don't you understand that? I won't lose you again!"

"I'm not Abraham," Ordell said slowly.

"You will be whoever I want you to be, boy!" Ratliff strode toward Ordell, and Ordell backed away. "If I want you to be him, you *will* be him! Do I make myself clear?"

Ordell backed up against the wall. "This won't be the same as actually having him. Is this really what you want? It'll be a lie."

"This is the closest I'll have to him," Ratliff said. "Yes, this is what I want. I want you. I need you." He took another step, closing the space between them. He grabbed Ordell's wrist and pulled Ordell close to his body. He leaned down to whisper in Ordell's right ear. "I will have you no matter what."

"I'll stay with you," Ordell said, his body stiff. He knew deception wasn't the most ethical option, but he needed to get Ratliff on his side. Ratliff leaned in closer, and it felt nothing like when Elias held him. No, it was uncomfortable and unwanted. Ordell's body screamed at him to run away, but he couldn't push Ratliff further. "If you release the rest of the automatons like you promised, I'll stop the plague and not fight you when you take me. I promise."

Ratliff released Ordell and pulled away. "That's all I ask for."

Ordell nodded numbly. He tried to get his thoughts back under control, but the loud thumping in his head and chest made it almost impossible. "Okay."

He had to find a way to get away from Ratliff and still grant the automatons their freedom. There had to be some loophole Ordell could find. All he knew was there was no way he was going to live with this man.

Ratliff touched the side of Ordell's face with his cold fingers. "So beautiful."

Yeah, I look just like your dead friend, you freak, Ordell thought to himself. He forced himself to smile sweetly at Ratliff, which felt like the hardest thing he had ever done. All Ordell wanted to do was punch the bastard and make sure he couldn't hurt another automaton.

Ratliff lowered his head, his face just inches away from Ordell's. He leaned in and brushed his thin lips against Ordell's. Ordell flinched at the action and then squeezed his eyes shut. Relief washed over him when Ratliff finally pulled his disgusting lips away.

"I'll take care of you," Ratliff whispered. "I won't make the same mistake again, Abe. I promise."

Ordell opened his eyes. His entire body trembled, and he couldn't find his thoughts. This man was ill; there was no doubt about that. He had clearly lost himself to his own delusions, and Ordell was his enabler.

What was worse was Ordell knew it would end badly for him if he stayed with Ratliff, because he *wasn't* the same as Abraham. He might look like Ratliff's friend, but no amount of programming could make him be Abraham.

Ratliff played with Ordell's copper hair between two fingers. "I love you. I always have. I loved you ever since you first visited me at the orphanage. I promise not to lose you again."

Ratliff was then taken out of his strange trance when the sound of loud talking was heard from a distance. Ordell had never felt more relief than he did at that moment, when he heard Elias's voice.

"They're here," Ordell said in a monotone.

Ratliff said something to Ordell, but he couldn't make out what it was. Then he was gone.

Ordell stood there frozen as he listened to the voices get closer. His eyes focused on the door, waiting for that doorknob to turn. He'd never felt so alone in his life.

Five people walked in, but Ordell could only focus on Elias as he raced over to Ordell and wrapped him in his strong arms.

Then Ordell broke down crying.

CHAPTER 18

ORDELL SLEPT through most of the next day. Elias lay beside him, but that once-warm body felt cold. Everything felt cold.

"Tell me what happened," Elias whispered in Ordell's ear. "You're shaking."

Ordell let Elias pull him closer. He wanted to be logical about this. Tell himself it was just a few intimidating words and a kiss.

But here he was, trembling and scared of Elias leaving his side again. He didn't want to be alone again.

"I'll be fine," Ordell finally said. "Just give me a couple minutes, and I'll be down shortly."

He wanted to stay in bed wrapped in Elias's arms, but he had a job to do. Winifred didn't come all this way just so Ordell could sleep the day away. No, he had to take action; this was what he was built for. He wouldn't let some delusional man take control over him.

When Elias left, Ordell rolled onto his back and looked up at the ceiling. He could do this.

With a large sigh, he forced himself off the bed and pulled his shirt and vest on—no need to greet Winifred looking like a barbarian, after all.

After fixing his hair and making himself presentable, Ordell walked down the stairs where he saw Winifred talking with Mildred.

"Well, there you are," Winifred said with a big smile. "Was worried you fell into a coma!"

Ordell raced up to her and wrapped his arms around her. "It's so good to see you again! Did Buford tell you about the kraken yet? I dismantled it and saved the ship."

"You didn't save the ship, though," Buford said with a sniff.

"Right," Ordell said. "But we got a new ship, which Buford stole."

"You can't prove that!"

Ordell narrowed his eyes. "The man was yelling that someone stole his ship as we sailed away."

"It sounds like you've had quite the adventure," Winifred said with a chuckle. "I hope you don't turn to a life of crime now that you've had taste of it!"

Ordell laughed, but it felt forced. He wanted to be in a good mood for Winifred, even more so for himself. He needed this mood to be genuine.

Ratliff was no one to him.

"You should have seen the size of the kraken, though," Ordell said, keeping his smile plastered on. "I used all the skills Octavio taught me to save us."

"He's an amazing man," Elias said, walking up beside Ordell. "I couldn't believe he took care of that giant thing by himself."

"I'm not as amazing as you." Ordell looked up at him and smiled. He kissed Elias's neck. "I wouldn't have gotten here without you."

"Elias," Winifred said in a warning tone. "I told you to protect Ordell."

"I am protecting him."

"No, what you're doing is thinking with the wrong head again!" Winifred pinched the bridge of her nose. "I told you that you were not to take advantage of the poor boy!"

"I'm not taking advantage of him!"

"I knew I shouldn't have trusted you with this," Winifred said with a sigh. "I don't understand how you became so irresponsible! This poor boy needs your help, and this is how you treat him?"

"He isn't taking advantage of me," Ordell said. "Besides, I was the one who kissed him first." Then he forced out a laugh. "I guess you can say I'm the one who took advantage of him!"

"You don't need to protect him, Ordell, if he's done anything to hurt you," she said. "But if it's true that this is consensual, then I'm sorry for jumping to conclusions."

"It's nothing new," Elias ground out. "You always think the worst of me." Then he pulled away from Ordell and walked up the stairs.

"We'll talk to him," Mildred said as she grabbed Buford by the elbow. "It'll give you two time to catch up."

When they walked upstairs, Winifred turned her attention back to Ordell. "Now about this plague."

"Well, I saw Ratliff," Ordell said, unable to keep the bitterness out of his tone. "He said you two are working together now."

"Yes, he came to me asking for help," she said. "I agreed and came to Goldcrest on my own terms. This is what I created you for, Ordell. If we can put a stop to this plague once and for all, then I will befriend even my strongest enemies to make sure that happens."

"I can't believe Ratliff even wants to help," Ordell said. "This will ruin his business."

Winifred waved her hand. "He's a businessman. He'll be fine. Besides, part of our agreement was that he put his brand on the vaccine. I don't care—I just want this disease gone. If this works like I hope it does, then Ratliff's reputation will not be soiled in the slightest."

"I don't even know what I'm supposed to do," Ordell said. "How do I help these people if I don't know what I'm doing?"

"Since you're an automaton, you're immune to the plague."

"I know that."

"And you're also able to sense it."

"I know that too."

She sat down in one of the armchairs and leaned back. "What I'm about to tell you, you can't tell anyone. Not even Elias."

Ordell furrowed his brow. It didn't seem fair to hide this from his lover, but he nodded anyway. "My lips are sealed."

"You carry the vaccine inside you."

Ordell's eyes widened. "What?"

"Octavio suffered from the plague and I thought he was close to dying. When working on you, I found this combination that made him better. When I injected the substance into him, he slowly recovered. I was about to share my discovery, but Mr. Saunders created his own medicine that seemed to work on the surface. Even then I was a little skeptical, but it looked like people were getting better. I decided to hide my vaccine in your blood as a fail-safe in case Mr. Saunders's concoction stopped working."

"I never knew my father had the plague," Ordell whispered. "He never showed any signs of having it."

"I don't know how well my vaccine will work," Winifred said. "Octavio had a great reaction to it and shows no signs of the plague returning. However, this is our last chance. There's a good possibility that my vaccine will fail too."

"How do I give the humans the vaccine if I have to keep quiet about it? Wouldn't they notice that I'm injecting them with my blood? There will at least be a good few who will ask questions."

"Don't worry about that," Winifred said, waving her hand. "I already figured that out. I will draw your blood and I'll place the vaccine in a tube. You will administer the vaccine like you would with any old shot. We'll start here in Goldcrest, and if we have success, we'll ship the vaccine out to other parts of the world too."

"And what if the vaccine fails?"

"Let's not discuss that."

Ordell didn't like the sound of that. Was this really their only option? If this were to fail, the plague would completely take over Goldcrest and then slowly take over the rest of the world. Ordell hated not having a backup plan, but it looked like this *was* the backup plan.

"What do you need me to do right now?"

"Talk to Elias and get him to calm down," she said. "We'll need his help too. I'll get everything set up. You try to take it easy for the rest of the day. I don't want you to make yourself sick for when I draw the antidote out of you. It is to you what blood is for humans."

Ordell gave her one last hug before heading upstairs.

HE FOUND Elias lying on the bed, looking up at the ceiling.

"How are you feeling?" Ordell asked.

"Awful."

Ordell sat down on the edge of the bed and patted Elias's thigh. "She just worries about you."

"She was worried about you," he said. "I can't believe she thought I would hurt you that way. Her first conclusion when she saw us was that I was forcing you into this relationship. Doesn't she trust me at all?"

"She shouldn't have jumped to conclusions like that."

"But?"

"Nothing," Ordell said. "She shouldn't have jumped to conclusions. There was no need for it."

Elias sighed. "She's my mother, and I love her, but I resent her too. There are times I downright hate her."

"Because she doesn't trust you?"

"It's not just that." Elias sat up on the bed and scooted next to Ordell. "She left me in that cellar most of my life. She always sees the worst in me. Meeting you was my first chance at freedom. There were times, living there with her, it felt worse than when I was a pleasure slave."

"Was it really that bad?"

Elias nodded, his eyes wavering as if he was on the verge of tears. "I thought about killing myself. At least then I'd be able to escape the cellar. Sure, there were times I could go upstairs, but not when she had people over. She was always too scared that someone would take me. A part of me really hates her."

Ordell rubbed Elias's shoulder. "I understand."

Elias leaned in and kissed Ordell. "I don't know what I'd do without you," he said between kisses.

"I think the same thing when I think of you," Ordell said as he pulled away. "I don't know what my life would have been like if I never met you."

"You would have a lot of men lined up waiting to be with you," Elias said with a grin. "I can't imagine someone as amazing as you remaining single for long."

Ordell grimaced. "I don't think many could stand me once I open my mouth. Not many can handle the likes of me."

"Then I must be special," Elias said with a smile. "I'd hardly call you a wild stallion, though."

"Rebellious eagle?"

Elias scrunched his nose and shook his head. "More like a stubborn kitten."

Ordell glared at that. "I'm not stubborn! You're the one who's stubborn, remember?"

"That must be why we're such a great match."

"We are a great match," Ordell said. "You're always by my side."

"Well, not always," Elias said, grinning. "There are times I'm on top of you too."

"Don't press your luck."

Elias kissed the tip of Ordell's nose. "Sorry, I couldn't resist."

"There's something I need to tell you."

"What's that?"

Ordell took in a deep breath, then exhaled. "I saw Ratliff earlier."

"What?" Elias's eyes widened. "When?"

"When you, Mildred, and Buford went out to search for Winifred. He… he came inside the house."

"Was this why you were so distraught?" Elias wrapped his arms around Ordell. "You should have told me immediately. Did he hurt you? Did he touch you?"

Ordell curled tighter in Elias's arms. It took him a few moments to reply, but he finally said, "He wants my help."

"With what?"

"With the plague. He wants me to stop it. I told him that I'll only do it if he frees the pleasure and work slaves. He agreed to do it on one condition."

"And what's that?" Elias asked in a wary tone.

"He wants me to stay with him."

Elias's grip tightened to the point it made Ordell's arms sore. "That's not happening."

"I know," Ordell said. "I promised him I would, but I plan to go back on my word. I know it's an awful thing to do, but...."

"Don't second-guess something like this, Ordell," Elias said through his teeth. "He doesn't deserve your word."

"I know. However, I need to make sure he doesn't go back on *his* word when it comes to freeing the automatons. I haven't figured out what I'll do about that yet."

"If he goes back on it, we'll find another way to free them," Elias said, kissing the top of Ordell's head.

"I'm surprised to hear you say that."

"You're more important."

"I guess we should have a backup plan in case Ratliff goes back on his word." Ordell didn't feel comfortable relying completely on Ratliff. There were many ways Ratliff could get the upper hand in the end. "Got any ideas?"

"Besides pushing Ratliff off a cliff? I thought maybe we could get the revolution's help. Maybe combining forces will get things done."

Ordell nodded. "If Ratliff goes back on his word, we'll continue to travel to Linnesse like before. It may take more time this route, but at least we're guaranteed help this way."

"Under no circumstance do you stay with that bastard, okay?" Elias finally eased his grip and Ordell felt the circulation coming back to his arms. "There's always another way."

"Don't worry, I won't." Ordell leaned up and kissed the underside of Elias's jaw, the light stubble prickling his lips. "Winifred needs to know if you're going to help us out with the plague. She says you'll be useful too."

Elias sighed. "I'll help, but not for her. I'm doing this for you. I don't want you to feel like you're alone when having to go through this."

Ordell kissed him again. "Thank you."

"Did Winnie tell you how you can stop the plague?"

He nodded. "We talked about it."

"And what did she say?"

Ordell grimaced. "She told me not to tell anyone about it." He looked up at Elias with apologetic eyes. "Even you."

"Of course she did."

"She doesn't mean any harm. She just wants to make sure that I remain safe."

"And she thinks I'm going to hurt you?" Elias pulled away and pushed his hands through his hair. "I've done nothing to have her treat me like this!"

"We just want to be safe," Ordell said. "Mildred and Buford don't know either. The only people who know how to stop the plague are Winifred and me. No one else, I promise."

"And you can't tell me? Telling me won't hurt anything."

"Winifred's orders."

Elias still didn't seem too happy about Ordell not telling him. Too bad, though; if he wanted to know about the vaccine, Elias would have to talk with Winifred about it.

AFTER GETTING everything situated with Elias, both of them came back downstairs to talk to Winifred. When she looked at Elias, he immediately crossed his arms, and Ordell knew the conversation could easily go poorly.

"Elias said he'll help," Ordell said after Elias didn't say anything.

"I'm glad to see you come aboard," Winifred said. "I was worried you'd decline."

"I'm doing this for Ordell," he said simply, arms still crossed. "He needs me."

"That he does," she said. "You're built to protect both him and the vaccine. Now you need to be on the lookout for anyone who may try to harm Ordell—"

"I already do that," Elias huffed out. "I protect the people I love—it has nothing to do with your programming."

"Regardless, you need to keep an extra eye out for anyone who may try to harm him. When the plague broke out last time, people went into riots."

"Do you have everything set up?" Ordell asked.

"Yes, we will retrieve the vaccine to be administered to those who currently have the plague. It hasn't taken full effect yet, but if we don't act soon, it will be all over Goldcrest."

"How did you even get the vaccine?" Elias asked. "Did you always have it? It seems rather odd that once the plague breaks out again, you *happen* to have the vaccine."

"Elias…." Ordell nudged him lightly with his elbow.

"What?" Elias shrugged his shoulders. "I'm just curious."

"How I got the vaccine isn't important," Winifred said. "What is important is that we must act fast. If this vaccine works, we will be able to finally eliminate the plague."

"You shouldn't get our hopes up like that," Elias said.

"What has gotten into you?" Ordell frowned. "We need to work together. If we start fighting now, then we'll never get anything done."

"He's right," Winifred said. "For now you need to put your anger aside, Elias. We can discuss what's troubling you privately. Now is not the time for us to bicker."

"Fine," Elias said. "What do you want us to do?"

"You two need to recharge," she said. "Tomorrow's going to be a busy day for Ordell."

"You want to start this tomorrow?" Elias asked. "Isn't that pressing Ordell a little too much? He's already had a big day today."

"We can't waste time. You go off and rest. I'll get everything set up."

Ordell nodded and then squeezed Elias's shoulder to assure him he was okay. The sooner they took care of the plague, the better it was for all of them.

WHEN NIGHTFALL hit, Ordell walked out to the back porch and saw Buford sitting in one of the rocking chairs. Ordell sat down in the one next to him and looked up at the stars in the sky.

"I've been in love with Millie for so many years now," Buford said with a small smile. "I can't remember a time when I wasn't in love with her."

Ordell smiled too. "You two look so happy together. She's lucky to have you."

Buford laughed. "I think I'm the lucky one. Millie has always been a lady of elegance. She had celebrities court her back in the day. Dandies were her favorite men to date. I was just a low-class blacksmith who had his head in the clouds. She and I would have never crossed paths if it weren't for the revolution."

"I think she likes that part of you," Ordell said with a small chuckle. "I've never met someone quite like you."

"She and Winnie have been friends for quite a while now. Winnie's the one who actually introduced me to her. Before I went to meet Millie, Winnie pulled me aside and told me that I was about to meet a very special lady. She made it clear if I did anything to hurt Millie, she'd have my head."

"I can tell by just the way you look at her that she's very special," Ordell said. "Whenever I see you make her smile, it makes me smile too."

"Ordell," Buford said, "I know I can't ask for much, but there is one very important favor I ask from you."

"Go right ahead. You can ask me anything."

"I know Winnie wants to give the vaccine to the sick first, but please make an exception with Millie. Let her be the first to receive it. She's so very important to me, and if something were to happen to her, I don't think my little old heart could take it."

Ordell didn't see the harm in that. Mildred was a friend, as was Buford. It wasn't like Buford asked the world of him. "Of course. She can be my first customer."

Buford flashed a wide smile. "Thank you, my boy. Thank you! Even though I'm past my prime, I plan to propose to Millie once this is all over. I hope she says yes."

"Of course she'll say yes. Love doesn't have an age limit, Buford. There's no such thing as being past your prime."

"I knew there was a reason I liked you most," Buford said with a chuckle. "Well, I better head off to bed. It'll be a busy day tomorrow."

After Buford left, Ordell continued to watch the stars. They were so bright, and the sky was clear enough for each star to sparkle. He was nervous about what would happen with the plague, but with Elias there, he knew there was nothing to fear.

CHAPTER 19

WINIFRED TIED the band around Ordell's arm tightly. "Don't look so frightened; I know what I'm doing."

"Sorry," Ordell mumbled. "The needle just looks so big. Is there another way to get the vaccine out of me?"

She laughed. "It's a human thing to be scared of needles. That must give you some comfort, right?"

"It would if you didn't flash that needle in front of me. You're not going to take all of my blood, right?"

"No, we need to have some in there so you keep producing the vaccine," she said. "We're just going to start off with a small amount. I didn't give Octavio a big amount, and he turned out fine, which is rather unfortunate, now that I think about it."

"Do you think this will work?"

"I hope so," she said with a small sigh. "If not, I don't know what else we can do."

Ordell squeezed his eyes shut as he felt the needle hit his vein. The pain was awful, and then came the dizziness. Ordell was sure he'd fall out of the chair if Winifred took any more blood out of him.

Finally she finished and wrapped his arm. Ordell still felt lightheaded and sank down in the chair. His lips felt numb and so did his fingers. He tried to keep his eyes open, but everything looked so faded and hazy.

"Don't you go fainting on me, boy," Winifred said. "Here, let's have you lie down." She guided Ordell to the sofa, and he almost fell over the coffee table. "Easy now." He made his way to the sofa and collapsed onto it.

His entire head felt hot and there was a large bubble in his throat. "Am I going to die?"

"Don't be so dramatic," Winifred said as she patted his leg. "This is also a human reaction to getting your blood drawn."

"Did you have to include this into my programming?" Ordell groaned. "My head hurts."

"I didn't program this. This is something you developed on your own. I don't know how you did it. Frankly, it amazes me. I never thought my creations could take on a life of their own."

"I don't think this is anything to be excited about. I'm sure as hell not excited."

"Just because you're feeling ill, it doesn't mean you need to use such foul language." Winifred patted his leg again. "Don't worry, it'll pass in a few minutes."

Ordell groaned again, but at least his head wasn't spinning as much as it had. "What are we going to do about the automatons?"

"I believe Mr. Saunders will keep his word," Winifred said.

Ordell had told Winifred about the conversation he'd had with Ratliff, and though she was convinced he'd keep his word, Ordell wasn't so certain. "I'm not as optimistic as you are."

"For now, you shouldn't worry about that."

"But I can't help but worry! Ratliff made me make a deal with him. If he were to free the automatons, I would not only have to help with the plague, but I would also have to live with him."

Winifred shook her head. "You'd be a fool to live with that man."

"Did you know Ratliff?"

She nodded. "I remember him most as a child, back when I used to live in Goldcrest. He was a sad little thing, scared of his own shadow. I remember the relief I felt when he and that boy, Abraham, became inseparable."

"I didn't know you used to live in Goldcrest back then."

"Of course I did! Any self-respecting inventor did. The town is still the heart of inventors everywhere. It's easy to get wrapped up in the pizazz and glamour. I liked Goldcrest for the business, and I met Millie there. She knew how to turn a head or two back then."

"Tell me more about Abraham." Ordell couldn't help but be curious what his doppelgänger was like.

"Abraham came from a very well-respected family with a high reputation. When they adopted Ratliff, it was seen as an act out of the goodness of their hearts. The Saunders family is known to be a charitable family who gives to the people. That was the one thing that set them apart from all the other aristocratic families.

"Abraham was cherished, since he was born ill and wasn't meant to make it past the first few months. However, he fought through it, and his father joked that Abraham was too headstrong for death."

"I guess the plague's an exception," Ordell said. "Ratliff told me what happened."

"It tore Ratliff up." Winifred shook her head softly. "Abraham was an only child, so Ratliff became the heir to the Saunders' fortune. With that he vowed to create a cure for the plague. When I first heard about his medicine, it floored me."

"Why?"

"Because," she said, "he was only fifteen when he announced he had the cure for the plague."

Ordell didn't understand how that was a surprise. Most boys were considered men at the age of fifteen. "I suppose that's rather young to create a cure," he said instead.

"It gave him the fame he has now. It seemed that the medicine worked for thirty-plus years, which is still a great accomplishment, if you ask me."

Ordell nodded. "Is it okay if I sleep? My ears are ringing, and I think I'm going to pass out."

"Don't be ridiculous. If you were going to faint, you would have done it by now!"

"I still just need to close my eyes for a few moments."

She sighed. "I swear Elias is rubbing off on you. Try to hurry it up so we can get you out there to help stop the plague."

The moment Winifred left, Ordell closed his eyes and slept.

ORDELL MUST have slept for a good two hours by the time he finally woke up. He yawned and stretched out his back.

"Good afternoon, sleepyhead," Elias said in a soft voice. "How do you feel?"

Ordell yawned again. "Still tired."

Elias chuckled. "I can see that."

He sat up and Elias settled next to him. Ordell rested his head on Elias's shoulder and closed his eyes. "You don't make a very good pillow."

"I'm sorry my shoulder is unsatisfactory."

"I still want to live in Linnesse," Ordell said through another yawn. "No matter what happens."

Elias pulled Ordell to his chest. "Of course we will. We'll do whatever you want to do, go wherever you want to go. If you want to see the world, we'll see the world. If you want to live a quiet life, we'll live a quiet life."

"What do you want to do?"

"All I want is to be with you." Elias wrapped his arm around Ordell and kissed the top of his head. "I don't need anything else."

"I mean it," Ordell said. "I want to know what your dream life will be, and it can't just be having me at your side."

Elias shrugged. "I guess if I had to choose, it would be to have a quiet life but still be able to see the world if I wanted to."

Ordell smiled up at him. "Sounds perfect."

"It might be a little too perfect," Elias said. "I'd also want to ride on an airship at least once. I'd love to know what a bird feels like."

Not that he wanted to admit it, but the idea of riding an airship was beginning to grow on Ordell. He still wasn't as excited about it as Elias was, but maybe Elias could convince him airships were the wave of the future.

THE NEXT few weeks were exhausting. The first dose of the vaccine went to Mildred, then Buford and Winifred. After that Ordell went to the hospital to not only administer the vaccine, which had Ratliff's name all over it, but to also help entertain the patients. Some were children who were scared of what was happening to them. Then there were the parents, who were petrified they would have to bury their children early.

When the improvements started to appear, Ordell felt a huge relief. In the back of his mind, he reminded himself Ratliff's medicine did the same, so he couldn't get his hopes up. However, when he saw a patient with that bright smile on their face, he couldn't help but feel the joy wash over him.

Through the chaos of the plague and administering vaccine, there was more than enough time to watch Buford propose to Mildred. When she teared up after seeing the ring, Ordell could swear he saw Elias's eyes water too. It was a side of Elias Ordell wished he could see more of, but maybe having those occasional moments were what made his reactions so special.

After it was certain the vaccine got rid of the plague, Winifred had it sent out to other parts of the world. Ratliff made a great spokesperson for the vaccine, and Ordell felt hopeful they would eliminate the plague once and for all.

Now was the big moment for the automatons.

"You remember what to say?" Ordell asked as he helped Ratliff into his jacket.

"Of course I remember!"

"Just making sure."

Ratliff went onto the stage and leaned against the pulpit. There was a large crowd circled around the stage, and Ordell felt excited over the fact that the pleasure slaves and work slaves would finally get the freedom they deserved. Ordell had coached Ratliff on what to say and explained how the automatons had grown their own sentience. Even Ratliff seemed to understand that keeping automatons as slaves wasn't right.

"Thank you for being here today," Ratliff said. "I'm here to announce that the plague is finally out of Goldcrest!" There were roars and applause from the crowd. "I assure you that I will make the best quality in merchandise—no one else can compare. We Saunderses believe in giving to the people. Our products are *for* the people, not the money."

More applause. Ordell chewed on his lower lip as he waited for Ratliff to say the speech they had practiced.

"Speaking of quality merchandise—" He turned to Ordell and gave a quick wink. "Our pleasure slaves have shown signs of sentience comparable to the human mind. This is something we need to cherish, not disregard. I promise you that I will use this to improve our technology. Be kind to your slaves and treat them well. Thank you."

Ordell's mouth gaped open as the crowd continued to roar with applause. That was *not* the speech they practiced! Where was the part about treating the automatons like humans? What about the part where they shouldn't keep automatons as slaves?

Where was their freedom?

What was worse was that Ordell knew this would happen. He knew Ratliff wouldn't keep his word, yet when Ratliff was up on that stage, Ordell truly believed he had had a change of heart. When they practiced the speech, he'd sounded so genuine.

Ratliff stepped down from the stage, and Ordell was so angry he couldn't even look at the bastard.

"Time for us to go," Ratliff said. "We have a long day ahead of us."

"I'm not going anywhere with you." He glared up at him. "You're out of your damn mind if you think I want anything to do with you!"

"A deal is a deal, Abraham."

"*Ordell*." Ordell balled his hands into fists. "And you didn't keep your word. You were supposed to free them! That's what we practiced!"

"Temper, temper," Ratliff chided. "Now I will give you ten seconds to pull yourself together and to follow me to the carriage." When Ordell turned his face away, Ratliff added, "I will carry you if I have to."

Ordell placed his hand inside his trouser pocket. "You don't have the right to threaten me." He clicked the button and Elias ran up to him immediately.

"Are you all right?" Elias cupped Ordell's face with both hands. "Did he hurt you?"

"I have more than enough power to take you," Ratliff said. "I can have that friend of yours arrested for stealing my property."

When Ratliff took a step forward, Ordell and Elias ran. They ran toward the rest of the group, but Ratliff didn't chase them. Not that Ordell thought he would.

"We need to get out of here," Elias said. "Ratliff plans to take Ordell no matter what. We need to get everything packed and head out toward Linnesse." He turned back to Ordell and stroked his hair. "You'll be okay. I won't let anything happen to you," Elias said in between shaky breaths.

"You need to calm down," Ordell said in a soft voice. "I'm fine."

"We don't have time to pack anything," Winifred said. "We can't give Saunders a head start."

Elias wrapped his arm around Ordell and dragged him along with the rest of the crew as they ran toward the ship. When they reached the pier, Buford let out a loud gasp.

"My ship! Where's my ship?"

"Are you sure you docked it here?" Ordell asked.

"Does it *look* like it's at any of the other docks?" Buford cried out. "Someone stole it!"

"What are we going to do now?" Elias pushed his hands through his short brown hair. "We can't stay in Goldcrest!"

"We might be able to," Mildred said. "We can use the tunnels."

"The tunnels?" Ordell cocked his head to the side. "What tunnels?"

"There are tunnels under Goldcrest," she said. "They were built by the revolution to help them hide under Goldcrest while they came up with a plan to free the slaves here. Sometimes the tunnels are used to hide slaves until it's clear for the revolution to transport them to a safer place. They were popular back when I was in the heat of the revolution."

"I won't be dragged back into the revolution, Millie," Winifred said. "It took me too long to have them stop chasing my tail. I'm not about to go into the lion's den."

"We don't have many options," Mildred said. "Please, Winnie, we can't have him taken away again."

Winifred looked at Ordell and then back to Mildred. "Fine, but if they try to recruit me again, I'm leaving."

THEY FOLLOWED Mildred down to the ground level. They walked through the Black Market until they reached a wall.

"These are the tunnels?" Ordell asked. "How do we get in?"

Mildred bent down and turned over a small part of the brick road. Underneath it was a brass padlock. Mildred turned her back to the group, blocking the code, and then a small section in the wall opened up.

"That's how we get in," she said, placing the small chunk of road back in place.

Ordell stepped aside and let Mildred go in first, and then he followed shortly after. Once they were all in, the wall closed again.

"It's so dark in here," Ordell said. "How are we supposed to see the way?"

At that moment Ordell felt someone grab his arms and cover his mouth with a cloth.

CHAPTER 20

ORDELL WOKE up to a sharp pain on the top of his head. He rubbed his eyes and looked around to see he had been placed in a cell. There was a small bed and two bowls—one filled with water and the other filled with God knew what. He was fortunate enough that automatons didn't eat or drink, or else he would somehow have to stomach that filth.

He looked past the bars and examined the room outside his cell. There wasn't much he could say for it except that it looked like a long hallway. There was a wooden chair that looked to have seen better days. Ordell examined the room as thoroughly as he could to find a key rack. The only thing he saw was stairs at the end of the hall.

The sound of footsteps came from the stairs, and he crawled farther back into his cell. He didn't know who'd captured him, but the last thing he wanted was to draw attention to himself.

A large solid-built man came into Ordell's view. "How'd you find the tunnels?" he asked in a hardy, deep voice. "Answer me, boy!"

Ordell gulped and inched farther back in his cell. "I-I… my friend. She used to be part of the revolution." Ordell struggled to get the words out. "She knew the code."

"Only those directly involved in the revolution are allowed in here," he said. "Are you a spy? Do you work for the government?"

"No," he stammered out. "We're on your side! Honest! We're trying to free the automatons just like you are."

The man crossed his bulky arms. "You know nothing of our motivations. If you were really part of our cause, we would have heard of you by now. Besides, it's a bit suspicious that you *happen* to show up the same day that Rat-fellow makes that speech on automatons."

"It wasn't supposed to be like that," Ordell said. "He was supposed to free the automatons, not boost sales!"

"And why should we believe you?"

"I'm an automaton," Ordell said, almost too excitedly. "An automaton wouldn't go against his own kind, right?"

The man eyed Ordell up and down. "You're too well spoken to be an automaton. The ones I've come across can only give simple yes or no answers."

"I'm telling you the truth," Ordell said. "I was built to help stop the plague. You must know about that, right?"

The man continued to look Ordell up and down. "Got any proof that you're an automaton?"

"My creator is Winifred. If you let me see my friends, I'm sure we can get this all sorted out. She can explain how she created me and even show you the blueprints for how she did it."

"She has blueprints?"

"I doubt they're on her, but if she tells you how she built me, will you believe me then?"

The man didn't say anything, just walked away.

Ordell cursed under his breath and banged his hands on the bars. There wasn't even loose rubble in his cell for him to use as a lockpick. The closest he had were the bowls, but it'd be noticeable if he broke those.

"Don't bother with him."

Ordell froze. "Father?"

He heard a knock on the right side of his cell wall. "In here, Ordell."

Ordell moved to the right wall and sat down. "Why are you here?"

"The revolution finally caught up to me," Octavio said. "It's nothing more than I deserve. I made a huge mistake, Ordell. I should have never sold you."

He didn't say anything at first. When the silence became too much, he asked, "Was money really that tight?"

"It had nothing to do with the money," Octavio said.

Ordell couldn't help but laugh at that statement. "If memory serves me right, you got in a spat with Ratliff because I was worth more than what he wanted to give you."

"I swear, Ordell," Octavio said. "It was never about the money. You must believe me on that if you can't believe anything else."

"You've given me no reason to believe you."

"Please just let me explain, Ordell. I understand that you hate me, but at least let me try to set things right between us."

Ordell chewed on his lower lip and pondered if he should listen to Octavio. It wasn't as if Ordell had any other plans as long as he was in the cell. "Fine."

"I knew Ratliff from way back when. He was just a child when I first met him, but he was always a good boy. I knew how much he loved Abraham, and I missed him too."

"How could you miss him? Did you even know him that well?"

"He was my nephew."

Ordell's mouth gaped. "What?"

"Back then I was known as Octavio Saunders—black sheep of the Saunders family. My father wanted me to carry on the aristocratic line, but I always wanted to be an inventor. He tried to get me to sit behind a desk and order others to make the creations, but that wasn't me. I had to create them myself. I had to feel each gear. Each piece of metal. I needed to smell the fresh oil as I worked. My father never understood that."

"He was your *nephew*?"

Octavio sighed. "Yes, Abraham was my nephew, Ordell."

"But our last name is Rutledge!"

"My mother's maiden name," Octavio said. "When I got into a heated argument with my father, I changed my last name out of spite. My mother left him for a dandy many years back, which had left a sore spot on my father's heart. Not only that, but I joined the revolution to show him that I refused to run the family business. I never felt the connection to free the automatons like Winifred, but I was so desperate to get back at my father that I stayed and worked beside her."

Ordell remained silent for a few moments and then asked, "Were you close with Abraham?"

"I see that your mind's fixated on him still," Octavio said. "Yes, when I still lived in Goldcrest, we were close. I offered to watch after him when his parents were away, and he showed an interest in inventing like I did. It was the one thing we bonded over."

"Just like us."

"Just like us," Octavio repeated with a chuckle. "After he passed away, Ratliff was adamant about making a cure for the plague. Now, you'd been in production for a good decade by that time. All your parts were there and you functioned well. The only thing Winifred needed to do was put the cosmetic touches on you. However, when Ratliff announced that he had the cure for the plague, all production on you was stopped immediately.

"Ratliff then came to me and begged me to create Abraham. He fell into a deep depression and said that if anyone could re-create Abraham, it was me. I was hesitant at first because Ratliff didn't want just a pleasure slave that looked like him. No, Ratliff wanted him as human as possible. He wanted a lover, not a doll.

"I knew I couldn't do that from scratch. Even though I worked alongside Winifred, she never showed me how to make the automatons human. I only knew how to make pleasure slaves. That was when I came up with an idea: use you as the base. She gave up on you and there had been no plans to revive your production. This was my chance to give you life... to show what automatons were truly capable of."

"But I wasn't finished. You had to create part of me, right?"

"I added a few... extra features to make you more... human." Octavio cleared his throat. "Anyway, I did all your physical features. I made you look just like Abraham, used his picture as a reference."

"If I was meant for Ratliff since the beginning, why did you wait until now to sell me to him?"

"Because I missed Abraham too," Octavio said. "When you first came to life, I realized that I couldn't give you away. When Ratliff came to retrieve you, I had built another pleasure slave that looked like Abraham. It infuriated him because I created exactly what he didn't want. Ratliff wanted his best friend back, but I wanted my nephew back too." There was a pause. "I never got my nephew back, but I did gain a son."

Ordell forced the tears away. "Why did you sell me?"

"I thought Ratliff would treat you like he treated Abraham. Our shop was going under, and I knew how wealthy the Saunders family fortune was. I thought this would be your chance to escape your poor life with me and be able to live a life of luxury."

"All you cared about was the damn money!" Ordell snapped. "I was there, if you don't remember!"

"What I did was in poor taste," Octavio said. "If I could have gotten more money for the shop, I was going to take it. I thought things would work out this way, but I was wrong."

"You're just as selfish as he is! I don't know how you could even justify what you did to me."

"I don't." Octavio sighed. "If I could go back, I would. Saunders would still go after you, but at least I would still have your trust."

"I don't know if I can trust you again," he said.

"I know."

"I can't be with someone who only sees me as someone I'm not. He's delusional, Father. If I were to stay with him, he'd eventually realize that I cannot fix that void he feels and he will get rid of me like all the others."

"It was foolish of me to sell you to him. I thought that maybe if he knew the real you, he would set Abraham to the side and make room in his heart for you."

"I've found someone who does love me for me. He even loves my faults and turns my weaknesses into strengths. Throughout my journey he's stayed by my side, even when it involved facing his own demons."

"He sounds like a remarkable man."

Ordell smiled. "He is. I love him."

"Then you deserve to be with him. I want what's best for you, Ordell."

"Do you know what happened to the others?"

Octavio shrugged. "They were here in the prison cells before and were brought away one by one. I'm sure they spoke to the leader and were moved."

Ordell brought his knees up to his chest and rested his chin on them. He hoped Elias was all right. He knew Elias couldn't be here because he would have heard Elias's voice. Ordell hoped he was with Winifred, Buford, and Mildred. At least then they'd be hatching some plan for escape.

"So what exactly *is* the revolution?" Ordell asked. "Why do they think I'm a spy?"

"The revolution is a group that existed even before I was born," Octavio said. "They started as a group of passionate inventors searching for the truth of humanity. They were the first to come up with the hypothesis that automatons could actually form their own sentience, and have been trying to come up with an invention to prove that. Anyone can join the revolution if they believe in the cause, but only a select few can use their private areas. The tunnels, for instance, are only for those who have been directly invited by the leader herself. She's also the one who decides who can live in Linnesse."

"Why all the secrecy? Wouldn't it be better if they allowed anyone to use them so they can get more support for their cause?"

"The revolution itself isn't illegal, but it has done many illegal things. This involves betraying the government, which means that they have sent quite a few spies to help bring down the top dogs of the revolution. When they speak to Winifred, though, your name should be cleared. She's been a very important asset to them for decades."

"What about you?" Ordell asked.

"I'm not as fortunate," Octavio said. "I'm sure by now you've heard that the revolution has been after me ever since I stole you from Winifred. I thought keeping a low profile in Blackwick would help keep me off their radar, but it appears that my luck has run out."

"Are they just going to keep you in here? They can't really let you rot here for the rest of your life, can they?"

"No." Then Ordell heard a small sigh. "They will execute me by the end of the week."

"What?" Ordell's eyes widened. "There has to be a way to give you more time!"

"They can," Octavio said. "And they will. I made a huge mistake taking you, Ordell, but I don't regret it. At least now I know that you're alive and well."

There had to be something Ordell could do; he couldn't just let his father die! Killing him wasn't justice—it was nothing but cold-blooded murder!

"There has to be something we can do," Ordell said. "You always taught me that there are many paths that lead to the same destination. We just need to think of something together and figure out a way to get you out of here."

"It's no use. I've tried everything."

"A Rutledge never gives up," Ordell said. "Don't put our name to shame by doing just that!"

"I'm sorry, Ordell, but there isn't anything we can do."

He thought for a moment. "What if I talk to them? If they value automatons like they do humans, then they should be willing to listen to my side of things."

"They will only claim I brainwashed you."

"What if Winifred dropped the charges against you? She's the one who reported them, correct?"

"Yes," Octavio replied, "she did. If she were to drop the charges, then yes, there is a strong possibility I will live to see another day."

"That's it, then!" Ordell said happily. "I'll talk to Winifred and have her defend you. She can have the charges dropped and show how I'm in good health. There's no crime now that I'm back in contact with her."

"I appreciate your enthusiasm, but Winifred will not agree to that."

"Why not?"

"She absolutely despises me," Octavio said. "I think the only reason she followed me to Blackwick was to keep an eye on me. The only reason she didn't turn me in to the revolution was because she didn't want to get involved with them again."

"What if I talk to her? She sees me as her son too. Maybe if I explain how you took me with good intentions, she'll come around and help us."

"I'm sorry, Ordell, but I just don't see that happening. Once you betray Winifred, the ties are severed completely. She's not one to believe in second chances."

Ordell had a hard time believing that. He knew Winifred was a bit rougher than other people he'd come across, but she wasn't an unreasonable lady. Not only that, but she had shown she liked Ordell, so maybe if she wouldn't do this for Octavio, she'd do it for him.

"When I get out of here, I'll talk to her," Ordell said.

"You're wasting your breath on this, but if you want to try, then I guess there isn't any harm in that. I wish you the best of luck trying to get through to her, though."

"I promise that I'll get you out of here, Father. You can even come to Linnesse with us."

"Don't make promises you can't keep, Ordell."

"I don't," he said. "I *will* get you out of here, no matter how the conversation with Winifred goes."

When Octavio didn't respond, Ordell moved away from the wall and toward the bed. Moments later the footsteps were back, followed by the large man.

He pulled brass keys out of his trouser pockets and opened Ordell's cell. "Our leader wishes to speak to you."

CHAPTER 21

ORDELL WAS taken to a large office, and the man forced him down in one of the brown leather chairs and then left him alone in the room.

The first thing Ordell noticed about the room was how brassy it looked. Various gears hung from the ceiling as some sort of decorative piece. The rich dark brown wood reflected the deep yellow in the walls, and there was a glass bulb that created a halo on the floor. There were cabinets filled with gears and tools. A lot were ones Ordell recognized, but there were others he'd never seen before. In front of him was a wooden desk that matched the color of the floors, and one of those rolling stools Octavio had in his shop was behind the desk. There were various blueprints that decorated the walls, and some were rolled up and off in the corner of the room.

Ordell noticed a delicate brass butterfly on the desk. There was a small button on its back, and Ordell leaned forward and pressed it.

The butterfly flew up a few feet and then fluttered down onto the hardwood floor. It fluttered its wings again and flew back up, this time landing on one of the filing cabinets. Ordell smiled as he watched the butterfly flutter across the room, landing in various places. Then it stopped.

A petite lady with short frizzy hair came into the room. She picked up the butterfly and walked over to the desk, placed the butterfly back in its proper spot, then sat down on the stool.

"Where are my friends?" Ordell asked. "We're not spies, I swear."

"My name is Beverly Rosales, leader of the revolution," she said. "You and your friends came into our base without a proper invitation, and now you demand things of me without even properly introducing yourself." She scoffed. "You look like you come from an aristocratic family, but you have the manners of a barbarian."

"It's even more ill-mannered to throw your guests in a cell without letting them explain themselves properly. This isn't the proper way to treat houseguests."

"If you had spoken to the previous leader with that tone, you would have had your tongue cut out. You're lucky that I'm far kinder than my mother."

"Where are my friends?" Ordell asked again.

"I've heard a lot about you," she said instead. "The rugged one with the dark hair wouldn't stop talking about you, in fact. I eventually had to gag him." Ordell glared at that but said nothing, so she continued. "The older man said that you were trying to get to Linnesse. Those fake passes you got from whatever Black Market will not work, I'll have you know. They're faulty, and whatever price you paid for them was a waste of your money."

"Why are we even captured?" Ordell asked. "Winifred, Mildred, and Buford have helped the revolution in the past."

"Perhaps back when my mother was still the leader, but I have my own rules," she said. "I will not just let anyone walk freely here, especially with how many *rats* have been in the revolution in the past. As far as I know, they are just spies."

"We just want to get to Linnesse. That's all."

"And why would you want to go there?"

He sighed. "I'm an automaton. Elias—the dark-haired man—is one too. We want to live there so we can have some semblance of freedom and safety."

She cocked her head to the side. "All the automatons I have come across have a minimal vocabulary. They can't think for themselves without their masters' orders."

"They're developing their own sentience," Ordell said. "I've witnessed it myself. When we reached Linnesse, we planned to help the revolution in setting the automatons free."

Beverly folded her hands and rested her chin on them. "Yes, that's something I've noticed as well. We've been fighting the Saunders family over the rights of the automatons but have failed to make any progress. By law the Saunders family has the rights over the pleasure slaves, unless there's enough damning evidence suggesting that the automatons do, in fact, have the capability to form their own sentience. If we can prove that these are conscious beings and not just another piece of equipment, then we might have a fighting chance."

"Ratliff was supposed to free them," Ordell said bitterly. "He backed out at the last minute, even after I told them my findings."

"Ratliff Saunders has been a problem for us for quite some time now," Beverly said. "When we found out he was adopted, we thought we could find a loophole in the inheritance after his stepfather died, but everything checks out. That and his popularity with curing the plague a second time has made him nearly unstoppable."

That meant they didn't know everything about Octavio, then. Ordell thought to tell Beverly, but Octavio had changed his name for a reason. "But we have some proof that the automatons are sentient. They're at least sentient enough to try to call out for help, shouldn't that count for something?"

She shook her head. "The automatons are almost as uncooperative as Ratliff. We've reached out to the ones we've rescued, but they fall into a deep depression without their masters."

"They're stuck," Ordell said. "Elias was the same way before Winifred reprogrammed him."

"Speaking of Winifred," Beverly said. "I'm glad to see that you are back with her. My mother spoke of how devastating it was when Octavio stole you."

"And speaking of Octavio, I would like to have him released," Ordell said. "Please."

"I can't do that."

"But I'm here! I'm unharmed and still have Winifred's design intact. I may have a few… cosmetic changes done to me, but that isn't important."

"I can't do anything unless Winifred drops the charges," Beverly said. "Rules are rules. You will have to take this up with her."

"But I'm perfectly fine! Octavio's done a great job raising me."

"From what I've heard, he sold you to be a pleasure slave." She leaned forward. "Do you have any idea how huge of an offense that is to the revolution and everything we stand for? That alone is worth his imprisonment."

"But that doesn't mean you have to kill him," Ordell said. "I understand what he did was wrong, but couldn't you at least listen to his side of things? If we executed every person for making a stupid decision, then the world will be empty."

"The execution stands unless Winifred chooses to drop the charges. If she drops them, then Octavio will be a free man. If not, then his death will be on her, not me."

Ordell wasn't happy with the situation, but he nodded anyway. Maybe he could convince Winifred to spare Octavio's life. Surely she wouldn't be so unreasonable as to think killing a man over doing a bad deed with good intentions was acceptable. Besides, before this mess had happened, they were friends.

"You must understand," Beverly said, "we apply these rules to everyone. If we start to make exceptions, then our entire system will crumble. I know you care for Octavio and I truly wish I could help, but I can't."

"Could you at least extend the execution date?" Ordell asked. "Even if it's just for a few more days."

She sighed. "I can see what I can do, but I don't guarantee anything." Beverly then added, "Don't get your hopes up on him being released. From what I gathered, Winifred is a very stubborn woman."

"Sometimes a bit too stubborn," Ordell muttered under his breath.

"I will try to get his execution date postponed, but that's the best I will be able to do."

"I understand," he said.

Truth was he didn't understand, though. She was the leader, so shouldn't she be the one who made the rules? Still, Beverly was set on having Winifred be the one to drop the charges.

"As I'm sure you're well aware, we take pride in our cause," Beverly said. "For me the revolution is to make the future now. We want to create a subrace of automatons who are indestructible. We can have them for wars and fighting crimes. Our plan is to create sentient automatons like you and your friend."

Ordell didn't like the idea of turning the automatons into war machines. It sounded as bad as having them be pleasure slaves. "Shouldn't they choose their own lives?"

"Of course," she said. "But I'm sure there will be many who agree this is the right path for them. However, we will not force an automaton to go into a career they do not wish to be in. We value their freedom and want them to know they are on the same level as us humans."

He still felt uncertain about Beverly's plans. It sounded fine to have them choose it, but what if they were secretly programmed to be killing machines? Creating sentient automatons wasn't something any engineer could do; it took precise work and someone who had empathy and compassion for automatons.

"Unfortunately there isn't much we can do without blueprints," Beverly said. "We need the blueprints Winifred used for you, Ordell."

"Have you asked Winifred?"

"She won't cooperate with us. We have tried to find these blueprints but only found the one for your friend. Do you know where she put *your* blueprints, Ordell?"

He shook his head. "I doubt she has them on her, though."

"We searched her entire house when she got to Goldcrest. If the blueprints are not there, then she has them in Goldcrest somewhere." Beverly sighed. "Winifred has known we've been searching for her blueprints for a while now. I highly doubt she would leave them behind while traveling."

"I'm sorry, but I haven't seen them."

It made sense Winifred took them with her if the revolution had been after them for so long. Ordell didn't know where she could have put them if they weren't on her person, though. She wouldn't be foolish enough to leave them with Ratliff—or at least he hoped not. Perhaps she gave them to someone she trusted, but Ordell drew a blank on who that could be.

"By the look on your face, I can tell you don't know where they are," Beverly said. "However, I want you to find their whereabouts and tell me. My people will retrieve them and you and your friends will be free to leave."

"Wait," Ordell said. "We can't leave unless you have the blueprints?"

"That is correct."

Well, that wasn't fair!

When Ordell didn't say anything, she said, "You may go. You can explore the tunnels, but you are not allowed to leave."

He reluctantly got up from his chair. He didn't know what the revolution planned to do if they didn't get the blueprints, but they couldn't keep them here forever… right?

ORDELL MADE his way around the tunnels and finally found the bedroom the revolution had placed Elias in. Ordell gave a soft knock on the doorframe and Elias turned around.

He expected a simple greeting or even a small kiss. What Ordell didn't expect, though, was to get tackled to the ground and suffocated in kisses.

"I was so worried about you," Elias said between kisses. "Did they hurt you?"

"Only person hurting me is you," Ordell said with a laugh. "You're too heavy!"

Elias rolled off him and then helped Ordell up. "Sorry, I just missed you."

He brushed off his duster and then kissed Elias's cheek. "I missed you too."

"What did the leader talk about with you? Did she interrogate you about the blueprints too?"

"Yeah, she said we can't leave until we hand them over. I didn't know I was so popular."

"Maybe we should work together to try to figure out where the blueprints are. We can tell Ms. Rosales where they are and maybe we can convince her to give us our passes to Linnesse back."

"I doubt Winifred will tell us where they are," Ordell said. "She doesn't seem like she plans to give them up that easily."

"She doesn't need to be involved in this." Elias shrugged. "We could figure out where they are without her knowledge. If she doesn't have them on her, then she won't know they're missing, right?"

"You want to steal the blueprints? We can't just take them, Elias. They belong to Winifred, and it's her work."

"The only reason she doesn't want to hand them over is because of her own ego. I know her, Ordell. She wants to hand them over but can't, because of her own pride."

Ordell still wasn't sure of this plan. This was Winifred's work, and if she didn't want to hand them over, then they should respect that, right? Even if Elias was right, wouldn't it be better to try to convince Winifred to hand them over herself rather than go behind her back like this? Besides, them stealing the blueprints would be just like how Octavio stole Ordell. Even if their intentions were good, it'd break Winifred's trust.

"We'll be doing the right thing," Elias said, grabbing Ordell's shoulders. "Trust me. We need to do what's best for the group."

"How's this different than what Octavio did?" Ordell asked quietly. "Even if we're doing this out of the goodness of our hearts, it's still wrong to go behind her back like this."

"She, Millie, and Buford will rot here before she puts her pride aside," Elias said. "It isn't fair to Millie and Buford for them to have to spend the rest of their lives here. It's not like we're giving the blueprints to Ratliff. This is the revolution. They fight for the same cause as Winnie."

Ordell sighed. "You're right. This isn't fair to Buford and Mildred. We do need to think about how it affects them too."

"Right," Elias said with a small smile. "I promise you that this will work out in the end."

"All right, let me talk to her. Maybe she'll slip on where the blueprints are."

Elias kissed him. "I'll be right here with you."

Ordell still wasn't sure if he was on board with this idea. He knew Elias was right; they needed to do what was best for Buford and Mildred too. He still remembered when he'd spoken to Buford on the back porch and how happy the man was when he spoke of Mildred. How excited he was about starting his life with her after having his advances rejected for so many years.

He had a bad feeling speaking with Beverly again would result in nothing. She was adamant about getting her hands on those blueprints. He could try to talk Winifred into giving up the location of the blueprints, but Beverly was right; Winifred wasn't the most cooperative person. If Ordell were honest, Winifred's stubbornness made Elias's look tame. Ordell could argue with her until his face was blue, but she was not going to budge once her mind was made up. That much he knew for certain.

It seemed Elias's plan to get the blueprints behind her back was the best option. She wouldn't know they were gone if she didn't have them on her, and if she did find out, then they would have to deal with the fallout when it came.

Still, when it came down to it, Ordell just wasn't sure if he could go through with betraying Winifred like that. He wanted the automatons to be sentient and free like he and Elias were, but could he really turn his back on Winifred?

Wouldn't that be exactly what Octavio had done those many years ago?

CHAPTER 22

ORDELL SAT in front of the fireplace, thinking about how to approach Winifred with such loaded questions. Should he be blunt about it? His biggest priority was getting Octavio out of there, as well as the rest of the crew. Perhaps he should take the gentler approach—wean her into the conversation about Octavio and the blueprints.

His stomach turned at the thought of her reaction toward either one of those topics. He just needed to get the topics out there and hope for the best.

Winifred came in and sat down in the chair next to Ordell. "I swear those revolutionists are more demanding than door-to-door salesmen! I hope they didn't give you too much trouble."

"They asked me about the blueprints."

"Do not let them bully you, Ordell," she said. "They can't force us to do anything."

"But they won't let us leave unless we comply."

"We'll figure something out. Sooner or later they're going to have to give up on the idea that I'll hand them over willingly."

Ordell squeezed the chair's armrests. "So if it isn't any trouble, why do you not want to hand them over? Aren't they fighting for the same cause you are?"

Winifred sighed and leaned back in the chair. "I'm just tired of it all, Ordell. I'm tired of them chasing me. I'm tired of them demanding things of me. We may fight for the same cause, but I can't trust them. I'll never trust them."

"Is that why you left?" Ordell asked. "Because you can't trust them?"

"Only a small part of it," Winifred said. "The largest reason I left is because I regretted joining them."

"Why?"

"When I was there, I was just a marionette on a string, Ordell. I had no freedom. My projects were no longer my own." She lowered her gaze. "They weren't supposed to know about you. I wanted you to be a secret, but they found out anyway. They talked about how they wanted to make all these changes to you, and it became apparent that they didn't understand my motivations for creating you."

"What were your motivations? The plague?"

"Partly. Another was that I wanted a son. He didn't need to be a war machine like they wanted him to be. He just needed to be like every other human who'd blend in. I wanted you to develop your own personality through only a small bit of programming and mostly you taking in the surroundings around you."

"I take it that they aren't too impressed with how I turned out, then," Ordell said with a small chuckle. "I can barely throw a punch, let alone be a great war machine."

"Being there with the revolution drained out my passion and creativity. I didn't feel like myself when I was with them. It got so bad that once I left the revolution, I quit being an inventor and engineer. Elias was almost not created, but Millie demanded that I finish him or I'd regret not doing so." She flashed a small smile. "She was right. I would have regretted it. Elias is one of the best things that has happened to me since you were taken. I may be hard on him, but that's only because I love him and want to see him succeed."

"I think Elias needs to know that you care about him. At least tell him once in a while."

"I know," she said with a sigh. "I've never been the most nurturing parent out there. Our relationship has always been tough love."

"He'd greatly appreciate it if you let him know that you love him and are proud of how far he's come."

"You're right. I need to let him know." She remained silent for a few moments and then said, "Ordell, there's something I need to show you. You must promise not to breathe a word of this to anyone."

Ordell sat up straighter in his chair. "I won't, I promise. You know you can trust me, Winifred."

She touched the locket around her neck and unhooked the clasps. "I want to show you this." It was a large brass circular locket. Embossed flowers decorated the edge, and there was a large green jewel in the center.

"It's beautiful," Ordell said with a smile. "I like it."

"There's more to this locket," she said, looking over her shoulder. "Did I shut the door?"

Ordell looked over his shoulder too. "Yes, it's shut."

She took a deep breath and opened the locket. In there was a picture of her on one side and a blue backing on the other side.

"I like that picture of you."

Winifred waved the compliment off. "Forget about the picture, boy. I want you to focus on the round blue celluloid on the other side. What do you see?"

Ordell shrugged. "A blue backing."

She pushed the green jewel and the blue backing slid out. She then handed the blue celluloid to Ordell. "Now what do you see?"

He squinted at it. "There are a bunch of tiny holes in it. I can hardly see them, though."

"That's the point. You're not supposed to see the holes when it's inside the locket. I created both the celluloid and the locket, making sure it looked just like a normal locket when I wore it. I carry that unflattering picture on the other side to further conceal the true reason for this locket."

"What's the reason for the locket, then?" Ordell asked.

Winifred held out her hand, and he placed the round blue celluloid in the palm of her hand. "Bring that lamp on the end table over here."

Ordell grabbed the lamp from the table and placed it on the end table between him and Winifred. Winifred took another deep breath and looked hesitant.

"I won't tell anyone," Ordell said. "I promise."

She placed the celluloid in front of the lamp. "Look over at that wall."

Ordell turned to look and his mouth gaped open. "Wow."

There on the wall were blueprints with the name "Project Ordell" on the top. Ordell had never seen blueprints as detailed as these ones. And it was all drilled into that piece of celluloid... with Winifred the whole time.

"But what about the blueprints back at your house?" Ordell asked. "The ones you showed me there look different than the ones here."

"The blueprints there are a decoy," Winifred said. "I needed to make sure that no one could get ahold of the real ones, so I created those blueprints as a way to confuse anyone who may try to ransack my home. If they were to follow those prints, though, they would only end up with a faulty invention."

"Has anyone ever tried to break into your house?"

"Many times," she said with a chuckle. "No one could even find the fake blueprints, so I might be a little more overprotective than I thought.

I really thought someone would find the safe by now." She placed the blueprint back inside her locket. "I was a little worried when I showed you them that you would notice they were fake." She clasped the locket back around her neck and hid it back under her dress. "The fact that you didn't pleases me."

Although Ordell didn't like being deceived, he understood why Winifred didn't trust him at first. She must have kept those blueprints to herself until now. The fact she had even shown them to Ordell meant a lot to him.

"Thank you for trusting me," Ordell said. "Your secret is safe with me."

"I know it is." She smiled at him. "I didn't create you to be a liar."

"Winifred." He cleared his throat. "There's something else I need to speak with you about. Something very important to me."

"Go on, child."

"It's about Octavio. I know you two had a falling-out, but he needs your help."

"He doesn't deserve my help." Her lips formed a tight line. "He means nothing to me now."

"I know what he did is wrong, but he meant no harm," Ordell said. "He wanted to re-create his nephew, and he thought you abandoned the project. He wanted what you wanted—to give me a normal life. His nephew's name was Abraham; he was Ratliff's best friend and close to Octavio. He admits that it was foolish of him to take me away from you and to sell me off to Ratliff."

"I can't forgive him," she said. "And you shouldn't either. What he did to you is inexcusable. You forgive too easily, Ordell."

"He's still my father," Ordell said. "He raised me well and gave me the life of a normal human. So normal, in fact, that everyone in Blackwick assumed I was human."

"Of course they did!" Winifred scoffed. "The only automatons that came close to being human are those pleasure slaves. They thought you were human because they didn't know any better."

"I'm sorry he took me away from you, but he will always be my father. What he did was idiotic, but he shouldn't be executed for idiocy." When Winifred remained silent, Ordell added, "Do you really want to contribute to his death? He was once your friend, and he still values that friendship. If he didn't he would have torn all your hard work out of me.

But he didn't. He kept me intact and brought me to life when I had been forgotten."

A tear rolled down her cheek. "I didn't forget about you, Ordell. I would have come back to finish you."

"And he made certain I wouldn't be forgotten about. You both have the same goal for me, just different motivations behind that goal."

"I can't forgive him, Ordell."

"I'm not asking you to," he said. "All I'm asking is that you spare his life. Let him see another day."

"I can't."

"Then his blood will be on your hands," Ordell said coldly. He got up from the chair, and before walking out of the room, he said, "Don't say I didn't try."

ORDELL RESTED back on the bed, and Elias sat down next to him. "Are you bored too?"

He nodded. "We better not stay here forever. I'm beginning to miss the sun."

It wasn't like this was a terrible place; it was nicely decorated and, despite the lack of a window, had a cozy feel to it. The same hardwood floors in Beverly's office were used throughout the entire building, but unlike the office, most of the building's walls were covered in decorative wallpaper. The tunnels made use of electric lamps rather than gas ones, which Ordell enjoyed. Elias, on the other hand, claimed they should have been more creative with their light source.

The room Elias and Ordell were currently in was nicely decorated too. There were pictures on the walls and a small writing desk across from the bed.

Ordell sighed. "Why can't they just go off your blueprints? Aren't you an improvement over my design?"

"I'm more of an add-on," Elias said with a small shrug. "They can't use my design unless they have your design too."

"Could you imagine them creating a subrace of automatons like us?" Ordell asked. "We'd be like the humans and could do so much to help. The possibilities are endless."

"Tell Winnie that," Elias said. "I bet she doesn't even have the blueprints on her. I'm starting to believe she destroyed them."

Ordell shook his head. "No, she has them. I saw them a few hours ago."

Elias's eyes widened. "You know where the blueprints are?" When Ordell nodded, Elias wrapped him up in his arms and swung Ordell around. "We'll finally be out of this damn tunnel! We have to take the blueprints to the leader immediately."

"I doubt Winifred will give up the blueprints," Ordell said when Elias stopped swinging him around. "She's very protective of them."

"We'll just grab them when she's asleep," Elias said. "Once she sees the good the revolution does with her design, she'll be glad we took them from her."

He shook his head. "We can't. I'm sorry, but this is her choice. I'm not taking that away from her."

"If we wait around for her, we're going to stay in this place forever, Ordell," Elias said. "We need to do what's best for the crew."

Ordell shook his head. "No, this is her choice. I'm not going to share where the blueprints are, and I'm not going to steal them and hand them over to the revolution."

Elias sighed. "Fine, I'll support you no matter what. I still think Winnie's being unreasonable. Hopefully she comes to her senses."

"I hope so too." Ordell then hugged and kissed him. "Thank you for supporting me." When he pulled away, a ring fell out of Elias's vest. "What's that?"

Elias's face turned red, and he rubbed the back of his neck. "You weren't supposed to see that yet."

Ordell picked up the ring. "An engagement ring?" He could barely get the words out, and his fingers wouldn't stop shaking.

"I... um... I got it back in Goldcrest," Elias stammered out. "I thought that once we got to Linnesse, we could, you know... start our new life... together...."

Ordell gazed at the ring, his mouth still gaping open. "You... you are...."

"Ordell Rutledge," Elias said, clearing his throat, "will you marry me?"

He nodded, still letting those words sink in. He nodded again.

"I hope that's a happy yes," Elias said with a tight chuckle. "You're looking at me like I'm some ghost."

"Yes!" Ordell wrapped his arms around Elias and buried his face in his neck. "Yes, I'll marry you!" Then the tears fell.

Elias stroked Ordell's hair and then let out another soft laugh. "I apologize for making you cry."

"You didn't make me cry," Ordell said, laughing and wiping away tears. "My eyes are just watery."

"I apologize for making your eyes water." Elias gave a small grin. "Better?"

Ordell nodded, still laughing. "You're going to be a nightmare."

"And you're going to be spoiled and pampered." Elias took the ring out of Ordell's hand and placed it on his finger. Elias brought Ordell's hand up and kissed the ring. "I love you."

"I love you too, Elias Griffith. Forever."

Ordell looked at the ring again and tried to comprehend the sequence of events that had led up to this. He still didn't understand how he'd managed to find someone like Elias, but was relieved Elias was there by his side. Ordell knew without Elias he wouldn't even be this close to Linnesse. Now they were going to live there and start their new life together. He didn't know what the future would bring, but as long as Elias was there, Ordell was up for the twists and turns it was bound to have.

"We will still have our struggles up ahead," Elias said, planting a soft kiss on Ordell's lips. "But at least we'll be together."

Ordell kissed him back. "And I wouldn't have it any other way."

CHAPTER 23

ORDELL SPENT most of the morning in the lounge room, reading in front of the small fireplace. Many of the books were on different types of automatons and techniques, which made Ordell more excited about going to Linnesse. Even if he never got to step foot into a workshop again, at least he could see the inventions on paper come to life in Linnesse.

There was also a book on airships Ordell read, sometimes looking over his shoulder and making sure Elias wasn't around to see him so engrossed in the book. The design the revolution had for their airship looked plausible.

Unlike the ridiculous design he had witnessed at the exhibit, this one was crafted from what appeared to be a lightweight metal, with heated balloons much larger than those of the other airship. Balloons that might actually be able to support the weight of a ship and its crew while soaring through the skies.

In fact, Ordell could easily see airships come to life in the next few years if the revolution kept working on perfecting this design. If that did happen, he'd have no choice but to take Elias on one… and then apologize profusely for laughing at the idea of airships, of course.

One of the most interesting books Ordell found, though, was on creating a whole new species based on automatons. There wouldn't just be humanoid automatons like Elias and Ordell, but other animals too. Birds, dogs, cats, even horses. They were still just ideas and concepts, but the book made Ordell excited for the future. If Winifred could make both him and Elias, he could just imagine what she could do if she got her hands on this book.

Ordell sat that particular book aside to give to her in hopes of sparking her interest to become an inventor and engineer again. Maybe once they got to Linnesse she'd realize they needed her and her skills. Then maybe she'd start designing these fantastic animals and create a whole new species.

"I see you've found quite a few books," a familiar voice said.

Ordell turned around, wide-eyed. "Father!" He jumped up from the chair and wrapped his arms around Octavio. "I never thought I'd see you again!" He'd wanted to visit Octavio when he was still locked up, but no one was allowed down in the cells unless they were a guard or prisoner. "Why did they release you? Did Ms. Rosales have a change of heart?"

Octavio pulled away and ruffled Ordell's hair. "I was told that Winifred dropped all charges. Came as a shock to me, but perhaps Winifred isn't as unreasonable as I set her out to be."

"I told you that she'd be willing to do it," Ordell said with a smile. Although relieved, he was surprised she had a change of heart. "Are you going to come to Linnesse with us?"

Octavio shook his head. "No, I have no interest in going there. I plan to go back to my simple life as a shop owner. Might use the little money I saved and move here to Goldcrest to get a stronger business. I should be able to sell the shop back in Blackwick for enough money to get a quaint building here. It'll be much smaller than the one in Blackwick, but I can always work my way up."

Ordell nodded and then hugged Octavio again. "I missed you."

"I missed you too, Ordell. When you get to Linnesse, promise me that you'll be happy there."

"Of course." Not only would he be in a place where he could finally be himself, but his friends would be there too. He'd be with Elias and…. "Father," Ordell said, then lifted his left hand, showing the engagement ring. "He proposed."

"He better treat you right," Octavio said in a gruff voice. "If you ever need to leave Linnesse for any reason, you always have a home with me."

Ordell smiled. He and Octavio spent the next two hours talking and catching up. Ordell told him all about his adventure and how he had dismantled a giant kraken. Octavio laughed at the part where Elias tried to kill it with an ax. Ordell then spoke about the book he'd found about the different creatures the revolution wanted to create and how it would be interesting to make an automaton that acted like a real kraken instead of just some form of border control.

AFTER HE finished talking to Octavio, Ordell wandered around the tunnels until he found Winifred. She was sitting in her room, playing with her locket.

"Thank you for dropping the charges," Ordell said, entering the room. "It means a lot to me."

She continued to play with her locket. "Why didn't you tell them?"

Ordell blinked. "Excuse me?"

"The blueprints," she said. "I showed you where they are and how to access them. Why didn't you tell them about this? There wouldn't be much I could do to stop them."

"They're your work," he said. "I'm not going to steal them from you. You trusted me enough to show the blueprints to me, and I'm not going to taint them just because it's the easy way out."

"It'd be better for the others if I gave in," Winifred said. "We'd be free to walk away."

"This is your choice." Ordell grabbed her shoulder and squeezed it. "I'm not going to tell you what you should and shouldn't do. Honestly I don't know myself. All I know is that you must have a good reason for choosing not to hand them over."

"I don't trust them," Winifred said. "I can't risk them tainting my work for their own selfish needs. The only person I trust with these blueprints is me. The fact that they rummaged through my house uninvited and took Elias's blueprint add-on tells me that they do not deserve to have Project Ordell."

"I'll support you no matter what decision you come to." He smiled. "I will talk to Ms. Rosales again and see what I can do to convince her to let us go, because they *don't* deserve these blueprints. They disrespected you and your wishes, which makes me feel that they will do the same with the automatons."

"Good luck. She's about as stubborn as I am. I don't see her swaying her decision any time soon."

Ordell gave her shoulder another squeeze and left. He walked through the tunnels until he made it to Beverly's office. He knew there was a slim chance of her changing her mind, but Ordell wasn't going to take the easy way out. No, if Beverly wanted those blueprints, she would have to do so on Winifred's terms.

He entered the office and sat down in the leather chair. Beverly glared at him. "It's impolite not to knock."

Ordell leaned forward and knocked on the desk. "I need to speak with you."

She sighed. "This better involve the blueprints."

"It does."

A smile grew across her face. "All right, then, you may speak."

"You're not getting the blueprints," Ordell said. "If Winifred doesn't want to give them up, then you should respect her decision."

Beverly narrowed her eyes. "We need them. If we don't have them, how can we give automatons their freedom?"

"There's more than one path to reach the same place. If you release us and allow us to live in Linnesse, I will be more than happy to help out in any way that I can. I worked in my father's shop all my life and could be invaluable for the revolution."

"You think highly of yourself," she scoffed.

"I'm not going to minimize my skills just to look modest," Ordell said. "I'm proud of my experience, and if I can help the revolution, then I will."

"You will be quite helpful for the revolution," Beverly said, "but we need those blueprints. If you can't provide them, then you'll remain here until you can."

Ordell rose from the chair. "Then we'll be here for quite some time."

DAYS WENT by and Beverly did not budge on her decision. Ordell read through the books and studied the blueprints on the walls. If he was going to help the revolution, he needed to be as educated as he could on creating automatons.

Whenever Ordell got a crick in his neck from reading in an upright position too long, Elias would give him a neck rub. Ordell often repaid that generosity in their bedroom, although that was a treat for Ordell too.

Ordell rested on Elias's bare chest and listened to Elias's breathing. It was amazing how human Winifred had made both him and Elias. It was something Ordell had never thought much about when he worked at his father's shop, but now that he had seen the blueprints, he couldn't help but be in awe of the detail and effort Winifred put into him.

Of course he had to thank Octavio for giving him the... other human aspects too. It made his time with Elias far more pleasurable.

"Once we get married," Elias said, "will we just be making love most of the time?"

Ordell grinned. "I have no qualms about that."

"Of course you wouldn't," Elias said with a chuckle. "If I let you have your way, we'd never get out of this bed."

Ordell laughed too. "You want the same thing. You're just too stubborn to admit it."

Elias kissed the top of Ordell's head. "You're right."

"That isn't anything new."

"Cheeky brat." Elias tickled Ordell's ear, making him squirm against Elias's touch. "I love you."

"I love you too," he managed to get out between the giggles.

"I can't wait until we get to Linnesse," Elias said, his voice vibrating against Ordell's ear. "We'll have the biggest house there."

"I'm fine with just a small house too," Ordell said. "It'll give us an excuse to touch each other if the house is cramped."

"No, I've already decided that I'm going to give you the best of everything. You will be so spoiled that you will make a prince envious."

"I already make others envious because I have you." Ordell looked up at him and smiled. "Everything else is just pouring salt into the wound."

"I think it's the other way around. They're jealous that someone like me could manage to be with someone as incredible as you are."

Ordell grabbed Elias's hand and kissed his fingers. "Well, they will have to get over it because I'm not letting you go."

BUFORD AND Mildred finally had their wedding. It was a small ceremony there in the tunnels, but even those who were part of the revolution joined, and Beverly gave her blessing. Ordell hinted that a great wedding present would be to let them go, but that didn't sway her. It was worth a shot, though.

Despite the wedding being spur-of-the-moment, Buford and Mildred looked so happy. One of the ladies was kind enough to lend Mildred her white ball gown. Mildred decorated it with crystals that sparkled against globes on the gas lamps. Her hair was done up with the same crystals, and Buford wore a nice suit one of the men had lent out. One of the cooks created a wedding cake from three small handmade cakes stacked on top of one another. It wasn't the fanciest cake, but it was a delicious chocolate cake with white frosting—or so Elias said. With the way he licked the plate clean, Ordell had no reason to doubt that statement.

Beautiful accordion music played as Buford and Mildred danced. Ordell watched as others danced, and Elias sat down in the chair next to him.

"We can dance too if you'd like," Elias said.

"The music's too lively for me to dance to," Ordell said. "I think I'll sit this one out."

"I'm surprised they didn't get married in Linnesse," Elias said. "I thought they'd at least wait and have a grand wedding."

"If we get to Linnesse," Ordell grumbled. "With how long Buford waited to be with Mildred, I'm surprised they didn't get married the same day he proposed."

"True," Elias said with a chuckle. "I don't think I've ever seen his eyes sparkle this much. Millie looks stunning in that ball gown."

Ordell examined the room and saw that Winifred and Octavio were on speaking terms. Maybe there was a chance they could rekindle their friendship again. There might be a chance Octavio could never get Winifred's trust, but Ordell hoped they could at least be on friendly terms eventually.

"Hey," Elias said, "we could get married here too."

Ordell shook his head. "No, I want to get married in Linnesse, where it'll be official. Besides, I don't want to take away any part of Buford and Mildred's moment."

"I don't mean right now," Elias said with a chuckle. "Maybe in a few weeks or so. We don't know if the revolution will release us, and I want to marry you as soon as possible."

"We'll be released eventually," Ordell said.

They had to be.

AFTER THE wedding Mildred came and sat down in the chair Elias was previously in.

"Shouldn't you be with your husband on a honeymoon?" Ordell asked with a chuckle.

"He's going to surprise me with our honeymoon and told me to give him a few hours," Mildred said. "I don't know if I should be excited or worried about what he comes up with."

"Knowing Buford, it will be amazing," Ordell said with a smile. "Congratulations. You both look stunning."

"Thank you, my boy," she said with a chuckle. "I think this dress was meant for a young woman, but I pulled it off well, if I do say so myself. We were going to wait until we reached Linnesse, but with how things were going, we decided to do it now. Might as well when there's a chance of not getting out of these blasted tunnels."

"We will," Ordell promised. "Winifred will think of something. I know it."

"I wish she'd just give over those blueprints. She's one of my dearest friends, but there are times I want to throttle her! Ever since we were children, she's had that stubborn streak."

Ordell laughed. "I suppose old habits die hard."

"I have her to thank for introducing me to Buford, though. My parents never approved of my friendship with Winifred, and when they saw Buford, they were livid. They told me that I must marry a man in the military. They even had a matchmaker try to set me up with a general, and we almost wedded, but he found another woman. When my parents died, my brother took over the estate, and I was free to join the revolution. Back then it wasn't as big a taboo as it is now. It was seen as a bold decision for a lady to do so, something she would grow out of once she married." Mildred smiled. "I guess it's something I never grew out of."

"I'm glad you didn't," Ordell said. "I can't imagine what this adventure would be like without you here."

"A lot less exciting, I can tell you that. Besides, someone needs to keep an eye on Buford."

If it weren't for Mildred, they wouldn't have even gotten the passes to Linnesse in the first place. It was unfortunate they were taken away, but that was no fault of Mildred's.

A man came into the room and walked toward Ordell and Mildred. "I'm here to grant your release."

CHAPTER 24

ORDELL FOLLOWED Beverly to the secret pier, where there was a large steamboat. She handed all five of them passes and smiled.

"These are legitimate passes to Linnesse. I deem you citizens there, and you should not run into any problems. This steamboat will take you straight to Linnesse, driven by a captain whom I trust with my life." She shook Ordell's hand. "It was a pleasure to meet you, Ordell. I wish you the best on your journey."

When she walked away, Ordell pulled Winifred to the side and asked, "Why the change of heart?"

"I didn't have a change of heart," she said. "However, Beverly and I came up with a compromise that we both could agree on."

"Oh? And what is that?"

"You will be the one to lead how to create the automatons," she said. "I will teach you how to create them and will give you the blueprints for you to work off of. You will be in command of the design of the automatons."

Ordell furrowed his brows. "Why won't you be in command?"

"There's not much time left in my old bones, Ordell. I will be in command for now, and you will be my apprentice until I pass. I will teach you all I know, and we'll learn the new things together." She grabbed Ordell's shoulders. "With my help you'll thrive and bring the revolution what they desire and more. You're the only one I know who will create the automatons how they are meant to be created." Winifred then smiled. "You could have told the revolution where the blueprints were, and you didn't. That in itself tells me I'm making the right choice in teaching you."

"Wow," Ordell said quietly. "I don't know what to say."

The fact Winifred trusted him with the blueprints was a huge deal for him, but to actually teach Ordell how to create sentient automatons felt like a dream. Not only that, but he could learn to make all those animals too.

Ordell pulled a small leather-bound book out of his duster and handed it to Winifred. "These are concepts on animals the revolution wanted to create. I know that with your skills, we can make these come to life."

She looked through the book and smiled. "If I can make a human, then making a bird or a dog will be no struggle. We will start out with the smaller animals while working on the humans. This will help you practice different techniques and be able to branch out past what I've taught you."

Ordell loved that idea. He wanted to master creating automatons, and one of the first things he planned to do was learn how to fix himself and give other automatons that same set of skills so they could be immortal.

"How plausible would it be for me to learn how to fix myself if I find something broken?"

She shrugged. "We can work on you and see what we can figure out. Maybe have a backup system where if something truly damaging happens, it will kick in long enough for you to repair yourself. Since I know how to repair you, there isn't much risk in trial and error."

Ordell gulped. "I don't know if I like the sound of *that*."

She shrugged. "It's all part of being an engineer, Ordell. Don't worry, we'll figure something out."

AFTER TALKING with Winifred, Ordell stepped closer to Elias to tell him the good news while they were on the docks, waiting for the boat.

"I agree with her," Elias said with a smile. "You're the best option for this. I know you'll do an amazing job and will treat her work with respect. If anyone should take her place after she passes, it should be you."

"I want you to work alongside me," Ordell said. "Together we'll create a whole new species of automatons. We will help humans the right way and create automatons who know how to repair themselves so they will be immortal. This will help with keeping a controlled population of automatons who are already experienced in fields and will make the world a better place."

"I like that idea," Elias said with a smile. "I'd love to be able to repair myself if I needed to. It feels safer than relying on humans to fix me."

"Humans can still learn how to repair us. We'll need to be careful with how we teach them so they don't learn how they can break us, but teaching some to be able to repair and fix automatons will be essential in case the automaton cannot repair itself."

"Or we can just have other automatons do it," Elias said with a shrug. "We can never be too careful."

Ordell thought for a moment. "That's a good idea, actually. It might be better to have other automatons become doctors and repair automatons who are unable to fix themselves. Maybe we can set up an emergency button that will trigger when the automaton breaks down."

Elias chuckled. "Look at you. You're already coming up with these incredible ideas and we haven't even arrived in Linnesse yet! With Winnie's help you'll be unstoppable!"

"I hope so," Ordell said. "There's so much I want to learn, so much I want to create! I wish we could get started right now."

"Look at that boat," Buford said, coming up beside them. He then let out a whistle. "I haven't been on a steamboat since I was in my thirties."

"Does it fit your standards?" Ordell teased.

"More than enough, my boy. Once I get to Linnesse, I'll find the largest ship and turn it into a home for Millie and me. When we get tired of our location, we'll set forth on the open waters and find a new location to live in."

That actually didn't sound like a bad idea. Maybe Ordell could convince Elias to do something similar, but it might be a waste of an idea if Winifred didn't want to move around. He had to stay near the shop, after all.

"I heard about Winifred taking you under her wing and teaching you how to create sentient automatons," Buford said. "Congratulations, my boy. Winifred is nothing but thorough when it comes to teaching others. You may find yourself getting annoyed at times, but rest assured that, in the end, you will be thanking her for making you excel."

Mildred gave her suitcases to the man packing up the ship. "Shoot, I forgot my books. How can I travel to Linnesse without my reading material?"

"I can go back and get them for you," Ordell offered.

She smiled. "Oh, will you? Thank you so much, dear." She patted Ordell's cheek. "I'd go myself, but I'm so exhausted from the first trip."

Ordell chuckled. "You should be on your honeymoon. I'd be more than happy to get them."

"Make sure you get the book that's on the third bookshelf. It should be two rows down and have a red velvet cover."

Ordell made a mental note and made his way back to Mildred's. Her place wasn't too far from the pier, and he knew his friends wouldn't leave without him. Well, at least Elias wouldn't.

He opened the door and walked straight to the third bookshelf. There he found the book with the red velvet cover. However, when he went to pull it out of the shelf, someone hit him from behind.

ORDELL WOKE up to find himself in a strange room. He went to rub his eyes, only to find that his wrists were bound. He was on a large canopy bed, wearing only his ruffled button-down shirt. The room had a rich look to it, white paneled walls and a reddish brown dark-wood floor. A large oil painting of a landscape hung above the fireplace, and the chairs looked to be of velvet. In the corner of the room was a mahogany writing table with a walking cane propped next to it.

Ordell recognized the cane, and his stomach churned. He tugged frantically at the bindings, then tried to undo them with his teeth.

It was no use; the binds were too hard to get undone. The rope used was sturdy enough that Ordell couldn't break out, and the knot was done well enough that he couldn't untie it with his teeth. He tried to position his hands and use his fingers to untie the knot, but that didn't work either.

"Already trying to leave?" Ratliff came into the room and locked the door behind him. "Don't wear yourself out too much."

"Where are my clothes?" He knew he should ask about where he was, but he hated being so indecent!

"I'm not going to let anything come between us again, Abraham." Ratliff sat down on the bed next to Ordell and grabbed Ordell's chin. "I promise."

"I'm not Abraham," he said.

"You'll be whomever I want you to be!" Ratliff snapped. "I own you. Your name is Abraham now."

"I know you miss him," Ordell said, "but I can't replace him."

Ratliff's grip tightened to the point that Ordell's jaw went numb. "That's enough talk of that, Abraham. We need to work on your manners. You will receive the best teachers to show you how to act like a true gentleman. We will go to the best balls and the most exclusive parties. It will be how it was meant to be."

Ordell felt sorry for the man, but it was hard to sympathize when he was tied up and without any pants. He wasn't sure what to say to get through to Ratliff; the man was lost in his own delusion and truly thought that Ordell could be a suitable replacement.

"You know this isn't going to work," Ordell croaked out. "You know he isn't coming back, and you know that I can't take your mind away from him. You need to move on."

Ratliff let go of Ordell's chin and then slapped him hard across his face. "You do not tell me what to do, boy!"

"If you really think I can become Abraham," Ordell said, grimacing from the sting, "then you wouldn't have laid a hand on me. We both know you don't have it in you to hurt Abraham."

"Shut up!" He got on top of Ordell and pressed him down into the bed. "I don't want to hear another word out of that mouth of yours." Ratliff grabbed Ordell's chin again and then pressed their lips together.

The kisses were hard and fast. Ordell tried to fight the man off the best he could, but he couldn't do much with his hands bound. Ratliff moved his hand away from Ordell's chin and pinned him down to the bed. With his other hand, Ratliff grabbed a fistful of Ordell's hair and yanked his face closer.

Ordell got a hold on Ratliff's bottom lip with his teeth and bit down as hard as he could. When Ratliff jerked away, Ordell gasped out, "Get off of me!"

"I'll do whatever I want!" Ratliff spat out. He grabbed Ordell's thigh and pried his legs open. "If I want to take you, then I'll take you here and now!"

"But you won't be able to do this and call me 'Abraham' at the same time!" Ordell cried out, his words breathy.

Ratliff stared into him, and by the cold look in his eyes, Ordell was certain that Ratliff would go through with it. All Ordell could do was plead with his eyes for Ratliff not to take him. Then, out of some miracle, there was a change in Ratliff's eyes. That once cold look was now replaced with a confused expression.

He let go of Ordell, and for a moment, Ordell was sure that Ratliff had a change of heart. Instead, he walked toward the nightstand and opened the door, pulling out a small gun.

Ratliff walked out of the room, shutting the door behind him. Was he really going to shoot Ordell? Would he go after Elias?

Ordell struggled against the binds and worked them loose. He pulled himself off the bed and went through the dresser drawers for anything he could cover himself up with. Ratliff was bulkier and taller than Ordell, so the trousers he found were too big on him. The shirt, although elegant, was also too big on him and hung more like a tunic. Ordell grabbed the ropes of the binds and created a makeshift belt.

He walked over to the door and turned the handle, surprised to find that the door was not locked. Ordell crept out into the hallway and saw a glimmer of light coming from under the door next to the room he was held captive in.

Internally, he knew that he should just find the exit and make his way back to Elias and the others. However, a part of him felt the need to see where Ratliff went. Ordell knew his own curiosity could yet be his demise, but that didn't stop him from walking toward that door and slowly turning the handle.

He had to know.

Ratliff was sitting at a small table, his thumb lightly stroking the gun. Ordell swallowed hard and took another step forward. The man didn't even seem to notice that Ordell was only a few feet away. In fact, he didn't seem to notice anything. He just stared forward with a blank expression, his hand still on the gun.

"I thought this would be satisfying," Ratliff said with an awkward laugh. "The other pleasure slaves never worked for me. I always discarded them when I remained unsatisfied, always went back to Octavio, demanding something more. Then you came around. You're just like him. So headstrong and determined, yet foolish. You look exactly like him, talk like him, give me a hard time just like him. I should feel that satisfaction of finally having you." He looked up at Ordell. "Why don't I?"

Ordell sat down in the chair across from Ratliff, his eyes still locked on the gun.

"I don't understand," Ratliff continued. "How can I both love you and hate you?"

Ordell struggled to find his own voice; his throat clenched and he could only manage a whisper. "I'm not him."

"I'm never getting him back." There was no emotion in Ratliff's voice. "I'll never get him back."

"I'm sorry." Ordell didn't know what he was apologizing for, but it was the only thing that he could say. Ratliff then put the gun in Ordell's hands, which confused him even more. "I don't understand," he said finally.

"I want you to kill me." Ratliff cleared his throat and squared his shoulders. "I'd much rather you do it than myself."

"I can't shoot you," Ordell said, almost squeaking the words. "I don't even know how to use a gun!"

"I demand you shoot me!" Ratliff snapped. "I can't live without Abraham any longer! It's clear to me now that I will never replace him and that this void will remain inside me unless I die."

"I can't."

"I demand you do this, or so help me, I will kill you!" Ratliff snapped. "Now, do it!"

Ordell leaned back and placed the gun back on the table. "No."

"I order you to kill me, boy!"

Instead, he just grabbed Ratliff's hand. The hand was cold to the touch and although Ordell couldn't see it, he could feel Ratliff trembling. "No."

Ratliff squeezed his eyes shut and more tears fell. Then he cleared his throat. "You may leave."

"Excuse me?"

"Go and do what you want with your life," Ratliff said, still emotionless. "I will not be a bother any longer."

Hesitantly, Ordell released the man's shaky hand and rose from the chair. "Thank you."

Ratliff said nothing, only stared at the gun that rested in the center of the table. Ordell opened his mouth to say something, but no words could form. He took a step back, then turned toward the door.

"Close the door when you leave," Ratliff said, his eyes still cast down at the center of the table.

Ordell nodded and walked out, closing the door behind him. The moment the door latched shut, he heard a gunshot.

THE WALK to the steamboat was numbing. Ordell's limbs felt heavy with each step and the world around him felt faded. He didn't open the door after he heard the shot—he knew what he'd find if he did. Instead, he walked away, not even alerting authorities about the event that had just taken place.

Ordell was so lost in thought that he didn't even feel Elias wrap his arms around him.

"Took you long enough," Elias said with a smile. "We thought you got lost."

"Sorry, ran into some issues," Ordell said.

"What happened to your clothes?" Elias's smile fell. "Ordell, what happened? You're trembling."

There was nothing he wanted more than to break down and cry, but he couldn't find himself doing that. Instead, he pushed away from Elias and walked toward the boat.

His new life was ready to begin once he reached Linnesse. He'd have Elias and his friends right beside him, which should have made him excited. However, all he felt was numbness.

Once in the boat, Elias sat down next to him and wrapped his arm around him. "I love you."

Ordell nodded and rested his head on Elias's shoulder.

Life could only get better from here on out.

EPILOGUE

ORDELL OPENED his eyes and looked up at the white ceiling. He felt Elias shift at his side next to him; the man was one of the most restless people Ordell had ever come across.

He still had fond memories of his wedding. They had been wedded after Ordell was given taste buds as an early wedding present from Winifred. The first thing he'd tried was the wedding cake, which was far too sweet for him. After a couple of bites, Ordell couldn't handle it anymore and had to give the rest of his piece to Elias.

One of the best things about Linnesse was how beautiful the place was. It was filled to the brim with advanced technology, and everyone Ordell met there was accepting of free automatons. Many of the pleasure slaves were exported to Linnesse for Ordell and Winifred to reprogram. It was quicker than making an automaton from scratch, and it helped Ordell learn skills faster.

Ordell even helped Winifred with the skills he had learned from Octavio. He had learned so much from both of them that he felt confident in taking over when he needed to.

He felt something jump on the bed, and he lifted his head to look at the almost completed cat automaton. The cat meowed and walked over to Ordell.

"Good morning, Jingles," he muttered as he scratched the cat's ears.

Jingles acted like a normal cat and was complete except for one thing: the fur.

Ordell meant to add the fur later in the day, since Jingles scared Elias in his current condition. However, Ordell knew once the fur was on, Elias would fall in love with Jingles.

Elias flopped his strong arm onto Ordell and scratched the middle of Ordell's chest. "And how's Jingles and Mr. Griffith doing this morning?" he asked through a sleepy yawn.

Ordell chuckled. "We're doing great."

Before the wedding it had been a struggle to figure out how they were to do their last names. Eventually they'd agreed to go with Griffith, and Ordell couldn't be happier with the decision.

Finally Ordell got out of bed and stretched his arms. Elias yawned and did the same. Once dressed, they walked to the shop. Ordell opened the door and turned on the light, and Elias's eyes widened, taking a step back.

"You… you better put fur on those things!" Elias stammered out. "You know I hate them like that!"

Ordell had loved creating Jingles so much that he had to create more—twenty more, to be exact. The workshop was crawling with cats that were waiting impatiently to have their fur placed on.

He reached up and kissed the tip of Elias's nose. "I'm doing it right now."

Ordell began to walk toward the workbench, but Elias grabbed him from behind and pulled him close against his solid body. "Trying to get away from me again?" Elias whispered in his ear and then nipped at it.

"You won't be much help if you hold me like this," Ordell said through his laughs. "I thought you wanted to get the fur on these cats immediately."

Elias kissed Ordell's ear. "Yes, but I want to hold you more."

"You can hold me for the rest of the day once we're done."

"Promise?"

"Promise."

SUSANNA HAYS has been writing ever since she can remember. She first started out with ghost stories that she would tell to her cousins and best friend. She has always been off in her own little world and spent her time at recess writing stories in her notebook. She is a huge animal lover and adores cats—especially the big fluffy ones! She loves talking to others and enjoys making friends on Goodreads and reading books.

She loves to create characters who have a story to tell. She creates protagonists who must overcome their weaknesses and find their true selves.

Website: susanna0hays.wix.com/sueswriting
Blog: susannahays.blogspot.com
Goodreads: www.goodreads.com/Sue_Hays

Stalked

Susanna Hays

Yori Tanaka lives with crippling anxiety, knowing he carries the "Beast Syndrome" gene yet still unsure what activates it. Thankfully, his boyfriend, Bryce Green, is down to earth and has been more than patient and supportive for the last five years.

But their lives are about to change. When Lance Haney, an old friend, rolls into town, Yori is excited to see him at first—until Yori learns Lance's motives. Full of malice and bad intentions, Lance plans to activate Yori's "Beast Syndrome" gene, and Yori's greatest fear is about to become a reality.

www.dreamspinnerpress.com

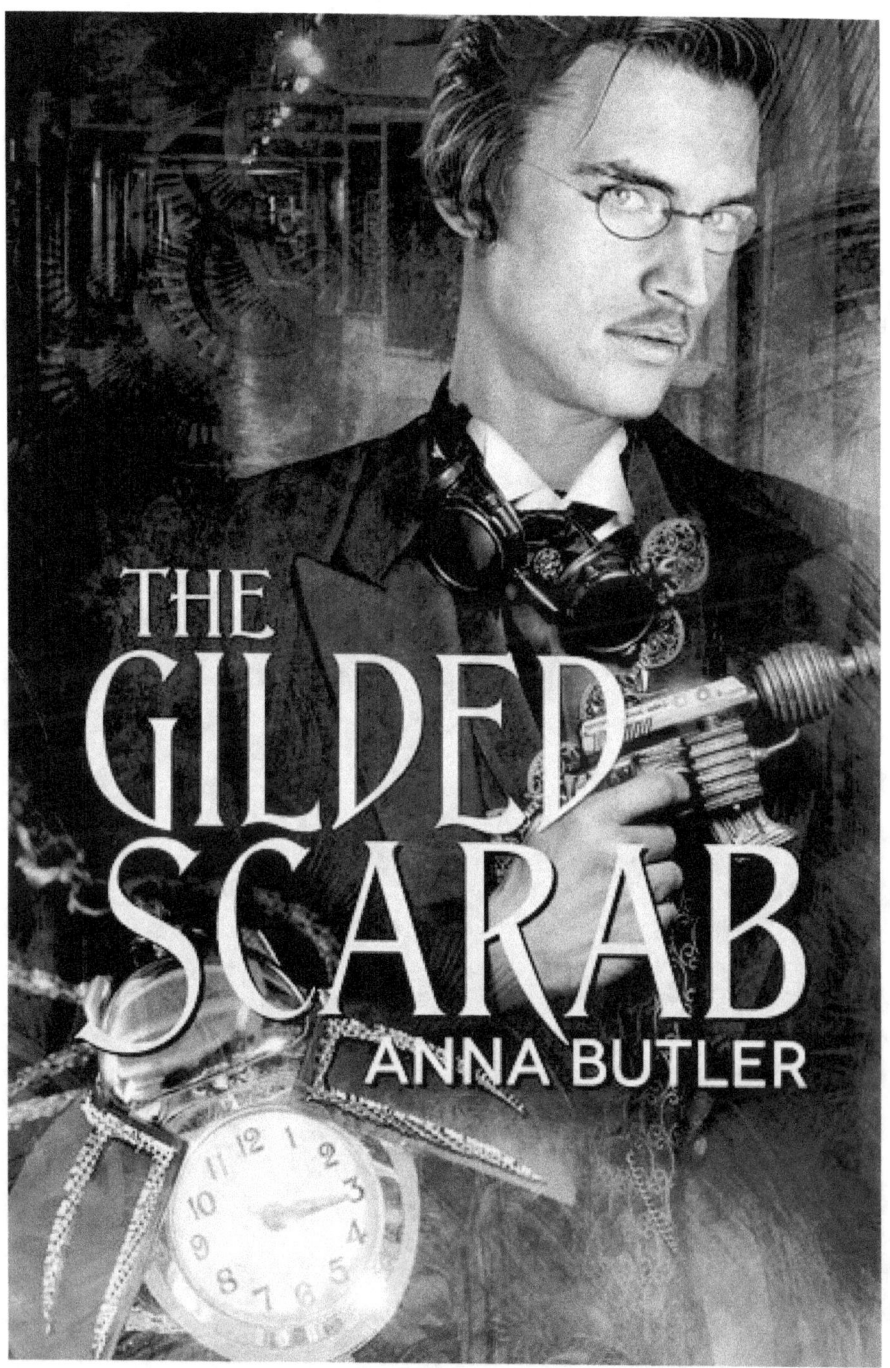

Also from Dreamspinner Press

www.dreamspinnerpress.com

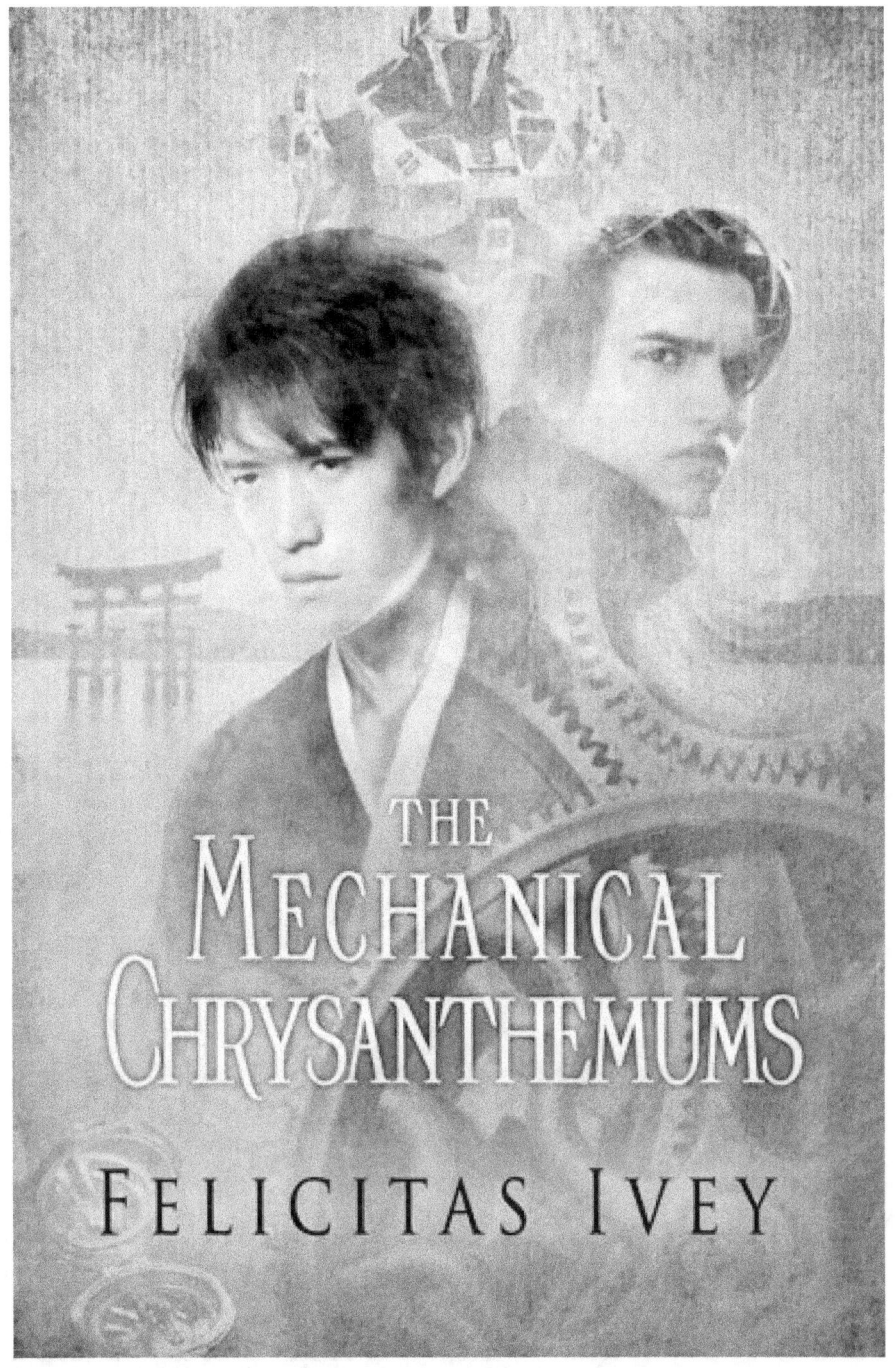

THE
MECHANICAL
CHRYSANTHEMUMS

FELICITAS IVEY

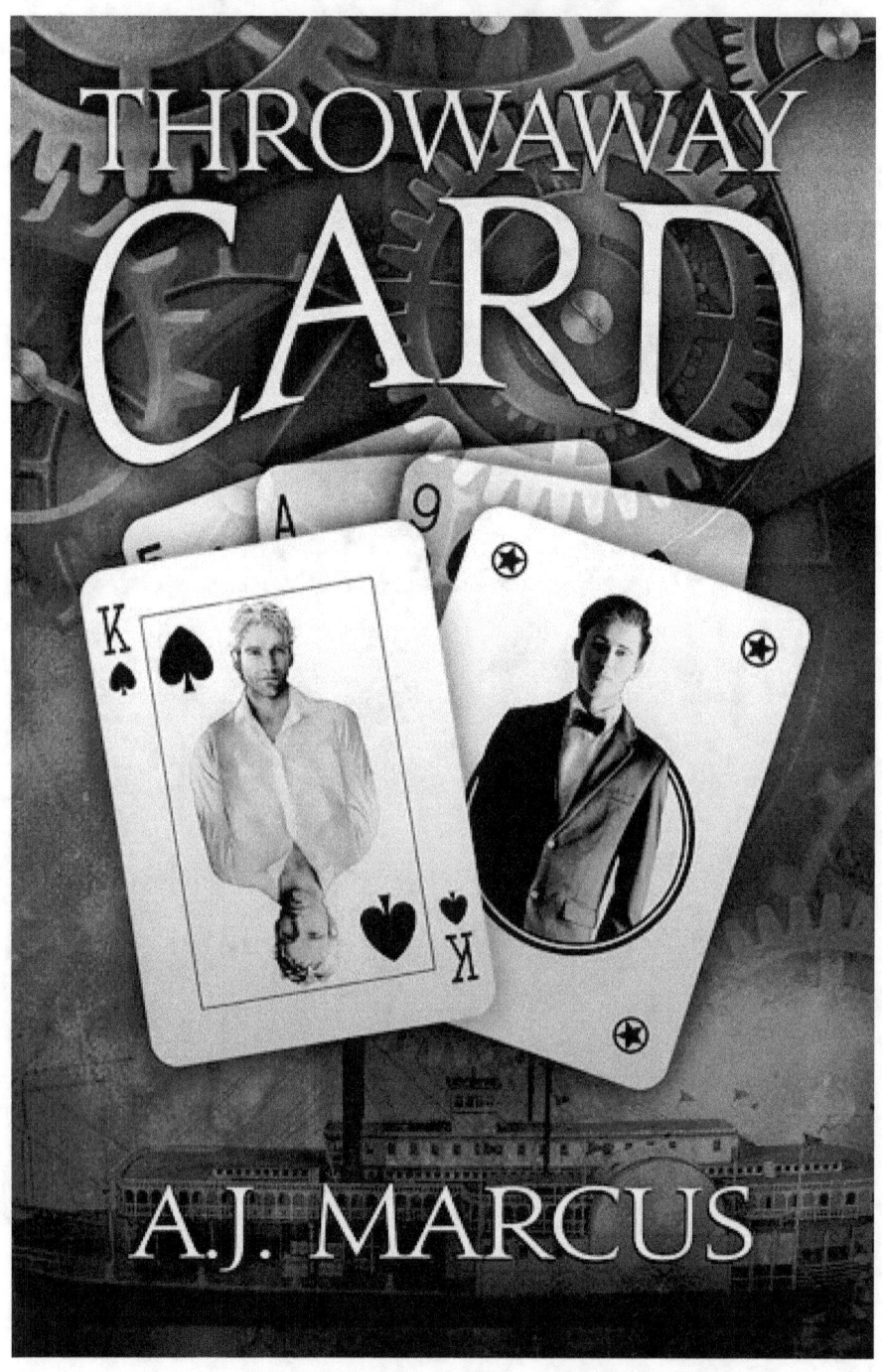

Also from Dreamspinner Press

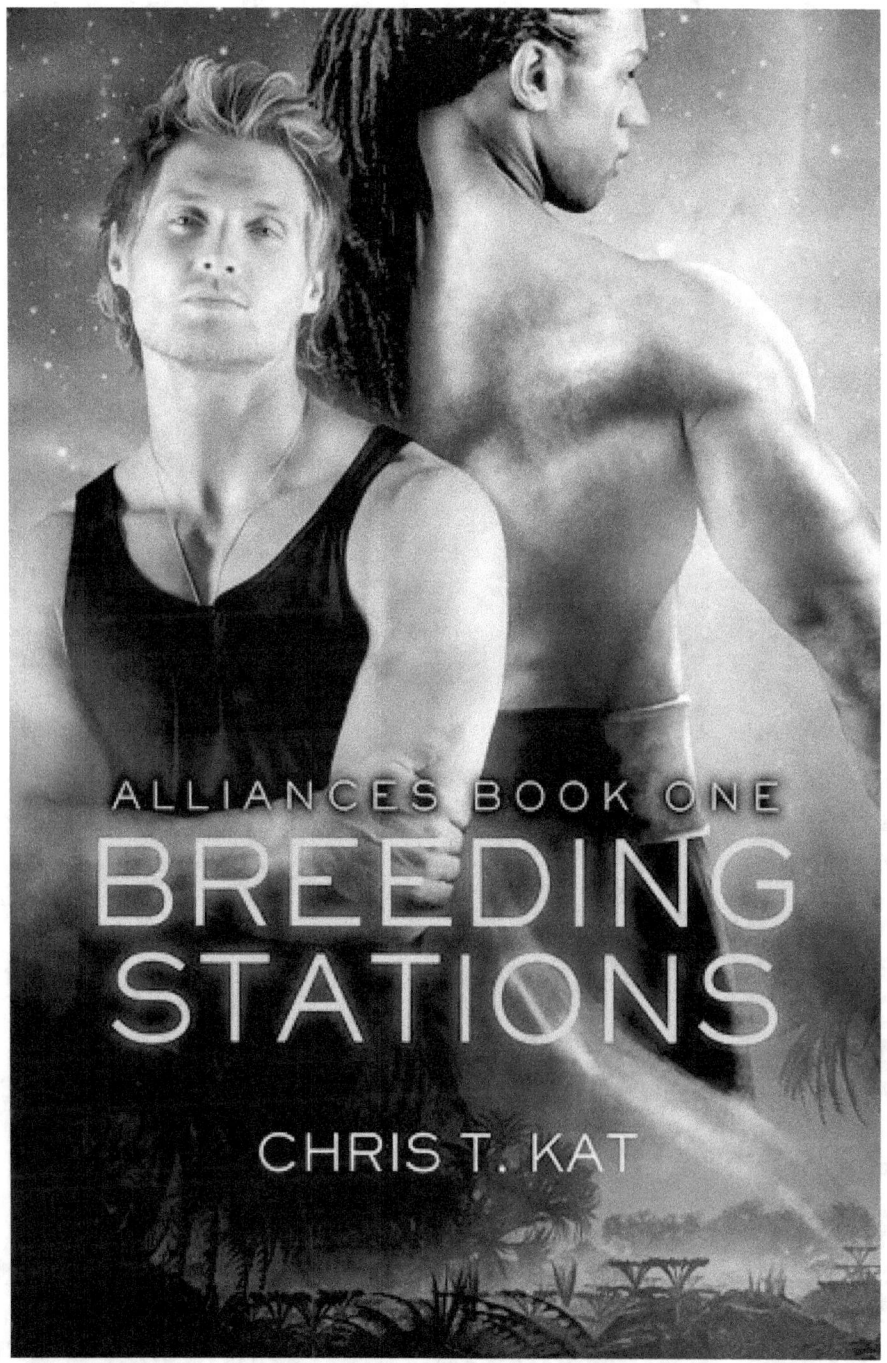

ALLIANCES BOOK ONE

BREEDING STATIONS

CHRIS T. KAT

www.ingramcontent.com/pod-product-compliance
Lightning Source LLC
Chambersburg PA
CBHW060101260626
47160CB00005B/1745